"You have to admit you feel the attraction."

Mark kissed her again and, under the water, wrapped his leg around hers, pulling her even closer. "Now, tell me you didn't feel what I felt."

"You know I felt it," Amanda confessed. "You know I feel the attraction. But I can't have anything to do with you. My number one rule is no fraternizing with the players."

"Damn the rules, Amanda. I'm no gambler. I only played last night because I wanted to see you. And aren't you fraternizing with me right now? All I want is to spend some time with you—to get to know you better. Look, I'm just asking for a date, not a lifetime commitment."

Amanda reached over and grasped the tiled edge of the pool. Acting so quickly that Mark didn't have time to react, she pulled herself out of the water and grabbed her towel. "If you're willing to accept only what I have to offer, meet me in London after the ship docks. I'll be at Sotheby's, 34 Bond Street, at noon."

Then she was gone.

ABOUT THE AUTHOR

"I lead the dullest life in Christendom," says Nancy Elliott, "and I've never gambled more than a penny at a time, but I've always fantasized about playing high-stakes poker and about charming heroes rescuing me from nasty villains. And being a romance author, I get to turn my daydreams into books. I just hope the readers like Amanda Kirk—gambler *extraordinaire*—and the dashing Mark Banning as much as I enjoyed dreaming them up." Nancy and her own hero, husband Donald, make their home in Carmichael, California.

Books by Nancy Elliott

HARLEQUIN SUPERROMANCE

303—MORE THAN BEST FRIENDS
367—THURSDAY'S CHILD

Blind Opening

NANCY ELLIOTT

Harlequin Books

TORONTO • NEW YORK • LONDON
AMSTERDAM • PARIS • SYDNEY • HAMBURG
STOCKHOLM • ATHENS • TOKYO • MILAN

Published October 1991

ISBN 0-373-70470-4

BLIND OPENING

To my friend,
Shirley Scott Campbell.
Thanks for being with me
on the trip to England.

PROLOGUE

THE THUDDING BANG of the front door echoed throughout the house. Susan Ross sat up in bed, instantly wide awake. She lay still, listening.

"I wonder what's keeping Susan. She should have been here by now."

Susan relaxed as she heard her mother's distinctively deep voice drift up the winding staircase to the second-floor bedroom. Felicia must not have noticed Susan's new Porsche in the three-car garage. She hadn't told anyone about her most recent purchase, a gift to herself for a lot of different reasons.

She focused on the bedside clock. Ten-thirty. Felicia's aerobics class must have gotten out late. Every Friday night she and Margo Buchanan worked out at a nearby gym, then swam for a half hour.

"I hope there wasn't fog along the coast," Margo said. She and Felicia had been good friends for years. They'd grown even closer after Susan's father's death six months before. She was glad her mother had had someone nearby to help her through that difficult time.

"Want a drink?" Felicia asked.

"I'll have a soft drink. I've got a complicated brief to review before court. At nine. Damn that early-bird judge."

"I'm going to have a large glass of white wine," Felicia said.

"We spend two hours working up a sweat at that damn gym, and you want to blow it all on alcohol."

Felicia laughed, a rare sound. "I deserve these calories tonight."

Susan could clearly hear every word that was being said. The large, open, marble-tiled foyer and the spiral staircase funneled the sounds to the second floor. As a child, she had lain in this same bed, listening to the jumble of voices emanating from the parties her parents gave. Even now she had a feeling of isolation, as if she were on an island, far away from the rest of the world.

Felicia began to tell Margo about the divorce of one of their mutual friends. Susan knew the two women would talk for hours. She got up and walked toward the door to shut it. The phone rang, making her jump. Before she could move toward the nightstand she heard her mother say, "Hello?"

Susan stayed near the door, wanting to hear who was on the line.

"Oh, hi, Bill," Felicia said. "I just got here. What's up?"

Susan was surprised her uncle would be calling this late. It was one-thirty in the morning in New York.

"What?" Felicia shouted. "Oh, my God. How did it happen?" "Where is he now?" "You're sure he's safe?" "How could he be that careless?" After each clipped sentence, Felicia waited a few moments for answers.

Susan knew she should run downstairs to see what was wrong, but somehow couldn't seem to make her muscles move.

"No, don't do anything," Felicia said. "Margo's here." She paused. "Damn it, Bill, I've got to tell her. She knows about the problems we had with the company. Maybe she can help." Another pause. "No, Susan hasn't gotten home yet. It's so late. She probably won't come till morning." She listened a moment, then said, "I know it was stupid not to tell her about Craig. Now she'll have to know. But I'll handle that when I have to. I'll call you later. Are you at your apartment? Okay. I'll get back to you." She slammed the receiver down.

Fear paralyzed Susan. She remembered another phone call in the night... informing her of her father's plane accident.

"What's the matter?" Margo asked.

"I... I don't know what to do."

The clinking bell-like sound of a heavy decanter hitting the side of a crystal glass filled the silence. "Here, take this," Margo ordered. "Sit down. Use both hands, damn it, or you'll spill it. Now tell me what's going on."

"Oh, God. I never dreamed he'd be spotted."

"Cut the dramatics, Felicia, and get to the point."

"Craig's been seen by someone who recognized him."

Felicia spoke so softly that Susan wasn't sure she'd heard correctly. She started down the stairs, then stopped when Margo spoke again.

"What did you say?"

"Craig—he isn't dead!"

Susan gasped and grabbed the banister to steady herself as she sat on the top step. Her father? Alive? How could that be? She'd read the newspaper accounts, seen the television newscasts. Craig Ross had been flying his plane and had disappeared somewhere over the ocean between Rio de Janeiro and Buenos Aires. No evidence of the wreck was found. Everyone who knew him had mourned the loss of a charming and brilliant man.

"What the hell are you talking about?" Margo was almost shouting.

"He wasn't killed in the plane crash. He had Bill announce to the media that Craig Ross was dead. He's been in hiding ever since."

At first all Susan could feel was joy that her father was alive. But then the implications of what she was hearing hit her. She clamped her hand over her mouth to keep from crying out. Felicia and Uncle Bill had lied to her. Her own father had been the instigator of the conspiracy. For six months her mother had let her believe Craig was dead. She and Felicia had even gone through the travesty of holding a private memorial service on a cliff overlooking the ocean.

Susan wrapped her arms around her waist. She felt sick to her stomach and tried to swallow, but her mouth was too dry. Tears spilled down her face.

"Felicia, tell me the rest of it." Margo's tone was a little calmer, but there was an underlying anger that left no doubt concerning her feelings about a man who would let his daughter think he was dead. "Why would he fake his death?"

Susan thought it was a pointless question. There were no explanations that could justify her parents' duplicity. What they had done to her was unforgivable. But still she couldn't make herself go downstairs to confront Felicia. All she'd offer her daughter were more lies.

After a long silence, Margo said, "Felicia, you've got to tell me. I can't help until I know what you and Craig have done."

"Re-remember two years ago, when the company was in trouble?"

Susan easily recalled that time. She'd been in Europe on an antique-buying expedition. When she arrived in Los Angeles to visit her parents for the Christmas holidays, Felicia and Craig had been so busy that she'd rarely seen them.

"You know what was happening in the computer business then. We were having a terrible time competing with Apple and IBM. We couldn't get the bugs out of the DOS, the disk operating systems. We were in deeper trouble than we let on."

"But you got capital from Chanticleer Investors. Bill and I worked on the contracts. You paid them back last— Oh, you mean, you got more money from someone else?"

"A New Jersey businessman."

"Knowing Craig as I do, he was probably a gambler. Right?"

"He gambled with a man named Septimus Garland."

"Garland! My God, Felicia, he's got his hand in every dirty deal imaginable." After a moment, Margo asked, "How much did Craig win?"

"Three million. I don't know all the details, except that later Garland tried to make a claim against the estate. Bill got rid of him."

Susan knew she should be having some kind of reaction to what her mother was saying. But none of it meant anything to her. All she could think about were the lies she'd been told.

"What happened after the plane crash?" Margo asked quietly.

"Craig was injured, mostly his face. He was picked up by a fishing boat and taken to a small village in Uruguay that had a visiting doctor. Susan and I were traveling through the Orient on a buying trip for her antique stop. At the time it was impossible to reach us." Felicia stopped speaking.

Susan started to stand, then sat back down as her mother continued. She would keep her anger in check, at least until she heard the rest of the story.

"Craig was able to contact Bill in New York. He flew down, bringing plenty of cash. Craig convinced him to accept his plan to change his appearance and to go along with the rest of the ruse. Before the media was notified of his death I was told the truth. For some strange reason Craig decided not to tell Susan. I guess he feared what her reaction would be. He said he'd rather let her think he was dead than to have her know what he was doing. Later he could make amends."

"Three million seems like a lot of money to win," Margo said. "Well, that is, without cheating."

"I know he won the money fairly."

"My God, Felicia, Craig did all of this just so he could save his company?"

"He was frantic to save it. The money pulled us out of the hole. We never made a claim on the insurance, so he's really done nothing illegal."

"He cut himself off from his wife and daughter, gave up his career and became an expatriot, living... where? Where does a moral coward live, Felicia?"

A moral coward. Yes, that was what her father was. And her mother had gone along with the plan. Susan bent forward, her head touching her knees. She had idolized her father. Now she felt betrayed by her parents, even by her uncle who was as close as a brother. Her whole life had been turned upside down.

"You don't understand," Felicia said. "There's more to all of this—"

Susan didn't want to hear her mother's rationalization. Standing, she ran to her room and shut the door. When her heart stopped beating so rapidly, and she'd managed to catch her breath, she tried to think about what she could do. Only one idea occurred to her: she must leave this house of lies.

With hands that wouldn't stop shaking, she dressed, making sure she made no noise. She had only gotten into her small overnight case, so she didn't have to repack her clothes. When she was ready to go, she waited in the dark room. An hour later Margo left. Susan next heard the low sounds of her mother talking on the phone, probably to her brother. What had they decided to do about Craig? Perhaps Susan would soon be reading about the scandal in the newspapers—all the more reason why she should leave. What her mother and father had done negated any sense of loyalty she might feel.

Another hour passed before Susan heard her mother climb the stairs and go to her room. When everything was quiet, Susan looked around, hesitating a moment. She was as ready as she'd ever be. Tomorrow, when she felt stronger, she'd call her mother. No, she'd leave a note now. That way she wouldn't have to listen to any more lies.

BY NOON THE NEXT DAY, after driving all night and morning, Susan's fatigue had blunted her pain. As she drove past the sparkling blue waters of Lake Tahoe, she felt her spirits lift.

When she had left her house ten hours before, she'd driven onto a freeway, not caring which direction it took her, just as long as it put distance between her and Felicia and everything she represented. Interstate 5 had brought her to Sacramento, where she turned east, following the American River toward the Sierra Nevadas.

She would stay a few days in South Lake Tahoe and perhaps look for a job, something totally unrelated to antiques. Tahoe was as good a place as any to start a new life.

CHAPTER ONE

MARK BANNING OPENED his eyes and glanced at the clock. "Five after five?" he groaned out loud. "Damn it all." Why had he awakened so early?

He stretched his six-foot-two-inch frame in the ship's five-foot-eleven-inch bunk and bumped his head on the backboard, an action that again reminded him of how much he disliked being on a ship. A trip to London on a luxury liner was a little too confining for his tastes. He was on board only because his aunt had broken her ankle by stepping in a gopher hole on the golf course and couldn't accompany his mother. The first-class room that had been reserved for his aunt couldn't be canceled. Connie's friends had been otherwise engaged and declined to join her for a free trip. Mark's sister, Diane, was at school in France. Their stepfather had flatly refused to go with his wife. Edward Quintero claimed he had too much work. He could be conveniently busy when there was an activity he didn't want to do.

Mark's mother had asked him to go with her, a request she'd never made before. After taking into consideration her aversion to traveling alone, he decided to accept. He now questioned whether his role as his mother's companion was absolutely necessary. She'd organized the details of the trip without his help, leaving him nothing to do except tag along. During their time on board, she'd acted happy and contented, more relaxed than he'd seen in a long time. Perhaps being away from her overbearing husband was good for her.

And he, too, was enjoying the trip, up to a point. He'd spent hours playing shuffleboard, backgammon and bridge; he'd dressed like a pirate for costume night, had danced with every available female and listened to descriptions and seen pictures of grandchildren ad nauseam. It wasn't that he didn't enjoy the company of people more than twice his age, but it would have been nice if a female in her twenties or thirties had been on board, preferably single. He had two more days to serve as courtly companion to his mother and the women friends she had made. Then he would spend two days in London, fly to Philadelphia and get back to work.

Work, he scoffed. For the past three months he'd been taking up office space at Orion Aeronautical Company. Nothing of importance came across his desk, giving him serious misgivings about the company his father had founded. For reasons Mark couldn't quite define he was feeling a growing distrust toward his stepfather and his son, Robert. Odd things had been happening that no one could explain: missing files and reports, interoffice memos that never reached Mark's office, meetings to which he wasn't invited.

One of the main reasons he was so impatient for the cruise to end was his plan to begin investigating the company's operations as soon as he got back. He was especially interested in learning what his stepbrother was doing. Why was he away from the office so often? What secret projects was he working on?

Mark stretched as much as he could in the short bunk, folded his arms behind his head and thought about how different the Bannings' lives had become with his father's death when Mark was fifteen. After waiting a disturbingly short time, Constance Banning had married Edward Quintero, an executive at the company. When they returned from their honeymoon, Edward had brought his nineteen-year-old son, Robert, with him and had assumed command of his new wife, her own two children and the house the Banning family had owned for a hundred and fifty years. Edward also took control of Orion, firing or retiring many of the longtime employees of the company founded by Russell Banning.

Robert was four years older than Mark and had immediately begun treating him as if he were an underling, useful only to do Rob's bidding. Diane had been five, too young to be part of the rivalry between the two stepbrothers that started the day they first met.

Edward had immediately given Robert a high-paying, responsible job at the plant. Mark was only fifteen and had to finish his education. To keep peace in the house, his mother had sent him to a boarding prep school near Washington, D.C. Not being around Rob suited Mark just fine. Even though the stepbrothers had tried to avoid each other's company as much as possible, their animosity had deepened into hatred.

Mark glanced out the porthole. The sky was the opalescent, washed-out blue of dawn. He shut his eyes and tried to relax. For weeks now the nagging doubts about the Quinteros and Orion had ruined his sleep, occupying his mind with unanswerable questions.

He should have gone to detective school instead of taking all that time to earn double doctorates in aeronautical engineering and business administration. Those

twelve difficult years had been aimed at one goal: preparing himself to take his rightful place as the chief de-
signer and one of the directors of the company. But
nothing seemed to be working out that way. Edward
had offered him a position that bordered on demeaning, implying a take-it-or-leave-it attitude. Even though
Ed had made Robert a high-ranking executive at nine-
teen, Mark, with years of education behind him, had to
start near the bottom. His contention that he was im-
measurably better qualified than Rob had been totally
dismissed as irrelevant.

Mark owed it to the memory of Russell Banning to
find out what was happening at Orion. But before he
could take any action he had to get off this ship and
back to Philadelphia.

He sighed. Only two more days before they landed in
Southampton, he reminded himself. He could endure
anything for that long. He hoped.

But he couldn't tolerate lying in bed another moment. He'd go swimming in the smaller of the ship's
two pools. He hoped it had been refilled from the night
before. He wondered why they drained it at midnight.
A safety precaution in case of a storm? Or just so there
would always be fresh water for the swimmers? He'd
have to remember to ask someone.

He jumped out of bed and hurriedly got ready. Later,
after breakfast with his mother, he would tactfully refuse to participate in the social activities she had organized and find a protected corner in the sun where he
could read the reports the Pentagon had issued on Orion's last shipment of jet parts for the air force.

He grabbed a towel, locked his room and headed for
the indoor pool.

AMANDA KIRK STOOD by her stateroom door, waiting to leave. "Have a good swim," Cal called out. "I'll see you later."

"I won't be long," she said, checking to make sure she had her key. "I can let myself in, so you might as well go to bed."

Even after all the time they had operated under this same routine, it still seemed strange to talk about going to bed early in the morning and getting up during the afternoon.

Cal gathered a stack of plates and glasses used by their guests who had just departed. "No. I'll wait for you."

She smiled, knowing he'd say that. Caleb Norton was more protective of her than any father with his teenage daughter. Before she shut the door she hesitated a moment, feeling a strong urge to tell Cal how much he meant to her. Since she'd met him at South Lake Tahoe a year ago, he'd been her only friend. With Cal's help, Susan Ross had ceased to exist, replaced by Amanda Kirk. He'd helped at a time in her life when she needed his quiet, unquestioning support. He had given her an opportunity to mature, respecting her privacy. During their time together, she'd learned to handle her parents' duplicity, which, to a certain extent, had lost its power to hurt her.

She realized Cal was looking strangely at her. "Back soon," she said, shutting the door and hurrying through the empty passageway.

Again she thought about how much she owed her strange, quiet friend. More than any man she'd ever met, she respected and admired him. She suspected he was in love with her, though he'd never said a word.

Why didn't she let him know how she felt? Was it because her affections hadn't developed into anything deeper than friendship—at least, not yet?

She also wondered if she'd been afraid to change the relationship because she didn't want to lose her independence. Keeping Cal at a distance gave her the option of leaving whenever she wanted. More and more frequently lately she'd been asking herself if she wanted to keep the status quo or start making some changes in her life.

Perhaps when they got to Lake Tahoe for their vacation she'd reexamine her feelings and discuss with Cal how she felt.

She put her thoughts in the back of her mind, now looking forward to her morning swim after a night of hard work. She hoped she would have the ship's pool to herself. But to her disappointment she saw someone by the diving board. In the shadowed light she thought the intruder was a man, but she couldn't be sure. She hoped he wouldn't try to talk to her. Since eleven the night before, she'd listened to the low, murmuring voices of men. If the swimmer insisted on starting a conversation, she'd go back to her room.

Sunlight slanted through the windows. The warmth felt good on her back. July on the Atlantic was colder than she'd thought possible. She dropped her towel and robe on a deck chair and slipped into the water, swimming to the rope that bisected the pool, then diving underneath, reversing her course and returning to the shallow end. She was about to push off again when she sensed someone was near her.

"I can't believe it," a man's deep voice said.

Amanda felt resentment that this stranger was going to talk to her. Now she'd have to leave the pool. She swept her wet hair back from her face and slowly focused her attention on the man. Part of her mind told her not to stare, but she couldn't avert her gaze. Something about his manner and open smile told her that if she gave herself half a chance, she would probably like him. But she was weary of being charming to men she would never see after this cruise was over.

Before she could say she wasn't interested in talking, he spoke. "I'm sorry I interrupted your swim, but could you tell me if you might be a figment of my imagination."

She glanced down at herself, held her arms out of the water and watched the water drip off. "No, I'm real," she said. At least this man's approach was different.

He looked at her left hand. "You're not married?"

Before realizing what she was doing she shook her head.

"How old are you?"

"Are you the ship's census taker?"

He laughed. "No. It's just that you're the only unattached female under the age of fifty I've seen on board. This cruise seems to attract a large number of older married couples, retirees and elderly widows. Where have you been hiding?"

She had nothing to say in response to what she assumed was a rhetorical question. She smiled with cool politeness and positioned herself so he could swim away.

"Don't go. Please."

"If you're looking for younger women for companionship, perhaps you should have brought one of your own."

She could tell by his expression that her words had stung, as she had meant them to. If he didn't like being with the people on board, what was he doing here? She was beginning to wonder if she had badly misjudged his engaging smile. "I'm sorry, but I haven't got much time to swim. Nice talking to you."

She couldn't bring herself to be rude enough to tell him to get lost, but she'd made sure her expression and tone of voice informed him that the conversation was at an end. With an expert maneuver she dived underwater and swam until she was nearly at the end of the pool.

As Mark watched her come to the surface and continue the butterfly stroke to the other end, he cursed his stupidity. Not only had he inadvertently insulted all the wonderful people he'd met on the ship, but he had also offended this woman. Since she had made it abundantly clear she didn't want to talk to him, he would respect her wishes and, for now, leave without offering an explanation or an apology.

Considering all the time he'd been on board and all the people he'd met and observed, it was inconceivable he hadn't seen this woman—which must mean she didn't fraternize with the passengers. Somehow, even if he had to ask every man, woman, child and crew member on the ship, he would discover the name of the beautiful woman with the glorious red hair. Then he'd find out which room she was staying in and ask her why she'd kept herself hidden away since they'd left New York.

"Evan Rawlings called," Cal said to Amanda in his rumbling bass voice. He entered her bedroom, ducking his head to prevent hitting the top of the door. His six-and-a-half-foot frame seemed to fill the room.

"What did he say?" She began to brush her damp hair. She wore a nightgown and robe of silk and lace, garments that were totally feminine but in no way revealing.

"He asked if he could come again tonight."

"Who else will be here?"

"The same as last night, except Milkovski. He told me you'd cost him too much money."

"We can get along without him." Amanda rubbed the back of her neck, again feeling her fatigue. It had been a long, tiring night. She was ready for a good day's sleep. "When do we start tonight?"

"About eleven." Cal leaned against the wall, crossing his arms.

"What did you say to Rawlings about meeting him this afternoon?"

"I wasn't sure how late you wanted to sleep, so I haven't set anything up yet."

Right at that moment Amanda became aware of Cal's expression. He was staring at her in the same way as the man at the pool. Desire was revealed in Cal's eyes, but there was more: love and a hunger she'd never seen before. She was so disconcerted that she almost forgot what they were talking about.

Finally she asked, "Do you think we should bother listening to Rawlings's proposal?"

Cal shrugged and looked away. "Guess it wouldn't hurt."

Amanda peered into the mirror. She was still stunned by the way Cal had looked at her. Many times he had offered a compliment on her looks or admired a new dress or hairstyle. But never before had she seen such longing in his eyes.

"We've still got two more days before we land," she said without looking at Cal. "If we decide to refuse Rawlings's offer, there might be some bad feelings. Why don't we wait until the last morning?"

"That's a good idea. I'll call him later." Cal stood by the open door.

Amanda looked at him. His expression had changed to one she recognized. He reached out to the wall switch to turn off the overhead light. The room was now illuminated by the lamp near Amanda's bed.

"You mentioned you wanted to eat dinner in the dining room. What time should I wake you?"

Amanda thought about the man at the pool and his guileless attempt to be friendly. She hadn't been very nice. But it was pointless to encourage him. Also, she didn't feel like answering any questions about where she'd been hiding since the ship had left New York. "I've changed my mind." She pulled the spread back on her bed. "When I'm ready to eat, I'll order room service."

"Call me when you're up. We'll eat together." Before leaving the room, he added, "Sleep tight." He shut the door behind him.

Amanda sighed and stretched out on the cool sheets. As she floated in the half-conscious state just before sleep, the image of the man at the pool appeared in her mind. Something about his face intrigued her. Honesty and a charming, almost boyish openness provided a contrast to his masculinity. Somehow he seemed different from any man she'd ever met before—and in her profession she'd met hundreds.

But before she could analyze her reaction to the stranger she fell asleep.

"THIS IS DUMB," Mark muttered to himself as he stared across the water, watching the sunset. His actions had been so out of character that he still couldn't believe he had spent most of the day trying to find the beautiful redheaded woman he'd met in the pool. He'd asked dozens of people all over the ship, but no one had seen her. All he'd accomplished was to make his mother angry because he'd refused to play bridge or shuffleboard on her team.

One good thing had come out of his search. For the first time since he'd left Philadelphia he'd been able to forget his worries about Orion. Concentrating on finding the mysterious woman had pleasantly occupied his mind all day.

The signal announcing dinner sounded over the loudspeaker. Mark returned to his deck chair, picked up the Pentagon report, which he still hadn't read, and went to find his mother.

All through the meal he paid little attention to her, the other people at the table or his food. His gaze roamed around the room, constantly seeking the woman he knew wouldn't be there.

"Mark!" his mother said in a commanding voice.

Connie Quintero was a petite woman who had kept her figure by eating a nutritious diet and playing tennis and golf. Her beautiful face was now flushed with excitement or possibly with anger directed at him.

"Are you or are you not going to play bridge tonight?" she demanded.

"No, thanks. I didn't get my report read. I think I'll stay in my room—"

"You had the entire day to read it. Instead, you roamed around the ship like a tiger in a cage."

"I'll get it finished tonight and devote *all* my attention to you tomorrow."

"Don't be impertinent," she said, speaking to him just as she had when he was a sassy teenager.

After his mother left the dining room to look for a fourth for her bridge game, Mark stayed at the table to see the floor show. He closely studied all of the dancers, the band members and the magician's assistant. A red-haired woman wasn't part of the entertainment, nor did one work the evening shifts at the casino or the gift shop.

By eleven that night he'd almost convinced himself that she really was a figment of his imagination. He was on his way to his room when he noticed a steward he hadn't seen before carrying a tray of food down one of the passageways in the first-class stateroom located on the topmost deck.

"Pardon me, but I'm looking for a woman—"

"Yeah, ain't we all?" the young man said with a leer, and readjusted the heavy tray on his shoulder.

The ship's registry was Greek, and most of the crew spoke English with heavy foreign accents. But this steward was unmistakably an American. Mark slipped a ten-dollar bill out of his pocket. Holding it in front of the young man's face, he said, "I met her at the pool this morning, but I haven't seen her since. She's got red hair and is—"

"Gorgeous," the steward finished. "She's staying in the ritziest suite on board. But then, in her line of work she can afford it."

"What do you mean, line of work?" Mark asked.

The steward looked as if he regretted his remark. "I didn't mean nothing." With a deft maneuver he extracted the bill from Mark's fingers, then resumed his hold on the tray. His voice dropped to a whisper. "One-A." He dipped his head to indicate the direction. "Deeluxe suite. Two bedrooms and a sitting parlor in between. I'm taking this tray of hors d'oeuvres there now."

"What's her name?" Mark pulled out another ten-dollar bill and shoved it into the man's jacket pocket.

"Amanda Kirk. But she ain't alone. Mr. Norton's bigger than you and me put together, so watch yourself. They do a lot of late-night entertaining in the suite, with lots of food and drinks, but I ain't seen no women visitors."

"What do you mean?"

The steward said nothing, just glanced down at his feet.

Mark wanted to ask more questions, but he could tell by the man's expression that he'd reveal nothing more. "Okay, thanks."

The steward began to walk down the corridor. "I ain't talked to you, have I?"

"I've never even seen you," Mark said. He stepped out of the way while the man knocked on Amanda Kirk's door and disappeared inside. After a few minutes, he returned.

"Good luck, pal. You've got a lot of competition."

Before Mark could ask the man to explain, he ran down the flight of stairs.

Mark started to go toward Amanda's door, then stopped, reviewing what he'd learned from the steward. When all of the facts were added up, there was one possible inference to be made: Amanda Kirk was a call girl. She worked all night. He hadn't seen her before because she slept during the day. Only men went to her suite. Her oversize friend, Norton, was her liaison, to use a polite job description.

Mark spent the next few minutes trying to deny his conclusion, until the sound of men's voices coming up the stairs made him move away from Amanda's room. He felt like a house detective snooping in a hotel corridor. The image didn't appeal to him. He started to return to his room but couldn't help overhearing what the men were saying. They came to the top of the stairs and began to walk down the passageway.

"This is going to be my lucky night," a short, balding man said in the soft, slurring drawl of a native of one of the Gulf States. Mark had noticed him in the casino throwing money around at the crap table. "It's my turn to make that Amanda Kirk sit up and take notice." The man straightened the collar of his white linen sport jacket and adjusted his belt under a bulging stomach.

The second man laughed. He was younger and even rounder than his friend. "Just like you tried to do last night, huh? Come on, Coleman, you couldn't do it then, what makes you think you can tonight?"

"I tell you, I'm feeling good. Melva went to bed early. She's snoring away in our room right now. I had a chance to have a quiet drink in the bar away from all those chattering women, and now I'm raring to go. Amanda's not going to know what hit her.'' The man knocked on the door, which was opened immediately. Both men entered and the door was shut.

Two at a time? Mark asked himself, stunned by the implication. He was surprised by the anger he felt. But why should he feel so resentful? He'd met Amanda Kirk for only a few minutes. She'd amply demonstrated she didn't want to talk to him. There was no reason why he should react so strongly... unless he considered his masculine vanity, which had been sorely wounded. At the pool she had shown absolutely no interest in him as a person, man or potential client.

Whatever the reasons for his strange reaction, he had to admit he was deeply disappointed to have his suspicions confirmed.

All day the image of Amanda had stayed in his mind. He visualized how she'd looked that first time he'd seen her, standing by the pool, when the rays of the early-morning sun had touched her, lighting her flaming hair, revealing her glorious body.

With a sigh Mark turned and walked back to his room. He had a premonition that he wouldn't get much sleep tonight.

CHAPTER TWO

AT FIVE-THIRTY, as if an alarm clock had rung in his head, Mark awakened. He got up and looked out the porthole. The morning sun was just high enough to illuminate the whitecapped waves of the blue Atlantic. He knew sleep wasn't going to return. After showering and shaving, he thought about going for a swim, then changed his mind. As he dressed, he decided he would walk around the deck and get some fresh air.

Once he was out of his room, he faced the truth. He was going to find Amanda Kirk and he had a good idea where she'd be. He hurried to the pool. She was concentrating so intently on her swimming that she didn't see him standing near the edge. He analyzed his motives for wanting to talk to her and decided his only reason was an intense curiosity about her. It would be fun to talk to a true demimondaine and the most beautiful woman he'd ever met. Perhaps he'd learn how she had ended up being a sister in civilization's oldest sorority.

He walked over to the chair where she'd placed her towel and short lace coat and sat down, holding the items on his lap.

Fifteen minutes later Amanda made her way to the top of the stairs and began to walk across the deck.

When she saw him, she stopped so suddenly that she almost stumbled.

"I thought you'd be in a better mood for talking today," he said. Trying not to be too obvious, he looked her up and down. Her one-piece suit molded her shapely torso like a second skin.

"No, I'm not." Amanda reached for the towel that Mark handed her. He continued to hold her coat. She silently wiped her face and rubbed her shoulder-length hair. Mark handed her the comb that had slipped out of the jacket pocket. She accepted it, smoothing the tangled curls. When she saw he was carefully studying her body, she avoided looking directly at him, pretending he didn't exist.

"I'm much better informed about you than I was yesterday."

Amanda said nothing. Her silence didn't stop him from continuing on the course he had set.

"I don't even care if the dialogue is one-sided." Mark watched as she rubbed the towel along her arms, across her shoulders and down the length of her legs. That sight made him stop breathing for a long moment. When he recovered enough to speak, he said, "I know your name is Amanda Kirk. Mine's Mark Banning." When she didn't respond, he continued. "I searched for you all day yesterday. About eleven last night I just happened to be outside 1-A. I was told you share the three-room suite with a giant named Caleb Norton."

Amanda stopped drying her legs. She straightened her back and focused her attention on the man's face.

"I'm such a super sleuth that I figured out why I haven't seen you during the trip."

"Oh?" The word escaped her lips before she could stop it. She didn't want to encourage him in any way.

"You work all night in your room and after a morning swim you sleep all day."

"How clever of you," she said, hoping her sarcasm would discourage him. She tried to get her coat, but he held it out of reach.

"Please join me. I want to talk to you." He stood and pulled a chair away from the table. "I know you're not going to believe me, but I've never met a woman like you."

"What does that mean?"

"You're beautiful enough to be a goddess or a model or an actress, but that's not how you make your living."

Amanda frowned. "How do you think—?" Then it dawned on her. If he had been near her room last night about eleven, he would have seen Coleman and Dix arrive. A few minutes later Evan Rawlings had tapped on her door. The most logical conclusion Banning could have drawn was that she rented by the hour. She bit the side of her lip to prevent her smile from showing. A plan was already forming in her mind. Sitting on the chair, she said, "You're right. I'm not a goddess, actress or model." She paused while Mark sat down. "I suppose you're just like all the other men I've met." She tried to sound a little weary of telling her life story. "You want to know how I got started."

Her statement disconcerted Mark. Now he wished he hadn't mentioned his suspicions. What had started out as a fun way to satisfy his curiosity had now become serious. He had pried into something that was none of his business. Instead of a man and a woman spending time together, getting to know each other, a whole new element had entered the picture.

"Well?" Amanda asked. "Do you want to know?"

He couldn't think of a graceful way to change the subject. "Oh, sure. Why not?"

Amanda had her plan all formulated. She inhaled deeply and said, "My father taught me everything I needed to know. Now I consider myself a pro."

"Your father?" Mark asked, trying to hide his shock. After that initial reaction, he forced himself to stop and think about what she was saying. Why would she be so open with a stranger, revealing such personal facts of her life?

"When I was a teenager," Amanda said, "I learned the basic tricks of the trade from him. Then I left home." She was thoroughly enjoying herself. She felt no remorse for what she was doing. Perhaps she could teach Mark Banning not to make erroneous assumptions about people. Looking at him from under lowered eyelashes, she offered a meaningful sigh. "But, of course, I had to earn my living. I decided, since this was the only work I knew how to do, I'd go where the profits are the highest. I got a...uh, a manager, bought some fancy clothes and started doing business with the big-time spenders." She hoped she wasn't being too melodramatic. Mark Banning's expression was one of serious interest, but she couldn't be certain of his level of gullibility. She didn't want to overact and give away her hand. But he appeared to be believing everything she said. A discreet cough covered her laugh. "So here I am, riding the waves, so to speak. No one in my family knows where I am or what I'm doing. Not that they'd care," she added for effect.

But the words created an unwanted image of that fateful night she'd learned about her father. During the year since then, she had tried to seal her memories in a locked compartment of her mind. But more and more often lately something or someone reminded her of the past. That was one of the reasons she'd been feeling a need to examine her life and to think about what she wanted to do in the future.

She looked up and saw that Mark Banning was watching her, waiting for her to speak again. She averted her gaze and smoothed an unruly curl from her cheek, letting the silence drag on.

Mark, too, was willing to keep quiet. Now he had a chance to think. Was she telling the truth? He couldn't be sure. Just then the sun slanted through the large windows, highlighting her hair, turning the color to various shades of reddish-gold. Mark watched with fascination. Her skin wasn't white, but a pale bronze. She truly was one of the most beautiful women he'd ever met.

Until he was proved wrong he had to go under the assumption she was being truthful, mainly for the simple reason that no woman would be willing to sully her reputation like that. His logical mind told him she wasn't lying, but he had to admit there was something...

"That's enough of my life story," she said, straightening her shoulders as if a weight had been lifted.

"Thank you for telling me about yourself. I appreciate your candidness."

Amanda glanced over at him. His sincere expression goaded her on to more flights of fancy. "Since I started being a pro, I've met hundreds of men. I think just about every one of them has been curious about me and my career. I rarely meet any women, but I suppose they'd be curious, too." She smiled to prove the questions no longer bothered her.

"Where did you meet your... business partner, Mr. Norton?"

"In one of the clubs at South Shore." She realized he didn't understand. "South Lake Tahoe, Nevada." When she and Cal met, he'd told her that he'd been looking a long time for someone with her unique combination of qualities. She and Caleb Norton had entered a relationship she'd never regretted. "For months Cal worked with me, making sure I understood all the rules, how to avoid trouble and, most of all, how to make the most money. We've been traveling together for about a year now." The ironic aspect of her revelations to Mark Banning was that everything she said was true. "Our partnership's been very profitable," she added with pride evident in her voice. "We never stay too long in one place. After we've made the big money circuit, we take a couple of months off and go somewhere quiet to rest. The work I do is very tiring, you know."

Her blasé attitude amazed him. "I bet it is tiring—especially since you aren't able to take advantage of the *other* games available for the passengers." Again he wondered if she were putting him on. But when he studied her face, he could see no sign she was deceiving him.

Amanda rose to her feet, followed immediately by Mark. She took her jacket out of his hand.

"I have to go now."

"Meet me later," Mark said, surprising himself. "Please."

"Why? Are you so lonely that you'd be willing to be seen in broad daylight with a woman like me?"

"That's a demeaning statement to both of us." His voice sounded angry. "I would be proud to be seen anywhere with you."

"You mean that, don't you?"

"Of course I do. I always try to say what I mean."

She almost changed her mind about continuing this charade any further. And yet he should learn not to judge people by circumstantial evidence alone.

She searched in the pocket of her jacket. Her voice changed, becoming husky with what she hoped was promised passion. "Let me show you just exactly what my speciality is." Taking his hand in hers, she held it, moving her fingers on the palm. Then she placed her room key on his outstretched hand. "Use this to let yourself in."

Mark stared down at the key, marked 1-A, not believing what he was seeing. If she were trying to fool him, she wouldn't go this far. Or would she?

"Come at ten-thirty tonight." She let her fingers lightly brush across his hand. She had never acted this way before, so she wasn't sure whether her amateurish attempt at being a seductress was effective. But when she saw the look in Mark's eyes, she knew she was doing just fine. "I'll be waiting for you."

He said nothing, just gazed intently at her, trying again to see whether she was serious or laughing at him.

"Don't you want to come?" she said in the same low tone of voice. "Or are you only interested in theory and not practice?"

At that instant he decided he wanted to be with her, if for no other reason than to make sure she truly was a call girl. And, damn it all, he was lonely. The twelve years he'd devoted to his studies hadn't left much time for women. His social life had consisted of an occasional movie or play. Only after he'd graduated had he dated on a regular basis, but no lasting relationships had developed with any of the women. And, to be totally honest with himself, he had to admit there was something about Amanda Kirk that fascinated and intrigued him.

His smile was full of meaning. "I'll be there," he said. He might as well go the whole way. "But I prefer staying the whole night."

"That would be expensive," she warned.

"Are you worth it?"

"I could get testimonials about my field of expertise, but I'm sure anyone with your boundless curiosity would rather find out for himself." She put her coat over her arm and began to walk away.

"All night, Miss Amanda Kirk, or nothing."

Without turning around she called back, "I'll try to arrange it, Mr. Mark Banning, but I can't make any promises."

MARK HAD ALWAYS considered himself a man in total control of his emotions, but knowing he had to wait all day and evening to be with Amanda made him realize his iron will could easily be destroyed by a beautiful redheaded woman.

Despite learning some new facts about Amanda Kirk today and the doubts he'd been feeling about what he was going to do tonight, the anticipation of being with her generated the same panicky yet euphoric feeling he'd had when he first soloed in a jet.

To fill in the hours until he could go to Amanda's room he spent the day with his mother, but she complained that he wasn't paying attention to anything she said. As her partner at bridge, he committed the worst possible sin. He trumped her ace on the last trick when they were vulnerable and their grand slam bid had been doubled and redoubled. After dinner he excused himself and headed for his room.

Once he was alone he forced himself to lie on his bed, waiting until it was time to get ready to go to stateroom 1-A. His mind kept reviewing his plan for how the evening would end, envisioning various scenarios. He couldn't wipe the smile off his face.

At ten he showered and shaved for the second time that day, then stood before the small wall closet, trying to decide what to wear for this kind of occasion. Finally he chose loafers, slacks, an open-collar sport shirt and, because the nights were cold, he carried a camelhair jacket. At twenty-five minutes after ten he slipped his room key into the left pant pocket, Amanda's into the right. He didn't want to fumble with the wrong key at her door. He left the room and walked up one flight of stairs. When he got to her room, he pulled his shoulders back, inhaled deeply and inserted the key. The door noiselessly opened. He entered, expecting to find Amanda. Instead he was totally alone.

A bar had been set up on a side table, complete with champagne in an ice bucket and a large variety of liquor bottles and glasses. Also present were small covered chafing dishes containing hot hors d'oeuvres, plates of pâtés and crackers and a large bowl of fruit. There was enough food for an army... or a large-scale orgy.

"Hello, Mark."

He turned to find her standing just inside the room. He didn't think anything could look better than Amanda in a bathing suit. But she had just proved him wrong. She wore her hair swept away from her face, the curls cascading to her shoulders. Her pastel-orange silk dress teasingly outlined her body. He could think of only one word to describe her—stunning.

"I wasn't sure you'd come," she said softly. Cal had gone to the purser's office to get cash out of the safe, so the time alone with Mark would be limited. Seeing the obvious desire in his eyes, she was glad Cal would be arriving soon.

"I decided I like practice more than theory." Mark set his jacket on a nearby chair. It was difficult to describe the mood he was in—excited at being with Amanda, savoring the anticipation of what was to come, yet cautious. His plan could backfire, or his information could be wrong. "I never shirk any duty in my quest for knowledge."

She laughed, a delightful sound that made him smile. She seemed so different from the first time he'd seen her. Then she'd been coldly indifferent, totally opposite of the impression he was getting now. He kept his gaze focused on her face as she walked toward him.

"It's all arranged. You can stay as long as you want." She passed him and continued toward the table.

Oh, yes, Miss Kirk, I'm sure I can. Mark hid his smile.

"Can I fix you something to eat or drink?"

"Scotch, ice, no water." The scent of her perfume tantalized him to follow.

She poured the liquor into a large ice-filled glass and handed it him. "I want you to know there's still time for you to change your mind. Being entertained by professionals can be expensive."

"Are you worried about my ability to pay?" He spoke in a low, teasing voice.

With an approving glance she carefully looked him up and down, an action that matched the way he'd studied her when she entered the room. She noted his well-cut, expensive clothes. When her gaze returned to his face, she smiled. "You look like you can afford to spend some money." She led him to the small sofa. They sat beside each other.

Mark sipped his drink. "You didn't check to see if I could afford a night with you, did you?"

"Cal did." She'd told her partner to learn everything he could about Mark Banning, especially information about his personal life. Luckily Cal hadn't asked for her reasons, probably assuming she was investigating Banning as one of the men who would be invited to come tonight. "I heard you're partners with your stepfather and stepbrother in a huge privately owned aeronautical company that your father built from scratch."

"You're right, up to a point." Mark wasn't a partner, more like a newly hired employee with the lowest-possible base pay for a man with his education and credentials as a test pilot. All of that was going to be changed and soon.

Amanda smiled. "With that kind of background we don't even have to discuss money until later."

"I'm glad that's not a problem. What else did you learn?" He placed his arm along the back of the sofa.

His fingers were close to her shoulder, but he didn't touch—not yet.

Amanda adjusted a strand of pearls so the ruby and diamond clasp was just above the top of her dress. "You're here with your mother, which I think is commendable of you. Not many men are willing to travel with their mothers."

He suspected she was teasing him, but he didn't care. He'd explain his reasons for being his mother's companion later.

"I guess you got your information the same way I did," he said with a grin.

"Stewards on a ship are mines of information, aren't they? Cal also tapped another helpful source—the passengers. According to his report, all of the women just simply love Connie Quintero's son. You're a good sport and a hell of a lot of fun. They were especially enthusiastic about your pirate costume. I'm sorry I missed it."

"A pirate suits my character perfectly." He set his glass on a nearby end table.

"That's what one woman said. According to her, you're handsome, charming and an expert at all sorts of games." One of Amanda's eyebrows rose, giving her an impish look. "I offered to provide testimonials about my field of expertise. Could that woman provide the same?" She wondered if she was going too far, but she couldn't seem to stop. There wasn't much time left before Cal came in.

Mark shook his head. "I haven't shown my true talents to any of the women on board. I've been waiting to demonstrate what I can do until the right woman came along." He moved closer to Amanda. "I've found the right woman." His voice was husky with passion.

Amanda experienced a sense of panic. She'd been totally aware of the supercharged ambience of sensuality that had been intensifying since Mark had entered the room. Now his mood seemed to have changed—becoming more intense, more sexually focused on her. Everything about his manner proved just how much he wanted her. When he brushed his fingertips across her cheek and down her neck, coming teasingly close to the top of her dress, she gasped at the exquisite shock that transfused her body, a sexual response that left her breathless. Mark's fingers continued their exploratory journey across her shoulders, up to her earlobe, then across her lips. When he did that, her senses took over, making it nearly impossible to think logically. She couldn't look away from Mark's steady gaze.

It was impossible for Mark to tell what she was thinking. Her expression revealed a variety of emotions. When he placed his hand on her waist, he saw a flash of passion, but the next instant she hesitated, drawing back. He moved closer and began to pull her toward him. She came, albeit a little unwillingly. He took her hand and placed it along the side of his neck. Her lips were slightly open, seemingly ready to accept his kiss. His right hand slipped to her back. He pressed her body against his, noting the location of the top of the zipper.

When their lips met, Amanda knew she was letting this get out of hand. After a moment, she pulled back, took a deep breath to steady herself and said, "We've got all night. Let's not rush into anything."

"Are you having doubts?" Mark used his finger to outline the contour of her brow, noting her long, arched lashes.

"No doubts," she murmured, forcing herself not to move away from his intoxicating touch. "I just think anticipation can be an exciting stage." She felt a little safer as long as they were talking.

"The slow buildup?" Mark asked, running his fingers through the ends of her hair. After a moment, he let the fine-textured strands slip through his fingers. Too many sensual signals were hitting his brain at the same time. He had to keep a clear head. "Okay," he said with a sigh, "we'll spend a *few* minutes getting to know each other."

Amanda smiled, feeling relieved. "Yes, I'd like that."

Mark got his drink, sipped a little of the Scotch, then leaned back against the sofa and tried to relax. "You know more about me than I know about you. Where are you from?"

"Born and raised in California. Los Angeles." She didn't want to get too specific. "I know you're from Philadelphia. Tell me about your home." She had learned a long time ago how to adeptly maneuver a conversation away from herself. Few people noticed the change of topics.

"I live in an apartment now, but I grew up in a house that's been in the Banning family since before the Civil War." Mark still resented the idea that the Georgian-style mansion was occupied by his stepfather and stepbrother. After Rob's divorce, he'd moved back in, a fact that added to Mark's sense of frustration. The Quinteros had taken everything he valued, including his mother's affections. When she married Edward Quintero, she'd drifted away from Mark, a state of affairs that he'd only lately been able to change.

"Anything wrong?" Amanda asked.

Mark forced his thoughts to the back of his mind and again focused on Amanda. Her hand lay on the cushion between them. He lifted it and examined her slender fingers. In comparison to his hand hers looked like a child's. He kissed the palm.

"Have—" she cleared her throat "—have you ever been married?" Amanda knew the best way to control Mark's passion, and her own, was to keep him talking about himself. He didn't respond to her question but ran his fingertips up and down her arm. "You aren't carrying out your part of the bargain. We're supposed to be conversing."

"Sorry." He released her hand. "What did you say?"

"Divorced? Widowed? Children?"

"Never been married. No children. I just spent twelve years getting my education. I've become such a dedicated bachelor that I don't know if any woman could adjust to having me around for long."

"Why do you think no woman would have you? You're rich and handsome." She almost added exciting and virile but shut her mouth in time. "Doesn't that make you a perfect candidate for marriage?"

"I'm not very neat," he said ruefully.

Amanda found that hard to believe. He was too meticulous about his appearance to be much of a slob. "Don't tell me you're the kind of man who lets the dishes pile up in the sink and the dirty socks and dust balls gather under the bed. What do you do? Let it get too thick, then hire someone to come in and clean?"

"That's right. I use my apartment as a workplace. Instead of furniture in the living room I have a drafting board and filing cabinets. Hanging from the ceiling are dozens of balsa wood models of airplane prototypes. Engine parts are lying all over. They're impossible to dust. I've had women tell me the place looks more like a factory than a home."

"Have there been many women to see your apartment?" His answer was important to her, much more than it should be.

"A few. Nobody steady. When I'm thinking out a problem, I'm not very attentive." He fell silent, staring at her.

"Are you thinking out a problem now?"

"Yes. But I've solved it." He set his drink on the table, moved closer to her and slipped his arm along the back of the sofa. "I can only be patient for just so long."

"And then what happens?" She wasn't sure she should have asked that question. She quickly added, "Remember what I said about anticipation of pleasure. Take each moment as it comes and enjoy what life offers." *Where was Cal?*

Mark smiled and came closer. It was time to increase the pressure. In one smooth motion he had turned her so that she lay across his lap. One arm supported her head. "Now we can continue to talk." She tried to protest, but he ignored her. "You aren't doing your part. All the information you've offered is that you come from L.A. Are you single?" He wanted to ask about her relationship with Cal Norton, but didn't dare. There would be plenty of time to learn the business arrangements between them.

Amanda forced herself to concentrate on what she was saying and not on the sensations that flooded her mind. "I've never been married." She thought about the past months with Cal. Only then did she realize what an unusual relationship they'd had. To an outsider, it must seem unbelievable that an adult male and female could be in such close company for all that time and not become intimate. She had been the one to set the rules; Cal had unquestioningly accepted them. Perhaps the way he'd stared at her that morning was a signal he wanted to change the relationship. She glanced at the door. If he entered the room right now, she'd have to do a great deal of explaining.

"What's the matter?" Mark said. "You're shivering." When she tried to sit up and move away, Mark tightened his hold.

"I'm all right." How much longer was she going to have to carry out her charade? She had lost control of the situation and didn't know how to extricate herself. She could again see desire in Mark's expression. "Why did you come on this cruise?" she asked, hoping to distract him.

"My mother asked me. She doesn't like to travel alone. My aunt was supposed to come, but she broke her ankle playing golf. I'm a companion by default."

"I see." Amanda didn't know what else to say. She sensed Mark was a much more complex man than he appeared. She let herself relax as she studied his face, wondering what kind of person was behind that affable facade.

For Mark, holding Amanda in his arms was a true test of his self-control. But he was enjoying himself for a number of reasons. "Since I met you, I've wanted to tell you how beautiful you are." He'd spoken in a soft, soothing voice, determined that they should return to the earlier mood. His hand lay on the side of her neck, the fingers buried in her hair.

"Thank you," she said, and dropped her gaze. Her appearance and sense of style in clothes had certainly been a plus in her choice of work. She'd learned more from her clothes-conscious mother than she'd realized....

Mark's kiss jolted her out of her memory. A rush of desire shot through her. This was all wrong. She wasn't supposed to be responding with such passion and pleasure. Her control had quickly vanished, leaving her only with a wish that their time together wouldn't have to end.

"I want to make love to you," Mark said, hoping his words didn't sound like a line from an old movie. He watched as her eyes opened wide, revealing fear and a surprising degree of excitement. He knew she had no idea just how telling her expression was. Knowledge of her vulnerability didn't deter him from his goal. "Let's go to my room."

"No! Uh, that is, not yet." When were Dix and Coleman coming? Why hadn't she heard Cal come back from the purser's office? She tried to control her rising panic. "We've got plenty of time." Her voice quavered.

Mark murmured his assent and continued to kiss her. Moving as carefully as possible, he shifted her weight, freeing one of his hands.

When the unmistakable sound of a zipper being pulled down penetrated her consciousness, her breath caught in her throat. *No! This couldn't be happening.*

She tried to end the kiss while at the same time attempting to reach behind her to see if her dress was open at the back. Because she was lying in Mark's arms, she quickly discovered the planned maneuver was impossible.

"Mark!" At last he'd ended the kiss and she could talk. "What are you do—?" A loud knock interrupted her.

The timing couldn't have been more perfect, Mark thought, as he continued to hold her, wanting to see her panic. After only a moment, though, he knew he had to relent. He released her.

When Amanda was at last standing, she started to reach for the top of her zipper. Her hands and knees were shaking.

For Mark, Amanda's reaction had been even better than he'd hoped. His plan of revenge had worked perfectly. "The zipper's closed," he said with a grin. He stood and smoothed his shirt inside his waistband. "I ran my thumb down the teeth, a trick I learned in high school."

"You . . . you . . ." She couldn't say what she wanted so she clamped her teeth together and straightened her hair.

When the knock came again, Mark asked with a wicked twinkle in his eye, "Aren't you going to let the other poker players come in?"

CHAPTER THREE

WHEN AMANDA HAD at last registered Mark's words, she realized what was going on. Somehow he'd discovered she was a gambler and not a call girl. The sexual advances had just been a big act. A myriad of conflicting emotions flooded her mind, dominated by anger. "You rat," she whispered, just as Cal walked in from his bedroom.

He glanced at Amanda, then nodded an acknowledgment toward Mark. "Sorry I was gone so long. It's taken me all this time to find the purser." He headed for the door that led to the outside passage.

"When did you find out?" Amanda whispered to Mark.

Before he could respond, two heavyset men entered the room. He had seen them the night before. Next came a tall, muscular man with piercing blue eyes. He walked with a limp, as if he had a stone in his shoe.

Caleb Norton introduced himself and the other men to Mark, and they shook hands with each other. He didn't listen to any of their names, his attention still directed at Amanda. She looked composed, but Mark wasn't fooled. She was a good enough actress to hide her feelings, but he could still sense she was infuriated.

As Amanda greeted her guests, the return of reason forced her to accept what Mark had done. Her anger turned into wry amusement. She had tried to teach him not to make assumptions about people, and he'd turned the joke on her. But it just couldn't end there. She wasn't finished with Mark Banning yet.

Dix and Coleman went to the sideboard, poured drinks and began filling their plates with food. Cal joined them and listened as the men talked quietly. Rawlings stayed by the door.

Mark moved closer to Amanda. "Was everything you told me at the pool a lie?" He kept his voice low.

She purposely looked as if she were having difficulty controlling her temper. "I told you the truth. You just put the wrong interpretation on my words."

"What about your father?"

Amanda straightened her shoulders and put one of her hands on her hip. "He taught me everything I know. Ever since I was old enough to count, we played cards." She intended to maintain her facade of indignation as long as she could, wanting him to believe just how upset she was at the dirty trick he'd played on her. "You could have told me you knew what I was up to *before* the big love scene."

"What? And miss out on kissing you and seeing you respond?"

"I wasn't responding." When she saw Cal looking at her, she lowered her voice. "I was acting, just as you were." The sound of her voice was covered by the other men talking.

"What I was doing wasn't an act," Mark whispered. "And don't tell me you didn't enjoy every minute you were in my arms. You might have the world's best poker face when you're playing cards, but I know a passionate response when I see one. When you're aroused, your eyes are very revealing."

"No they're not!" Then she realized what they were arguing about. No longer could she contain her laughter. Mark joined her, making her laugh all the harder. The other men in the room turned to stare, but neither Amanda nor Mark bothered to explain what they found so hilariously funny.

"Do you agree I was right in leading you on?" Amanda asked Mark. With her fingertips she wiped away the tears of laughter that had formed at the corners of her eyes.

"Only if you'll acknowledge that what I did was justified." She nodded her agreement. He held his hand up in a pledge. "Then I swear I'll never make the same mistake again."

"Amanda!" Cal's voice indicated his disapproval of her rowdy behavior.

She turned in his direction. "What?"

"Are you ready for me to bring in the table and chairs?"

She forced herself to be serious. "Yes, please." As long as she didn't look at Mark, she could keep a straight face.

Cal walked into one of the bedrooms. Mark again noticed the man with the cold blue eyes. He still leaned against the closed door, his arms folded across his chest. Since he'd entered the room, he'd steadily watched Amanda, as if he had some kind of claim on her.

Mark turned toward her. "I didn't catch everyone's names."

"Mr. Dix and Mr. Coleman are at the table. Dix has on the loud plaid sport coat." Amanda continued to speak in a low voice. "Mr. Evan Rawlings is by the door." She had noticed how Rawlings had been staring at her and Mark. Obviously the professional gambler didn't like having a new player in the game. Milkovski had been a known element. Banning's abilities would have to be discovered.

Partly to spite Rawlings, Amanda purposely stared at Mark, offering him a warm, intimate smile that excluded everyone else in the room. "Now that we've gotten our little misunderstandings straightened out, are you still interested in participating in an all-night session?"

"I wouldn't miss seeing you in action for anything."

"Do you know how to play poker?"

Robert Quintero's face formed in Mark's mind. More than anyone he had ever known, Rob liked to gamble and had taught his unsuspecting stepbrother every game imaginable. Poker had been Rob's favorite. For months he'd played with Mark, winning all of his allowance until Mark finally became good enough to win more than he lost. By the time he was in college he was able to earn a little extra money gambling with his fraternity brothers.

"It's been a long time," he said, "but I think I can remember a few of the finer points of play." He moved closer, letting his voice drop. "Perhaps later, when you're off work, we could pick up where we left off?" He placed his hand on her back, again running his thumbnail down her zipper.

Amanda's breath caught in her throat. She straightened her spine. Before she could reprimand him, Mark quickly stepped away, looking totally innocent. The way she kept responding to his touch stunned her. It was going to be difficult to play poker against him.

Mark again looked at her. "I'll even wait until after you've had your morning swim."

She shook her head at his offer, regretting that she had to refuse. "Thanks, anyway, but I think I've had enough excitement for one night. Besides, poker's the only game I play."

"I could teach you some new ones. I bet you're a fast learner."

"I think I've heard that line before."

Rawlings pushed away from the door and walked across the small space that separated him from Amanda and Mark. "Where's Milkovski?" he asked gruffly.

"He said he didn't want to play. Mr. Banning will be the fifth player."

Rawlings's response was interrupted by Cal coming back into the room, carrying four dining-room chairs, two in each hand. Next came a wooden semicircle. Amanda, Mark and Rawlings had to move out of the way. With an economy of motion, Cal unfolded the two halves to make a circular table, opened the extension legs and set it on the floor. An insert of green baize covered the top. In front of each player was a well to hold chips. Even though this suite was one of the most spacious on the ship, the room's furniture, the extra tables, five large men and a woman, made the space extremely cramped. It was impossible for two people to move around at the same time. Cal made a return trip to the bedroom and came back carrying the fifth chair, a leather case and about a dozen sealed decks of cards stacked on top. Amanda sat at the table, opened the case and began to count out the chips.

Cal turned to stare at Mark. "House rules, Mr. Banning. Amanda is allowed to play any hand she chooses, and she's the only dealer. Do you have a problem with that?"

Even though the dealership was usually on a rotating basis among the players, Mark had no argument with the arrangement. It gave everyone a better opportunity to concentrate on the cards rather than the deal. "Okay by me," he said.

"We'll be playing for the same stakes as last night," Cal declared to all the men in the room. "Blues are a hundred, reds fifty. Five hundred's the maximum for each bet. Minimum is fifty."

Mark realized he would need more money or he'd be out in one round. Since he had learned what was going to happen earlier that afternoon, he should have gone to the purser's office. He glanced at Amanda, who continued to count out stacks of chips. "Will you accept a check," he asked Cal, "or should I see if I can...?"

"The purser was on his way to bed when I finally found him," Cal said. "A check's okay."

If the Banning financial background hadn't been investigated, Mark doubted he would have been offered that privilege. He sat down at the table and began filling out the check in the amount of five thousand. He purposely used Amanda Kirk's name as the payee.

"Where's a good place to eat in London?" Dix was asking Amanda.

She responded to his question by describing the various ethnic restaurants in the city, but her thoughts remained focused on Mark. She wished she knew why, of all the men she'd met in the past year, Mark Banning should excite her so. Her reaction stunned her, filling her with doubts.

After she finished with the chips, she checked that everyone had what they wanted from the bar, then took her seat at the round card table.

Mark sat next to Amanda. There was no doubt in his mind that she was in command here. He had to admit he was impressed with Kirk and Norton's floating poker game. So far everything had been handled with cool efficiency. When Amanda said she was a professional, she hadn't been exaggerating.

"Would you tell Mr. Banning the rest of the rules?" Cal asked.

Amanda nodded and began to explain about the three percent of each pot that belonged to the house, the schedule of breaks and the time the games would end. Smoking was allowed only out of the room and at break periods. She could take the long hours of sitting at the table, concentrating not only on dealing, analyzing her own hand and trying to outguess the other players, but she couldn't tolerate the smoke.

"There's a hundred-dollar ante." Amanda again spoke directly to Mark. "You can check and raise later, if you want. We only play three types of games—five-card draw and five- and seven-card stud. On a rotating basis each player can choose the game."

She had repeated the instructions so many times that they had become a mantra, a verbal incantation that required no thought. The next stage in the ritual was the opportunity for each player to inspect the deck of cards. This usually was just a formality, but some professional players, men like Rawlings, took it seriously.

After he checked the cards for holes and shaving along the edges, he spoke with his usual economy of words. "First game's draw. Anything to open."

"Fine." Amanda shuffled and allowed Rawlings to cut. With long manicured fingers he divided the deck, then joined the two halves. His nails had been buffed so that they gleamed. On his little finger he wore an ostentatious diamond ring.

Everyone fell silent. After Amanda began to deal, unnecessary conversation wasn't encouraged. In smooth, graceful movements she let the cards fly across the table. They landed exactly in front of each player. No matter how many times she performed these duties, the minute the game started she felt her excitement grow. Part of the thrill was the multifaceted tasks she performed. As dealer and player, she had to make sure the pot was correct at all times, keep track of her own and everyone else's revealed cards and assess their value, determine her opponents' chances of winning, try to read the players' body and facial language for clues about what they were holding. The analytical study of human nature appealed to her. She enjoyed the elation she felt when she won and had learned to accept losing with composure, a lesson carefully taught her, first by her father, then later reinforced by Cal.

She had played often enough with Coleman, Dix and Rawlings to know their strengths and weaknesses. But Mark Banning was the unknown factor, which made tonight's game more interesting. She considered herself a good judge of men. Something about his unassuming, watchful manner told her he would be a skillful player. Whenever their gazes met, he would smile, relaying a message meant only for her. She felt a warm glow radiate throughout her body, a sensual reaction that surprised her.

"That calls for another drink," Coleman declared in a loud voice after winning the first hand.

While they waited for the next round to begin, Rawlings leaned closer to Amanda and asked, "Are you going to stay in London long?"

"Just a few days." She placed the cards so that Dix could cut.

"When you're not working, where's your home?"

From the first moment she'd met Rawlings, she'd decided she didn't like him or his dandy ways. He said he had taken this cruise just for the privilege of playing against the legendary Amanda Kirk. The night before he had told her he had a proposition he wanted to discuss with her. He probably wanted to join the Kirk and Norton partnership. A number of times in the past they had been approached by other gamblers with a similar plan. Most of them had made it clear that part of the deal was Amanda's willingness to offer certain fringe benefits to the new partner. Cal had efficiently dealt with all the opportunists, leaving no doubt in anyone's mind that the partnership wouldn't be altered and that Amanda was off-limits.

Rawlings repeated his question, forcing her to answer. "We don't have a permanent home," she said at last. "We're either working or we go to quiet out-of-the-way places for a vacation." She was aware that Mark's gaze was on her, which made her all the more conscious of what she was saying. "We're going to Lake Tahoe this year." After she said the words, she regretted them. Where they were going was no one's business. Cal was especially secretive about their plans, saying the less people knew, the better. "Or there's a good chance we'll stay in England," she quickly lied.

"Are you two married?" Rawlings asked.

"No." Evan's question couldn't be taken at face value. He also wanted to know if she and Cal were lovers. Their arrangement was purely business and had been from the first time they'd met. She glanced over at him. He winked, his signal that she was doing fine.

Amanda picked up the cards. "The game is starting," she said, cutting off any more conversation. She forced her mind away from Cal and Rawlings and his probing questions and again divided her attention between the cards and her study of Mark. Now that she could compare the two men she saw that he outclassed Evan on all counts. At the pool, when she saw Mark in his swimming trunks, she had learned he was built like an athlete, yet with a sinewy slenderness that appealed to her more than Evan's overdeveloped muscles. Mark's hair was dark brown, worn a little long at the neck and had a slight wave. Above perfectly sculpted cheekbones his blue eyes were full of contrasts, one minute contemplative, the next amused at some private thought. His face was saved from being beautiful by a slightly crooked nose, undoubtedly broken a long time ago. It added a nice touch to his interesting face.

Rawlings won the hand. As Amanda dealt, she relied on her training to carry her through her duties. Out of the next six rounds Mark won four, a phenomenal accomplishment considering his opponents. He played a masterful yet cautious game, seeming to know instinctively when to be aggressive and when to fold. He presented a challenge both to her and to Rawlings, whose frowning countenance proved how much he disliked losing. He seemed especially resentful whenever Mark won.

"We'll play seven-card stud," Amanda announced when the center of the table had been cleared of chips. "Mr. Dix, would you cut?" The formality of addressing the players by their surnames had always amused her, but she could see the logic behind it. Everyone involved in the business of poker was an adversary.

The rolling motion of the ship seemed to have become more pronounced. The lights formed flickering shadows on the table, making it difficult for Amanda to focus. She dealt the first three cards, two down and one up. When she saw she had little possibility of winning the hand, she declared, "Dealer's out."

Except for distributing the cards to the other players after every bet and making sure the pot was correct, she was free to analyze what was happening around the table. The atmosphere seemed much more tense than on the other nights she had played with these men. Coleman and Dix were quieter, concentrating more on playing than on drinking and eating. They were under a great deal of pressure, knowing they were up against three excellent gamblers. Rawlings, too, was much more intense, acting even more resentful whenever Mark won. Perhaps Evan didn't like the competition, either in the game or for her attention. The thought amused her. He had no reason for jealousy. Once they landed she would never see either man again.

As she continued dealing, she became conscious of the strange and powerful effect Mark was having on her emotions. Since he had arrived at her room, her physical awareness of him had intensified, a fact which disturbed and mystified her. The memory of his kisses continued to remain vivid in her mind. Her usual indifference toward members of the opposite sex, especially her opponents at the poker table, seemed to have disappeared. Always before, she'd made it a point never to learn anything about the players' personal lives or to become interested in them as individuals. After the games, she quickly forgot their names and faces.

During the year she'd been a professional gambler, she'd categorized men into certain types. Some of them were like Coleman and Dix, amateurs who didn't mind losing money for the privilege of being involved in what they considered an ultramasculine sport, made all the more exciting and challenging when played against a woman. Other types were men like Evan Rawlings, the smooth-talking, intelligent professionals who gambled on the poker circuit, just as she and Cal did.

But Mark Banning didn't fit in either category. Perhaps that was why her emotions were in such turmoil. Feeling any kind of attraction toward him was totally out of character. Instead of being interested in him as an attractive man, she should feel as neutral as she felt toward Dix or Coleman.

"Looks like you win again, Banning," Coleman said.

Amanda snapped to attention. She had been operating on automatic pilot, not really watching the game. After she extracted the house's cut of the pot and Mark collected his winnings, she began gathering the cards.

Rawlings's harsh voice interrupted her task. "I want a new deck," he demanded brusquely.

"You've played twenty games, Amanda," Cal said from across the room.

She was surprised the time had passed so quickly. "Let's take a fifteen-minute break," she said. "When we start again, we'll open a new deck."

All of the men stood and stretched. Mark quickly came behind Amanda's chair and held it so that she could stand. Rawlings started to approach her, but Mark grabbed his jacket and placed it over her shoulders, all the time maneuvering her toward the door.

When she realized what he intended on doing, she said, "Wait!"

"What's the matter?"

"I'm sorry, Mr. Banning," Cal said, "but the dealer can't leave the room with you. You can go outside together if you want, as long as you stay within hearing distance of other players."

Mark frowned, then the reason occurred to him. Collusion between himself and Amanda or among any of the players was always a possibility. He looked at Amanda. "Sorry," he said in a low tone.

"You couldn't have known," she said, slipping out of his jacket and handing it to him. "But you go ahead. The cool air will do you good."

"You mean like taking a cold shower?"

"Well, something like that."

Dix and Coleman walked past him, going through the door to stand near the railing. Rawlings hesitated, started to speak to Amanda, then went to stand with the others. All three lit cigarettes. Cal joined them. Mark and Amanda didn't move from the doorway.

The cool, salty air blew on her face. She inhaled deeply, savoring the scent. The light from the full moon on the water looked like a pathway of shimmering silver rocks, ready to be walked upon.

Mark ignored the view and leaned his back against the edge of the door. He studied Amanda's face in the bright moonlight. For a long time he didn't say anything, waiting until the men had started to talk. All four were slightly bent forward, leaning their arms against the railing, staring out across the water.

"I'm not making a moral judgment, but I always thought private gambling was illegal." Because the men were only a few feet away, Mark didn't speak in a normal tone of voice, but he also didn't whisper. If any of them tried, they could hear what he was saying. The last thing he wanted was to cause Amanda any problems.

"We're not doing anything illegal," Amanda said. She wasn't surprised by his question. Many people had misconceptions about games of chance for profit. "Gambling's illegal only in some places of the world. It just depends on where the games are played. Cal and I have always gambled where it's legal, or on private islands in international waters or ships that aren't owned by any citizen of the United States. We've kept our operations small, playing with men like Coleman and Dix, who enjoy gambling, especially against a woman, and who can afford to lose. Even their losing becomes a point of pride to be discussed among their cronies at the country club. It proves their financial status, like owning the most expensive house and cars in their hometowns." Amanda placed her back on the side of the door and tried to ease the tightness of her muscles. She turned to Mark. "For someone who hasn't played in a long time, you've done very well tonight."

"When I accepted your key, I was praying I was wrong about the poker game and that we'd be playing a different kind of game."

Amanda shrugged. "Just proves you can't win 'em all," she said, controlling her laughter. "When did you start not believing my sob story?"

"Oh, I don't know exactly. I had my doubts when you mentioned how your father taught you the tricks of the trade. Then I convinced myself you were telling the truth. Giving me the key really did it. I didn't think you'd carry a joke that far."

"I just couldn't resist. It was too much fun watching you accept everything I said."

The men's voices rose. They seemed to have forgotten Amanda and Mark behind them.

"You could have played fair and let me know," Mark said. "It wasn't until late afternoon that I learned your secret."

"How did you find out?" Seeing Mark's smug smile, she thought for a moment that he wouldn't tell her. Finally he spoke.

"As you said, ship stewards are mines of information."

"Cost you much?"

"Seventy-five," he said with a shrug, "and a few hours of time. Then I had to wait around all day, as jumpy as a . . . a, well, I don't know what."

"Your story really breaks my heart," Amanda said, again remembering how clever she'd felt when she was at the pool, knowing she'd pulled a fast one on him. But her own doubts had built until she'd regretted her actions. "You might as well know. My conscience did bother me. I didn't get much sleep all day."

The sound of laughter caused her to turn. Dix was now talking in a low tone, obviously telling an off-color joke, using an Irish brogue. Rawlings looked back at her and Mark for a long moment. When he seemed satisfied that nothing was going on between them, he resumed his position.

Amanda looked again at Mark. He was staring intently at her.

Stepping closer, he said, "You owe me. Someday I intend on collecting."

"I owe you?" she asked incredulously. "You're the one who made the first mistake."

"We won't argue the point now. Just remember, I always collect what's due me."

She could tell he wasn't joking. "Think of the money you're earning," she teased. "Your mother would be proud to know her son wasn't just frittering away his time having a good time. You've been engaged in a worthwhile activity that expands your mind and wallet."

Mark smiled and leaned back, wanting to put distance between them in case Rawlings or Cal turned around. When he spoke, he barely moved his lips. "Make some excuse—a headache or something—and end the game."

A shiver coursed down Amanda's spine. "I can't do that." Her voice sounded breathlessly excited.

"Why not?" He wanted to take her hand and get her away from the other men. When she didn't answer, he said, "Even if we went to my room, nothing would happen unless you wanted it to. Or we could find a quiet corner and have a drink."

"I have to finish the game. It's my job."

"After the game?" Mark urged.

She almost agreed to meet him, but then she remembered the Kirk and Norton partnership's ironclad rule:

no entanglements of any kind and most definitely not with a man who was a participant in one of their high-stakes poker games. Besides, no matter what her confused emotional and physical states were, she could do nothing that might hurt Cal.

"Shall we start again?" Cal asked as he turned in her direction.

"Has your headache gotten any worse?" Mark asked so that everyone could hear him. He knew she'd understand.

"No, I feel better, thanks." She smiled. "The fresh air helped. And I'm not the least bit thirsty," she added in a low tone. "I'm all ready to play," she said to Cal and the other men as they entered the room.

"Your enthusiasm seems a little forced," Mark muttered under his breath as he shut the door.

CHAPTER FOUR

EVERYONE AGAIN SAT at the table, resuming their original positions. Amanda was positive she looked composed, but just to be sure she kept her gaze averted from Cal, knowing how astute he was about her. She didn't want him to see the turmoil in her mind caused by being in Mark's company

She offered Rawlings a number of decks of cards. When the inspected deck was returned to her and everyone had anted, she said, "It's your choice, Mr. Rawlings."

"Draw."

She began to deal, letting her thoughts return to the excitement she'd felt since Mark's arrival in the room. He'd made it clear he considered her a desirable woman. But as much as she liked him, after they reached England in the morning she would disappear without saying goodbye. That way was so much less complicated.

Even though she'd never see Mark Banning again, she would remember him. Their meeting had made this voyage the most memorable trip she'd ever taken.

During the gambling junkets or when she and Cal were taking rest periods, he'd served as her protector, making sure the men clearly understood that she was a player in only one kind of game. Her bodyguard had done his job so well that the only males she met were adversaries in a game of cards.

She knew she was missing some of the joys of youth, particularly the elation of being courted and made love to by a man as sensually exciting as . . . as Mark Banning.

"Amanda!" Cal bent down beside Dix and picked up a card that had fallen to the floor.

"Sorry," she said. Cards were to remain on the table at all times. "New deck?" she asked the players.

"No," Rawlings said. "But in case you've forgotten, we're playing draw, not stud."

Amanda saw she had dealt part of the second round faceup. She nodded, gathered the cards, shuffled and began to deal, reminding herself she had better start concentrating. Playing high-stakes poker was no time to be thinking about having a man make love to her. Draw, which seemed to be Rawlings's favorite, was a difficult game to play and win. She preferred stud, where there was the advantage of being able to see some of the players' cards.

Rawlings won only a small pot. As soon as he had collected his winnings, he arranged two equal stacks of chips next to each other, then, using his index finger, he shuffled them together to form one stack. Over and over again he performed the trick, acting as if his mind wasn't aware of what his hand was doing.

Amanda was amazed at how quickly the tension was building again. Knowing she had to do something to lighten the mood, she decided to break her own rule about conversing with the players. "Mr. Dix?" She began to shuffle the deck. "Didn't you say you're from

Cherry Hills, New Jersey? Mr. Banning lives right across the river—Philadelphia.''

Before Dix could respond, Rawlings said, "Banning? Philadelphia?'' He had stopped playing with the stacks of chips; his eyes were bright with interest. "Orion Aeronautical, founded by Russell Banning?''

Mark frowned, surprised that Rawlings had made the connection. "Yes. How do you know?''

"You have a relative named Quintero?''

"A stepfather, Edward, and his son, Robert. Do you know them?''

Like a referee at a tennis match, Amanda watched the interchange between Rawlings on her left and Mark on her right.

Rawlings held his glass up and signaled to Caleb that he wanted a refill. Since the break he had been drinking vodka but showed no signs of being drunk. "I met Robert once. A couple of years ago after one of the Triple Crown races—Belmont, I think. I played poker with him. He's good, but that night he dropped about twenty-five grand in a game that lasted twelve straight hours. I made myself quite a bundle.''

Mark felt as if he'd been hit. He knew Robert liked to gamble but had no idea he had moved up to the big leagues. Mark wondered if Rob could be gambling and perhaps losing on a regular basis. That might explain his odd behavior and Mark's nagging thoughts that something wasn't right at Orion. "What else do you know about Rob?'' he asked quietly.

Rawlings didn't say anything for a moment. It was so quiet in the room that Amanda could feel and hear the vibration of the ship's engines. She tried to remember if she'd ever played with Robert Quintero. She was sure

she hadn't. It was a name she probably would have remembered.

"He's got quite a reputation at the racetracks,"
Rawlings said as he accepted the drink Caleb handed
him. "Likes to put on fancy spreads at reserved boxes.
That time in Belmont he had a real knockout of a
woman with him." He stared at Mark. "Hope I haven't
said too much, seeing as how he's married. Wouldn't
want to cause any trouble."

Mark thought Rawlings's disclaimer sounded false.
He seemed to be thoroughly enjoying himself. "You
haven't caused any trouble." Mark kept his voice
steady. "He's divorced now." His philandering had
been the cause. After seeing Rob's unhappy marriage
and how ill-suited Edward and Connie were, Mark had
frequently wondered if wedlock was for him.

He realized everyone was waiting for him to speak.
He forced a good-natured laugh. "I knew Rob gambled. He taught me how to play poker."

Coleman cleared his throat. "Speaking as one of the
two losers tonight, I wish he'd taught me. Both Dix and
I could use a few lessons."

Everyone except Mark and Rawlings responded with
a relaxing smile. Amanda silently thanked Coleman for
his well-timed speech.

"It's my turn to name the game," Dix said. "I sure
as hell haven't done anything with draw. Let's try seven-
card stud."

A cold breeze suddenly blew through the porthole.
Amanda turned to Cal. "Would you close that,
please?" She glanced around the table. "Anyone else
need something before we start?"

"Bring a plate of the pâté," Dix called out. His gaze returned to Amanda. "Been meanin' to say that you and Norton put on a mighty fine spread. Yes, mighty fine." His smile told her more than his words. "You must have an in with the chef. The dining-room food's good, but I haven't had anything to equal that pâté."

"We made arrangements ahead of time," Amanda said.

Dix looked around the large stateroom. "I tried to book this suite for me and my wife. Doris was sure disappointed." His gaze shifted to Amanda. He scanned the tight-fitting bodice of her silk gown, which showed just a teasing glimpse of décolletage.

Amanda hated the way Dix and Coleman and even Rawlings ogled her. She didn't mind having Mark look at her, a fact that surprised and puzzled her. But part of her job was enduring a man's stare. When she and Cal started their partnership, she had objected to wearing the gowns. Cal had pointed out that the way she looked was as important as her skill at poker. Her beauty served as a distraction for the other players, creating an advantage for her. Her clothes, face and body were part of the entertainment. She was no different from the singers and dancers who put on the musical revue in the ship's dining room.

Amanda began to deal the next hand, forcing herself to again concentrate on the interaction of personalities, the cards and winning and losing. They took two more breaks, but no one left the room. At four, Caleb said, "Time's up. No more deals."

Amanda sighed and set the cards down, then focused her attention on Mark. Standing in neat rows in front of him were stacks of chips—mostly blue ones.

During the last game, Rawlings had had to buy more from the bank. He had lost a great deal of money. Even Dix and Coleman had recouped some of their losses at Rawlings's expense. Amanda calculated she hadn't done too badly, either.

Rawlings turned his cold gaze on Mark. "My compliments to a semipro." His laughter sounded rather forced. "It's not often I lose or even get bluffed out. You learned Quintero's lessons well."

"Thank you, Mr. Rawlings."

Amanda released the breath she hadn't realized she'd been holding. Through the portholes she saw that the sky was milky gray, signaling the coming of dawn. She thought of being in the pool. Only this time she doubted she'd be alone.

But before she could leave she had to finish her work. Coleman, Dix and Rawlings stood and stretched. Everyone looked fatigued. Aware that Mark was watching her, she began to count the chips in the middle of the table, calculated the house's three percent and subtracted it from the pot. After Cal checked the count and moved away, she pushed Mark's chips over to him. He reached out and rested his hands on hers.

"Swim?" He asked so quietly that only she heard.

She hesitated, glanced over at Cal, who had his back turned, and said, "I'll meet you there." She stood and walked toward her bedroom. "Mr. Norton's in charge of settling the debts and paying the winners." With her hand on the door she bid them all a good-night.

"Amanda?"

She stopped and turned as Rawlings walked toward her. "Look, I'm very tired," she said, not wanting to hear what he had to say. She opened the door and stepped just over the threshold. He came closer.

"I'm sure you are, but I'll only keep you a minute." Behind him the men were settling their debts or collecting cash for chips, gathering their belongings, pleasantly discussing the various hands. The sound of the men's voices covered Rawlings's words.

"I wanted to tell you what Cal and I have worked out for our meeting tomorrow. I wired ahead and got a reservation for a suite at the Berkeley, where you're staying. The ship docks at seven, and it's supposed to be on time. Cal insisted on taking the boat train to London rather than drive with me. But he's agreed to meet me in my hotel room at four."

She wished she hadn't told Cal to agree to meet Rawlings. "What was it you wanted to talk about?"

"I'd like to join your business operation. I've got a plan that'll—"

"Mr. Rawlings, Cal and I don't need anyone else in the partnership, so I can't see any reason for us to meet."

Rawlings took her arm. "I'd at least like a chance to lay out my plan. When you hear it, you'll change your mind."

She extracted her arm from his grasp. Over his shoulder she could see into the sitting room. Cal had his back turned, but Mark was studying her and Evan. She hoped he wouldn't come over.

"Okay," she said unwillingly, "we'll listen, but no promises."

"I'd like to talk to you alone."

She shook her head. "Caleb's the business manager of this partnership. He's present at all meetings. We'll

see you at four at the Berkeley. Now, good night."
Again she tried to move toward the door.

"Wait. I lost tonight, but I won the other nights. It's
customary for the winner to tip the dealer. Please accept this."

She tried to step back, shaking her head. "No." He
reached for her hand, opened her fingers, laid a stack
of folded bills on the palm and then closed her hand
around the money. His action so surprised her that she
couldn't think of anything to say. Because she was a
representative of the house who took a percentage of the
pots and a participant in every hand, tipping her was
way out of line. Not only that, it was demeaning, even
insulting, in a subtle way she couldn't quite explain. His
gesture could only be an attempt to curry favor with her.

"I can't take the money." She tried to remove her
hand from his. "Tipping isn't—"

"The money is because I enjoyed the time I spent
with you. Just watching you was a pleasure." He released her hand, strode across the room and joined
Caleb to settle his losses.

Amanda quickly disappeared into her room, shut the
door, kicked off her high heels and threw the bills onto
the bed without looking at them. The money he'd given
her was a self-serving, grandstand gesture. Evan Rawlings could go to hell, she thought. Reaching behind her,
she yanked down the zipper, tearing the silk dress.
"Damn." She yelled the word so loud that she feared
she'd been overheard. But the subdued tones of the
men's voices next door continued without pause.

She let the gown slip down and land in a heap around
her feet. The digital clock on the nightstand clicked as
the numbers changed to four-thirty. Wearing her lace

teddy, she lay on her bed to calm down and to wait until all of the men had left. Her thoughts were a kaleidoscope of images. Mark's face was the most prominent. She was confused about how she felt toward him. The little time they'd spent together didn't justify the strong impact he had made on her.

Why did she feel such a throbbing ache deep inside her whenever she thought about Mark? No man had ever elicited such a response. Was she setting herself up to be hurt? Was she so vulnerable, so susceptible to a charming man's attention that she could forget Cal and everything he'd done for her? Was she experiencing a temporary aberration that would end as soon as the ship docked in Southampton?

None of those possibilities made any difference. She had to go to that pool.

When she heard the final good-night, she slipped on her swimsuit and short lace coat, grabbed her towel and the money off her bed and returned to the sitting room.

Caleb was gathering the dirty glasses, getting ready to move the poker table out of the crowded room.

"Here," Amanda said, "Diamond Jim gave me a tip. Include it in the take." She headed for the door. "I was right. He's going to propose joining us. I'm sure he believes that only with his help can we hit the big time. I guess he thinks we've been on the penny-ante circuit."

As she talked, Cal counted out the bills Rawlings had given her. "There's an even thousand here. You earned every penny. I'll put it in your room."

"Rawlings is a showboater."

"But a damn good poker player." Cal began putting the chips in the wooden box. "Don't let him get to you. We'll tell him we're not interested in his deal, and that'll be the end of it." He turned to look at her. "Have a good swim. I'll wait up for you."

"Thanks." She turned to leave.

"Don't make any commitments to Banning." Cal spoke in his usual quiet tone, his expression totally blank, as if he were discussing nothing more important than the weather. But she knew he was deadly serious.

"What do you mean?"

He took a moment longer to study her, then said, "About meeting him in London."

So he'd guessed she liked Mark. But she shouldn't have been surprised. Her partner was highly intuitive, especially where she was concerned. Sometimes he knew what she was thinking even before the thoughts had formed in her mind. And there was no denying he was right. She couldn't possibly let her feelings for Mark develop into anything deeper. She swallowed to ease the dryness in her throat. "Rule number one," she said, speaking like a child reciting lessons. "Contacts of any kind with the players are strictly forbidden." She opened the door, then looked back at Cal. He had turned his face so that she could no longer see his expression.

"We're leaving for Tahoe Tuesday night," he said.

That was three days from now. She had thought they were staying a week in Britain before moving on. "I'll be ready," she said quietly, and shut the door.

As she hurried down the corridor, she realized just how much Cal controlled her life. Since the beginning of their relationship, she'd let him make all the business and travel arrangements, had listened to his advice, had learned every lesson he could teach. She rarely made a decision on her own. Now that she thought about it, she realized she'd slipped into a submissive role she wasn't sure she liked. Meeting Mark Banning might be the catalyst she needed to change her life.

She began to run down the passageway, heading for the pool.

Mark was there, standing by a table. Amanda's feelings of joy were an unexpected, pleasant shock. Without Cal's warning she knew she would have agreed to do whatever Mark asked. Now all they had were a few hours before she had to go to her room to pack and get ready to leave the ship. So little time.

"Hi," he said softly, taking her towel and coat and setting them on the chair. Turning back, he reached for her hand and led her to the side of the pool. "For the past two days I've been thinking about being alone with you."

The sun again slanted through the windows, filling their world with a golden light, warming their skin. As if on a signal, they dived into the water, swam submerged, then surfaced, both laughing with sheer pleasure. They began to swim side by side, back and forth, until by unspoken agreement they stopped at the deep end of the pool. Clinging to the rim, they paused to catch their breath.

Amanda used the time to study Mark's face, seeing in his eyes a message of desire. She felt her own excitement heighten. How easy it would be to let him take her to his room....

Don't think about it. Just enjoy the moment, because it can't last.

"I'm glad you won," she said, turning to lean her back against the tiles of the pool. The water caressed her skin, an intensely sensual stimulus that didn't help her to control her thoughts. "Rawlings needed to have his ego deflated."

Mark's smile lit his eyes. When she remembered the hours she'd spent sitting at the poker table, the one image that was most vivid in her mind was his face and the way he would look at her, relaying an intimate message.

"Rawlings was concentrating more on you than the cards." Mark's gaze never left hers. "I had the same problem." With the lightest of touches he ran his fingers up her arm, stopped at her shoulder, then returned to the underside of her wrist.

A shiver coursed down her spine. She again tried to focus her mind on matters other than her physical awareness, but she was totally unsuccessful. Everything was happening too fast. "Mark, I think—"

"Don't think." He lowered his hand to her waist and drew her closer. But with a strength of will she didn't know she had, she tensed her muscles, slightly arching her back, trying to pull away.

"Just let it happen," he whispered, increasing the pressure to counteract her resistance.

"I can't let anything happen between—"

His kiss was meant to make her forget her denial and to force her to concentrate only on the passion he knew she was feeling. When he lifted his mouth from hers, his lips wandered down to the side of her neck. "Come to my room . . . please."

Amanda desperately wanted to go with him. She started to say yes, then remembered Cal and his words of warning. He must have suspected how vulnerable she was, how lonely she'd been. But then Cal had never allowed himself the pleasure of another woman's company. They had both made sacrifices—all for the good of the partnership.

"Amanda?"

"Mark, I can't go to your room."

He didn't release her, just leaned his head back to see her face. "Why?"

She was having difficulty making her mind function. Being in his arms, feeling his sinewy strength, having her naked skin touch his, conspired to undermine her power to resist him.

"You said you and Norton aren't married," Mark said. "Did you mean not legally married or not in any way?"

It would be so easy to lie and say she and Cal were lovers. But Mark deserved to know the truth. And beyond that there was an even more important reason for not lying to Mark. Years from now, when he thought about this cruise, she wanted him to smile with pleasure at the memory of the woman named Amanda Kirk and the short time they'd spent together.

She turned to look into Mark's eyes. "Right now my relationship with Cal is purely business. He's been my teacher and manager. When I needed a job, he worked with me until I learned my craft." She could have said that it was Cal who had created Amanda Kirk. He had shown her how to get a new birth certificate, the first step in assuming a different identity. He had never asked questions about her past. He didn't even know her real name. In return she'd never inquired about his former life, although she'd often wondered. The day they met became the first day of their lives. "Cal is more than my friend," she said.

"You realize he's in love with you, don't you?"

Amanda hesitated, then said, "Yes, I know."

Mark stared intently at her. "But you don't love him."

She almost denied his statement but then realized she did love Cal—in a complicated way she wasn't sure she could define. But she also had to admit that never once with Cal had she experienced the indefinable spark, the burning heat of passion that she'd always thought were preludes to deeper feelings between a man and a woman. Strange as it seemed, she'd felt that rush of excitement, a supercharged jolt of desire, when she first saw Mark, but she'd dismissed her unsettling feelings, blaming them on the strange mood she'd been in. Being with Mark these past hours had confirmed the validity of her first reaction.

"Am I right?" Mark asked. "You're not in love with him, are you?"

"I don't know how I feel about Cal. He's a wonderful man."

Mark tightened his hold on her, pulling her even closer. "Then there's nothing to keep you—"

Amanda placed her fingertips on his lips. "Please don't make this any more difficult than it already is."

"You have to admit there's a mutual attraction." He again kissed her, a long, leisurely kiss that left them both breathless. He wrapped one leg around hers, pulling her even closer. Her uncontrollable responses proved the point he was making.

"Tell me you didn't feel what I did."

She waited until her heart stopped pounding before she said, "You know I can't do that."

"We're both consenting adults."

"Mark, please."

"We just can't leave it like this. Meet me in London. We'll use the time to get to know each other... nothing more." .

Damn the rules, Amanda thought. After they arrived in London, she had until four in the afternoon before she had to meet Cal and Evan. What harm would there be if she and Mark explored the city together for just a few hours?

Once she and Cal got to Tahoe they could talk about the future of their partnership and their personal lives. She could ask Cal for some time alone to think about what she wanted to do. She had some decisions to make—whether to face her parents and again become part of the Ross family or to spend the rest of her life as Amanda Kirk and stay with Cal, either keeping the status quo or changing their relationship.

"Amanda?" Mark said softly, releasing his tight hold on her. He stared down into her face, trying to read her thoughts. "You agreed to come here with me. You let me kiss you, and you sure as hell responded. Why are you hesitating when all I want is to spend some time with you? Are you so much under Cal's control that you can't make a decision on your own?" When she didn't respond, he continued. "I want a chance to get to know you better. It's a date, for God's sake, not a lifetime commitment."

Amanda reached over and grasped the tiled edge of the pool. Slipping from his arms, she pulled herself out of the water.

Her actions were so swift that Mark didn't realize what had happened until he saw her lifting her coat and towel from the chair. He joined her at the table.

Without giving him a chance to speak, she said, "If you're willing to accept only what I'm prepared to give, meet me at Sotheby's, 34 Bond Street, at noon."

And then she was gone.

CHAPTER FIVE

As THE HOTEL PORTER put Amanda's cases on the racks and opened the drapes, she glanced at the small brass clock sitting on the bedside table. It was nearly ten-thirty, which didn't give her much time to pack, exchange traveler's checks for pound notes, call and reserve the only two rooms at the Black Swan Inn, place her picnic order with room service, rent a car and get from the Berkeley on Wilton Place to Sotheby's. Picking the auction house as a meeting point was a spontaneous decision. She'd used it because Sotheby's was the only address she'd been able to remember from the days when she came to London looking for antiques. In her rush to leave Mark she hadn't given him a chance to argue or even to ask what her terms were. She wasn't even sure he'd be there.

After making the rash commitment to meet Mark in London, she rationalized her actions by concluding that she deserved a chance to explore her feelings for this man. But to do that she needed more time than just an afternoon tour of the city. She didn't bother examining all of her motivations. She just knew she wanted to get away from Cal and Evan and to be with Mark. As Mark had said, they would use this time to get to know each other better. Beyond that she refused to conjecture what her true reasons were.

But she'd worried about how to tell Cal she wanted to escape for a few days. On the train coming from Southampton he'd made everything easy by asking what she thought about canceling the appointment with Rawlings. She'd readily agreed. Then he'd suggested she take their layover time and go to Oxford or even on up to the Cotswolds, her favorite place in England. They both needed some time to unwind. Without thinking, she'd asked his reasons. His comment again had proved how attuned he was to her moods. He'd said for the past few days she'd seemed especially tense, which hadn't improved her poker playing. She could have a rest while he stayed in London to contact some gamblers with the idea of organizing a game sometime in the future.

In thinking back on their conversation, Amanda decided that Cal must not have suspected she was meeting Mark. If he'd had any doubts she would break her word, he would never have suggested she go off on her own. She felt a little disloyal, but also independent—the same feeling she'd experienced when she ignored her parents' warnings about the failure rate of small businesses and had opened her antique shop. Right from the beginning the shop had made money, which proved to them and to herself that she could accomplish what she set out to do.

"Do you need anything else?" the porter asked as he reentered the sitting room.

"No, everything's fine." Amanda tipped him, closed the door and began to pack a small overnight case. Everything was working out in her favor, including a way to get even with Evan Rawlings for being such a show-off. During the poker game, she'd sensed a rivalry between him and Mark. Rawlings had not only resented losing to Mark but had also disliked the way the amateur poker player and the lady gambler had been so interested in each other. It made a nice, ironic twist that Evan Rawlings's thousand-dollar tip would help finance her trip.

Within thirty minutes she was ready. Just as she was about to leave the room, she remembered that Mark had no idea she intended on getting out of London. Perhaps he and his mother had made plans for this evening or tomorrow. Amanda shrugged. If he couldn't join her on an excursion into the English countryside, she'd go alone. No. Mark Banning would find a way— he just had to.

FROM HIS BEDROOM WINDOW Cal watched Amanda as she climbed into the rental car and drove off. Even from that distance he could tell how happy she was. Was she meeting Mark Banning? *"No!"* His shouted answer startled him, making him wonder why he had reacted so strongly. Was he trying to convince himself? During all the time they had spent together, Amanda had never once deceived him. He was almost positive she wouldn't this time. The element of doubt bothered him, but he couldn't rationalize it away.

He studied the sky, noting the gloomy overcast. He hoped the rain would hold off until she got to an inn. But it wouldn't make any difference to Amanda. She loved the rain and would spend hours out in a storm, either driving or walking.

The next two days were going to be a hell of loneliness, reminding him of the dark months before he'd met her. But he'd had to let her go off on her own. Since they'd started on this last gambling circuit, she'd been under a great deal of pressure. Never once had she complained. Sometimes he felt he'd been totally unfair to that scared and lost young woman he'd found in Tahoe. For her own good he probably should have asked her to reveal her past and encouraged her to return home. Instead of helping her solve her problems, he'd selfishly shown her how to establish a new identity, taught her the skills necessary to be a great poker player, then continued to use her unique talents for his own benefit.

If she ever left him, he wasn't sure what he'd do. By falling in love with her, he'd broken his own rule. But he'd been powerless to control his emotions. He'd been patient, giving her as much time as she needed. During the past month, he'd thought maybe her feelings for him were changing. Or was he deluding himself? Was he seeing what he wanted to see? No. He'd been sure their relationship was deepening.

And then, on the last night of the cruise, she'd met Mark Banning. For the first time she'd taken an interest in one of the gamblers.

Even if she did like Mark, even if she was meeting him right now, Cal vowed he'd pursue her. He couldn't lose Amanda—not ever.

He sighed and turned around, heading across the bedroom to start unpacking. He effortlessly lifted his huge, heavy suitcase onto the bed, but just as he started to unzip the leather case, he was interrupted by a knock. Hoping it was Amanda, he rushed out of the bedroom, across the sitting room and opened the door. Evan Rawlings stood there, holding a silver ice bucket, three glasses and a bottle of vodka.

"I got your message canceling our meeting," Rawlings said, heading past Cal into the sitting room. "I don't like to have promises broken."

Rawlings's limp seemed worse. Cal realized his left knee was the cause. Leaving the door partially open, Cal walked farther into the room. "There weren't any promises made." His deep, rumbling voice filled the room. He neither liked nor trusted Rawlings. Sensing the man's foul mood, Cal was glad Amanda was safely out of London. "I told you before that we don't want or need a new partner. So there's nothing to talk about. Now get out of here."

Rawlings set the bucket and glasses down on a low table in front of the sofa, then opened the bottle. After silently fixing himself a drink, he turned toward Cal. "I tried to find Amanda. She's not in her room. Where's she gone?"

"I don't know." And even if he did know, he wouldn't tell Rawlings.

Rawlings continued to stand by the table, clenching his glass tightly in his hand. "Look, I don't like being jerked around. Is she still in London?"

Rawlings's voice had been low, his manner controlled, but Cal knew just how angry he was. "No. She's gone away for a couple of days."

"Alone?"

"That's her business."

"Damn it, Norton, I wanted her here. When's she coming back? Or has she left you?" His tone was snide.

Cal didn't bother to comment but began to head toward the door. Just as he reached for the handle, Rawlings spoke. "I know who you are."

Cal turned to face him. "Just what the hell does that mean? Of course you know who—"

"Sit down, *William Bainbridge,* and I'll tell you your life story."

William Bainbridge! Cal's vision blurred. What he'd long feared had happened. Rawlings knew his secret. But how? And why had he gone to so much trouble to learn the truth? Blackmail was the only answer. Cal squared his shoulders, determined not to give Rawlings any kind of edge. He closed the door and slowly walked across the room. Both men sat down, facing each other. "You've made a mistake," Cal said in a steady voice. "I've never even heard of anyone called Bainbridge."

"Your memory's slipped, then." As if in pain, Rawlings rubbed his knee. "But I'll be glad to help you remember."

Cal said nothing, just gripped the arms of his chair. If Rawlings knew his real name, then his whole past had been revealed.

"You know," Rawlings said, "in the U.S. today it's damn easy for somebody to get a fictitious name. I make it an ironclad rule to always check out everybody I plan on going into business with." He acted as if he were proud of his suspicious nature. "I called every state's vital statistics department until I found a child named Caleb Norton, born thirty-one years ago in a little town called Lillie, Idaho. According to the state of Idaho and the United States government, *you* are Caleb Norton, with all the rights and privileges thereof, including a valid passport. But I still wasn't satisfied. To check you out I went to Lillie."

Rawlings studied Cal for a long moment, then smiled, an expression reminiscent of a crocodile.

"Those small-town people sure like to talk. When I asked about the Norton family, I learned their farm had failed and they'd moved away nearly thirty years ago. The Nortons' son Caleb died at the age of two in Nebraska."

Still Cal said nothing. He knew he should be feeling panic, but he was too stunned to experience any emotion.

"That whole Norton family always had bad luck, the lady in the post office said. Mrs. Norton had a second or third cousin who lived in Cheyenne, Wyoming, named Bainbridge. He died quite young, leaving a widow and a boy. When this woman's son, William, was eighteen years old, he killed a teenager and disappeared. Mrs. Bainbridge died from grief, everybody said." Rawlings had that same self-satisfied smile he wore when he won a hand at poker. "That's where you made your mistake, Bill. You should have found a name that had no possible connection to your family."

Cal remembered his panic when he fled Nebraska. All he could think about was changing his identity. He'd read about the young men during the Vietnam War who'd evaded the draft by using a deceased person's name. He'd remembered his distant cousin. Both Bill and Caleb had been born the same year. Cal never thought anyone would be able to trace him through his mother's distant relative.

He looked over at Rawlings. "Are you from the police?" That didn't seem likely, but he had to know for sure.

Rawlings laughed and shook his head. "Not bloody likely, as they say in England. The Reginald family, the parents of the dead teenager, posted a ten-thousand-dollar reward to help find the killer of their son. The bond is still in effect, but I'm not after it. I'm aiming higher than that."

The sound of ice dropping into a glass startled Cal. He had to keep his thoughts away from the past and think only about the danger that was present in this room. He accepted the drink but only sipped it. In dealing with a man like Rawlings he had better keep a clear head.

"So what do you want?" Cal's hands were surprisingly steady. The self-control he had worked on for so long hadn't failed him.

"I've got to hand it to you. You're a cool one."

"Come on, Rawlings. I don't like being jerked around, either. Tell me your deal before I throw you out."

"I don't think you want to do that. After all, one call to the Wyoming authorities and Amanda Kirk would have to get a new partner."

It had been so long since Cal had even contemplated the possibility of being discovered that it was difficult for him to consider Rawlings as a serious threat. And yet he knew it was stupid to underrate this smiling, quiet-spoken man. After a long silence, Cal asked, "What do you want?"

"Let's wait until Amanda gets back before I move on to the next stage." Rawlings reached over and poured himself another drink. "What I've got in mind takes careful timing and patience. I've gone to a lot of work and expense to pull this off. Nothing's going to screw it up. So sit back and relax. This is just the beginning of a beautiful friendship." He raised his glass in a toast.

"Here's to the three new partners, Norton, Kirk and Rawlings."

NEW BOND STREET was crowded with taxis, cars and buses. People darted in front of the traffic, reminding Amanda of downtown Manhattan. She managed to pull the rented MG in front of the building in a no-parking zone just as the rain started. Looking like mushrooms, umbrellas popped up everywhere, making it difficult to spot Mark. She leaned over the passenger seat and rolled down the window, oblivious to the water that splattered on her arm and the car seat. But Mark was nowhere in sight.

"Damn," she whispered. Wasn't he coming? Had he misunderstood the time and place? She swallowed and took a deep breath to ease the pain she felt. She had just started to roll the window back up when the door opened. Mark struggled for a moment to get his body into the bucket seat of the sports car. His long legs just barely fit into the space under the dashboard.

"I don't suppose you could have found a larger car?" he asked, and finished closing the window.

"I . . . I thought you weren't coming." She knew she was grinning like a teenager just invited to go to the prom, but she didn't care. Within the few seconds Mark had been in the car, she'd felt as if she'd come alive. It was as if no time had passed since he'd held her body next to his in the pool.

"You shouldn't have doubted me." He used his handkerchief to wipe his face and brush the drops of water off the sleeves of his jacket. "I told you that I like practice better than theory." He leaned over and kissed her lips, touching the side of her cheek with his hand.

With no hesitation, Amanda responded, giving in to the passion that filled her mind with a thousand pleasurable sensations.

A loud tapping made them jump apart.

"Sorry, madam," the uniformed woman in a little round hat shouted through the steamy window. "You've got to move. If you intend on continuing to— uh, that is, if you want to stay in the area for any length of time, there's a car park by the Leicester Square Tube on Charing Cross Road."

Amanda nodded, revved the engine, put the car in gear and shot away from the curb. A taxi behind her honked in protest.

Mark purposely kept his mouth shut about the close encounter with the vehicle. Instead, he forced the seat back to give his legs more room. "When you asked me to meet you at Sotheby's, you said I had to be willing to accept only what you're prepared to give. What are your terms?"

Amanda tapped her fingers on the wheel, stalling for time. Finally she spoke. "If you'd like, I thought we could spend a few days in a tiny town in the Cotswolds Hills, northwest of Oxford. Or we can find some other place to go."

Mark was utterly amazed by her suggestion, but he didn't want to show his astonishment. He tried to sound blasé about the whole thing. "If we go out of town, I don't have any clothes or gear with me."

She couldn't tell by his tone if he was agreeing or not. "Does that mean you want to go?"

Mark laughed, a low sound that seemed to rumble deep in his chest. "What do you think?" He laughed again. "Do you know where my hotel is?"

"I'm heading there now."

"Where are we going to stay?"

"I've rented a seventeenth-century thatched cottage that was once a woolen mill. The house has two bedrooms and is on a stream that feeds into a private pond. It's the permanent home to a pair of black swans. Mrs. Wilde, she's the new owner, so I haven't met her, said the... the babies have just hatched. Uh, what are swan offspring called?" She knew she was rambling, but her courage had failed her. What was Mark going to think about her? Even though she'd rented two rooms, it still sounded as if she'd planned the trip as a lovers' tryst. Was she now willing to admit that was what she'd unconsciously wanted all along? And what were her reasons? An attempt at independence from Cal? Wanting to prove she was a desirable woman and not just a coldhearted gambler? Or was it just that she was undeniably attracted to Mark Banning?

Well, she rationalized, nothing was going to happen unless she let it.

"Baby swans are called cygnets," Mark said in answer to her question, well aware that she had hurriedly glided past the mention of the two bedrooms. "What other rules have you got?"

"You're my guest. This is my treat, and I don't want any argument."

"Now, wait a minute," Mark said, turning to look at her. "I don't like that rule."

"That's the way it's going to be. I've got an extra thousand dollars of bonus money. When it's gone, we'll use yours."

"But I don't—"

"Cal suggested I use the money to go on a little vacation. It's mine to do with as I please." Now she wished she hadn't mentioned Cal. Damn this traffic, she thought. Once she was in open country she could think better.

"We can argue about the expenses later," Mark said, seeing the determined set of her jaw. "Does Cal know you're not going alone?"

"Well, not exactly. I mean, nothing was mentioned one way or the other."

"But he wouldn't like it, would he?"

Mark's voice was low and conversational, as if he were talking about the traffic that clogged the streets. He repeated his question, this time sounding more demanding. Why did he have to be so persistent? she wondered.

"No," she answered at last. "He wouldn't like it. But it's not just you. We have a rule: no fraternization with the players."

"Am I your first fling at fraternizing?"

Amanda stopped at a red light and glanced over at him. He was staring straight ahead. "Yes, you are. But all it means is two adults spending time together—*nothing more.* If you don't want to go, I can leave you at your hotel."

Mark's head slowly turned until he was facing her. "I didn't mean I wasn't interested in going with you." Amanda's hand rested on the stick shift. He placed his on top. "I'm pleased and flattered you asked me to go— no matter what your ground rules are."

Amanda released her breath. The bad moment had passed. "I'm glad you're coming, too. It'll be fun to show you the areas I love the most. And May is the perfect month to visit England."

When Amanda had to shift, Mark took his hand off hers and tried to stretch out his legs. He bumped his knees against the dashboard. "Did you rent or borrow this midget car?"

"It's all the hotel rental agency had. We can exchange it later, if you want."

"We'll see how I survive as a sardine." He turned in his seat so that he could look at her. She was even better than he remembered. Her fine wool slacks molded her thighs; the shell-pink silk blouse draped enticingly across her breasts. He forced himself to return his gaze out the front window, watching the flow of traffic. "I'd offer to take the wheel, but I've never driven on the left. You act as if you've done this before."

"I used to come to England often—a long time ago." Just a little over a year by the calendar, but it seemed like a decade.

"I see." Mark had spent the time since he'd last seen her thinking about what she had done before she'd become a professional poker player. Perhaps now she would answer some of his questions. "On business?"

"Yes." She negotiated a turn into a side street that she remembered was a faster way to get across town.

"What kind of business?"

For the first time since she'd left home she wanted to tell someone about herself. Perhaps she'd even reveal why she'd left her family. "I owned an antique store in California." Cal didn't even know that. She'd never told him anything about her life. "I came to England on buying trips."

"And how did you become a gambler?"

"When we've got more time, I'll tell you all about it."

Mark knew right now she needed to concentrate on her driving. Expertly she wove in and out between cars, taking every advantage to pass slower vehicles. It was raining harder than before, but even on the rain-slick streets she had perfect control of the car.

"Pull in here," Mark said, pointing to a portico in front of the hotel. "I'll be right back."

Ten minutes later he climbed into the car, threw a small overnight case into the back and said, "Onward to the Cotswolds."

Amanda smiled and silently shifted into gear, heading toward Kensington Garden and the M-40, the motorway that led to Oxford.

"SHOULD WE BYPASS Oxford and stop on the way back to London?" Amanda asked. "Oxford will be nicer when it's not raining." They were well out of the city by now, but the countryside with its rolling hills covered in green grass and the golden-yellow fields of rape were only dimly visible, obscured by the rain and low-lying clouds.

She entered a roundabout that had tulips blooming in the middle section. Mark didn't answer her question but held his breath as cars seemed to come from all directions. She only slowed her speed a little. The first time they'd used one of the traffic circles that had streets radiating out from it like spokes on a wheel, Mark had gripped the armrest, trying to act composed, even though he was visualizing the multiple accidents that could happen in that seeming free-for-all. But Amanda hadn't hesitated as she maneuvered around the outside edge, found the right road and took off, totally oblivious to the danger.

When they were again driving on the straight road, Mark said, "You're the tour leader. And since we're using your hard-earned money, whatever you decide is fine by me." He again thought about asking what would happen when Cal found out about this little excursion. But he knew pushing her on the subject would accomplish nothing and just might ruin their time together.

"What's your mother doing these next few days?" Amanda asked.

"She decided to fly to Paris to visit my sister. I said I'd rather stay in England."

"Did you tell her why you didn't want to go?"

He smiled. "No. I said that without me she and Diane would be free to shop and sightsee to their hearts' content."

"Then both of us have secrets."

Mark nodded but said nothing. When his mother told him her plans, he'd felt like a man let out of prison. Not that he hadn't enjoyed being with her. But this way she was off doing what she wanted. As for himself, he could temporarily forget Orion and his problems. Spending any time with Amanda was pleasurable, no matter what happened between them.

He sighed in contentment, leaned his head on the back of the seat and crossed his arms, thinking about the coming evening and night. For a long time he let his mind dwell on the possibilities, becoming mesmerized by his erotic thoughts and the hum of the tires on the wet pavement.

Amanda shifted down as she passed a truck and wished Mark would end the long silence. She still felt a little shy and unsure of herself. She'd never done anything like this before.

"Hey," Mark said, "why are you so quiet?"

"I was just wondering why *you* haven't said anything for the past ten miles."

"You mean, you're doing all the work, the least I could do is entertain you?"

"Well-l-l, I wouldn't put it quite like that, but in essence, yes." Laughter underlined her words.

"I like your honesty. I like *you,*" he added in a low voice. "I like everything about you—your hair and the way you absentmindedly brush it back from your cheek when you're concentrating. Your body that so perfectly fills a bathing suit. I like the way your skin felt when I kissed you in the pool...."

Amanda was having difficulty keeping her mind on her driving. She knew his words were overtures to the romantic scenarios that might take place at the Black Swan Inn. Her excitement was already building. Right at that moment she wondered if she'd be strong enough to insist on their having separate rooms.

When Mark didn't continue, she asked, "Is that all you like? What about my brilliant mind and mathematical abilities?"

"Einstein had those qualities, but nobody raved about his beauty. When it's too dark to see you, I'll think about what a good intellect you have."

"That's rather a sexist statement, Mr. Banning."

"Yes, I guess it was," he said with a grin. "I sincerely apologize. At a time like this the last thing I want to be is sexist."

"Just keep that in mind." Amanda looked out the side window. Only a few drops of rain still fell. "Look." She pointed toward the west. The clouds were lifting, allowing the sun to peek through, lighting the landscape. For the first time it was possible to see flocks of sheep sheltering under the huge oak trees. The rolling hills of green and gold were crosshatched by untidy hedgerows. A brilliant rainbow arched against the sky.

"All those paintings by Constable didn't do this scene justice," Mark said.

"He was from Suffolk. That's in the East."

"Well, if he'd lived over here, he wouldn't have been able to paint hills that particular shade of green. And those fields covered by the yellow flowers—what are they?"

"Oilseed rape, a member of the mustard family. The plants become cattle feed and the oil from the seeds is used in industry."

Mark turned toward her. "How do you know all that?"

"From Cal. He's got an encyclopedic memory." Again she'd mentioned Cal's name. For the next two days, was he going to be like a specter, an unseen presence that served as a constant prick to her conscience?

"Whenever you mention Cal you go all quiet. What's troubling you? A bad case of doubts about what you're doing?"

She knew it wouldn't do any good to lie. "My doubts aren't bad enough to make me want to go back to London. It's just—well, since I've been partners with Cal, I've never broken the rules."

"And he hasn't, either?"

"Never."

The relationship between Amanda and Cal continued to confuse Mark. It was like a marriage, but with one big difference. They didn't share a bed. How could Cal be with the beautiful Miss Kirk for all those months and resist the temptation of making love to her? He must have a will of tempered steel.

Mark turned toward Amanda and studied her for a long moment. "I'm not uncomfortable when you mention Cal's name. You don't have to be, either." He paused. When she didn't speak, he said, "We might as well be honest with each other. I know just how important Cal is to you. I think you've come to rely on him more than you even realize. This is your first flight out of the nest."

"Yes, that's true." Amanda's voice was barely audible. She gripped the wheel, keeping her eyes on the road ahead.

"More than anything I want to be with you," Mark said. "But I don't want you to be constantly worrying about Cal. Do you think you can forget him and the partnership for a little while?"

"Yes, I can." Amanda had purposely made her voice sound confident. And yet, despite her assurance, a little niggling doubt remained. What would Cal do when he found out about Mark? Would it be the end of their partnership?

Of even more importance right now was the confused state of her emotions. Since Mark had joined her, she'd become more and more excited. She was experiencing a sensual awareness that predominated her every thought. Now she wondered if it had been such a good idea to come with Mark. Was she making the biggest mistake of her life?

CHAPTER SIX

THE BLACK SWAN INN was even more charming than Amanda remembered. The small two-story Tudor building, with its white plaster panels and distinctive black diagonal support timbers, was nestled at the pond's edge. Since she'd last been here, the roof had been rethatched, the straw still golden-yellow. Along the ridge line was a design of sticks on top of a border of scallops cut from the thatching material. The building, with its rotating waterwheel and multiflowered gardens set against a backdrop of gently rolling hills, created a picture worthy of a full-color postcard.

Amanda was pleased she'd chosen this particular inn, one of the most picturesque places she'd ever seen . . . certainly the most romantic. Her thoughts made her cheeks feel warm. She realized why she'd never forgotten the Black Swan. When she visited here before, she'd been alone. She must have stored the memory of its unique beauty, unconsciously hoping she could return to show it to someone special.

They drove over the wooden bridge that spanned the sparkling river and onto the crushed-rock road leading to the inn. "This is a perfect place for a tryst," Mark said, his voice low and intimate.

She'd used that same phrase when she tried to justify her own motives. Now the term had connotations she didn't like.

"Shouldn't I use that particular word?" he asked when he realized what he'd said.

"I prefer vacation. It sounds less..."

"Illicit?" Mark offered. She remained silent. "Is the way I describe our time together that important to you?" He'd purposely made his tone light and teasing. He would have to remember how insecure she felt about herself and what she was doing.

She didn't answer as she pulled into the area reserved for a single car. It was too pretty to be called a garage. The arbor was made of latticed boards covered with honeysuckle in full bloom. She shut off the engine but didn't make a move to leave the car. Staring straight ahead, she said, "I suppose my asking you to go away with me seems, uh, strange and a little calculating." She inhaled deeply. "The way I acted on the ship, leading you on, letting you believe I rented by the hour..." She cleared her dry throat. "And then to ask you to come with me, well, I can see why you're thinking this is a tryst."

"But I was just—"

"Wait. Let me finish. I acted impulsively...in defiance of Cal, I guess." She shook her head. "To tell you the truth, I still don't understand my reasons."

The car was getting too warm. Amanda rolled down the window and breathed in the sweet scented air. Bees were noisily buzzing in the flowers.

"Amanda." Mark's voice was quiet and serious. He placed a finger under her chin and turned her head toward him. "I want you to stop worrying about what might or might not happen. Our making love isn't what's important and certainly isn't the reason we're here. We're supposed to be relaxing and having fun. We're giving ourselves a chance to become better acquainted. It's the same when any man and woman first meet. It takes a certain amount of time to get past that preliminary awkward stage of getting to know each other. That's what we're doing right now. We're trying to establish a basis for our friendship."

Mark bent over and brushed his lips against hers, a restrained, neutral kiss meant to reassure. "Forget what I said on the ship. Sex is much more enjoyable when the two people know each other well, when the act can be a sharing instead of just a mating. Let's just take each moment as it comes and—"

"Is that you, Miss Kirk?" The voice was coming from outside. "Are you in there? Is anything wrong?"

Amanda glanced in the rearview mirror. A white-haired woman, most likely the new owner, Mrs. Wilde, stood in back of the car, looking concerned.

Mark waved at the woman. She tentatively waved back. Before he opened his door, he asked Amanda, "Has the storm passed?"

She thought a moment before answering, desperately wanting everything to be perfect for these next few days.

"Amanda?" Mark said again, wondering what she was thinking that made her look so serious.

She inhaled and turned toward him. "No more clouds. The sun is shining brightly." Her tone was supposed to relay a lightness of heart that she didn't really feel. She would have to be careful not to let her self-doubts ruin their time together.

"Everything will be fine. You'll see." Mark opened his door and climbed out, his muscles stiff from sitting too long in one position. He grabbed the two cases from the back and exited the arbor. "Hello." He spoke to the woman. "I'm Mark Banning."

"I'm Sheila Wilde. Welcome."

Mark went around to Amanda's side and helped her get out of the car.

"How do you do, Mrs. Wilde," Amanda said as the two women shook hands. The last time she'd been to Black Swan Inn she'd been Susan Ross. She wouldn't have come if the previous owner had still been here.

"Welcome to Black Swan." Mrs. Wilde straightened her apron. She glanced at Mark and then Amanda, studying them for a moment with a puzzled expression. "Your two rooms are all ready. Would you like to go on up? Then I'll serve tea." She headed across the driveway and nimbly stepped onto the flat stones that led past the pond.

Amanda followed, trying to see everything at once. All around the cottage door was pink clematis. Clusters of wisteria flowers hung from the fences. Along the path tall hollyhocks nodded their multicolored flowers. She paused to stare as a memory formed in her mind. She saw herself as a child, using the bell-like flowers as ball gown skirts for clothespin dolls. Her father was playing the piano, providing the music while the tiny debutantes danced around the floor....

"Amanda?"

She blinked away the images. Mark stood beside her, staring intently at her face. She smiled. "I was just remembering something." She turned and walked toward Mrs. Wilde, who was waiting for them by the door.

"You said you'd been here before, Miss Kirk," she said as she entered the small entryway. The odors of baking bread and spices filled the rooms. "So I'll leave the decision on the room assignments up to you." At the foot of the stairs she paused. "Both have beautiful views, but one room is larger than the other. The bath has to be shared, I'm afraid. Everything's all prepared for you, so just go on up. I'll put the kettle on." She walked toward the back of the house. "When you're ready, why don't you go into the sitting room that faces the pond? I'll meet you there." She walked through a door and shut it behind her.

Mark carried both cases up the narrow, twisting stairs. Amanda had purposely not mentioned that they would be alone in the house. He could find that out later. At the top landing she said, "I'll take this room. It's smaller and the ceiling is lower than the other one. The doorframes are made for— Watch your head!" she shouted just as Mark cracked his forehead.

"Damn," he said, setting the cases down. He rubbed his already reddening brow.

"For short people," she finished lamely. "I'm sorry you hurt yourself." She reached up and ran her fingers across the small bump.

"Thank you for being sorry." He grabbed her hand and kissed the fingertips.

It was such a simple act that at first Amanda didn't comprehend his intent. Unlike the kiss in the car, this time his touch was meant as a subtle message—an unspoken promise that there would be more intimacies.

She hid her strong reaction, slipped her hand out of his and stepped past him into the sunlit room.

Mark ducked his head, entered, then placed Amanda's case on a luggage rack by the wall. The wallpaper was pale yellow with a repeat pattern of tiny white flowers. Through the open window a breeze wafted the lacy curtains, carrying the myriad scents of grass and flowers, of earth and water. Amanda sat on a padded seat in front of the window, gazing down at the pond.

"Look."

Mark joined her on the cushion. Below them the swans, their graceful necks held high, were swimming side by side, followed by a string of cygnets, each creating a pattern of overlapping Vs on the smooth surface.

Mark sighed deeply, feeling utterly content. "Thank you," he said, turning to see Amanda's face.

"What are you thanking me for?"

"For bringing me here. I've never allowed myself much time to do anything like this. I've been so determined to take my place at Orion that I kept myself buried in my studies." Orion. He had hardly thought about it since he'd met Amanda. She seemed to have driven out all thoughts of his crusade to find out what was going on there. "And now that I've seen all of this—" he pointed out the window "—I don't have enough time to enjoy it. Soon I'll have to go back and face reality."

Amanda watched Mark as he spoke. His eyes narrowed, as if he were worried and frustrated, reminding her of the time he'd been talking to Evan Rawlings at the poker table. She wondered then if something might be wrong at Orion. When he talked about his stepfather and stepbrother—the Quinteros—there had been an emotion akin to hatred in his expression.

"Have you been given a place at Orion?" she asked.

"Oh, I've got one. But it's a job that could be handled by an engineer with a correspondence school degree. As soon as I get back to Philadelphia, I'm going to start making some changes." He got to his feet, took Amanda's hand to help her to stand and said, "Enough of that. Get ready. Tea is waiting for us." He headed for the door. "Then after tea I hope we're going to find someplace to eat dinner."

"Dinner's all arranged."

"I wish I'd thought about bringing something stronger than tea to drink."

"I did. At an outrageous cost I got the hotel to sell me champagne and a bottle of Scotch, glasses and Brie and crackers. All of it's in a small ice chest in the back of the car."

Mark laughed. "I like your style, Miss Kirk. I should have known you'd be resourceful." Just at the last second he remembered to duck his head.

"How OLD DID you say that place was where we ate dinner?" Mark held Amanda's arm as she walked on an uneven footpath not made for high heels.

"It was built in 1610. It had been a stagecoach stop for a hundred and fifty years before the railroad line came through. Then the building became a private home. Now it's an inn and a restaurant."

Mark carried a full bottle of champagne. A car robe lay folded over his arm. Amanda held the two stemmed glasses she'd gotten from the room service waiter at the hotel.

They were nearing the stream that fed the millpond. For the next few minutes neither spoke; speech seemed extraneous in the beautiful setting. On the distant hills no houselights were visible, giving the appearance that they were totally alone. The muted shades of night slowly stole over the land. Even though it was past nine, light lingered in the evening sky, as if the sun didn't want to lose its battle with darkness. The lingering twilight, the balminess of the floral-scented air, the trill of a skylark's evening song, combined to create a sensuous experience that was unlike anything Mark had ever known.

When they neared the brook, they could hear the music of the water spilling over rocks. On a grassy knoll overlooking the river they stopped. "How about here?" Mark asked, already spreading the blanket on the ground.

"Looks good to me," Amanda said, setting the glasses in a protected place on the grass. "Shouldn't be too much stinging nettle." Across the stream were slow-moving shapes that could only be cattle and sheep. Now she could hear the cows lowing to each other. "I don't see any bulls or rams that might defend their territory from us two-legged interlopers."

Mark thought for a moment about what she'd said. He looked behind him, trying to see past the huge oak trees to the field beyond. He peered at the bushes and shrubs nearby. "Tell me you're kidding."

Amanda laughed and sat on the blanket, arranging her full skirt around her legs and tucking the silk blouse into the waistband. She had to shift her position to avoid a rock. "Had you worried, didn't I?" She kicked off her shoes.

"Yes, you did."

"I asked Mrs. Wilde. She said to watch out for the nettle if we walked off the path, but all the animals on this side of the river are kept in fenced areas."

"And those over there won't cross?" He pointed to the low-lying hill opposite them. In the dying light the unmistakable silhouette of a bull could be seen.

"I doubt it. The river's too swift and rocky."

"That's reassuring news." Mark pulled the flashlight from his rear pocket, sat down next to Amanda and opened the champagne bottle. After he poured the wine into the glasses, he raised his and said, "Here's to my trusted guide, Amanda Kirk. May she continue to keep well informed about the flora and fauna of England."

They drank their champagne, then Amanda raised her glass. "Here's to Mark Banning, the perfect gentleman. May he continue to be the paragon of virtue and strength he's been today."

Mark's laughter agitated the cattle. Their bells clanged in the silence. "That was certainly a subtle message." He set their glasses out of the way. "But are you absolutely sure that's what you want?" Pulling her toward him, he cradled her in his arms. "And what happens if I stop being a perfect gentleman? What'll you do when I kiss you like this?"

Amanda proved exactly what she would do. Her response was instantaneous, as if every nerve of her body had been waiting a lifetime for his touch. And then, as abruptly as it had begun, the kiss ended, surprising and disappointing her.

Mark looked down at her face. The full moon had just crested the hill behind them, allowing him enough light to see the dreamy expression in her eyes. "What? No angry outburst? No demands to be taken back to the inn?"

"Not yet. I'll let you know when it's time." She placed her hand on the back of his neck and pulled him toward her until their lips met. She lay on her back while he bent over her. This time she was the aggressor, using feminine wiles she hadn't known she possessed, wanting Mark to experience what she was feeling. It had been such a long time since she'd been intimate with a man. She'd forgotten what it was like to be kissed, to let her mind and body be dominated by sensations that threatened to engulf her.

Mark let his kisses wander down to Amanda's neck and around to her earlobe. His fingers searched for and found the top button of her blouse, loosening it to reveal the top of a lacy bra. He caressed the warm, fragrant skin, reveling in the sensations that engulfed him.

Then common sense returned. Mark realized what could happen if he didn't put a stop to this most pleasurable activity. His excitement was beyond description and nearly beyond control. And that was the main problem—he knew how easily he could make love to Amanda. But they were supposed to be getting to know each other, becoming friends, not lovers. Too little time had passed. And, of course, there was Cal. Mark didn't want to do anything that would make Amanda regret her first bid for independence.

"Amanda?" he said when the kiss ended.

A shiver coursed down her spine. "What?" The word was muffled as she continued to press her lips against his neck.

His breathing slowly returned to normal. He leaned on his elbows, looking down at her. "You want me to make love to you, don't you?"

She didn't answer his question, just reached up and touched his cheek.

"But remember what I said?"

She inhaled deeply and sighed. "What did you say?" Her voice was dreamy.

"Sex is much more enjoyable when the two people know each other well, when the act can be a sharing instead of just a mating." Amanda continued to lie on her back, her hair fanned out around her face.

It took her a moment to comprehend what he was trying to say. "Yes, I see what you mean," she whispered. For some surprising reason she didn't feel resentment. Instead, she was glad he'd reminded her that they were both losing control. "You're saying we haven't spent enough time getting to know each other."

"Well, I have learned a few things about you."

Amanda changed her position, sitting in front of him. "We've only been together a few hours. What could you possibly have learned about me in that amount of time?" She pulled her hair back from her face, then adjusted her blouse. More than anything she wanted to hear what he had to say.

"You'd be surprised just how much you've revealed to me."

She decided to call his bluff. Crossing her arms, she lifted her chin and said defiantly, "Okay, tell me some of your observations."

The moon had risen even higher, making it possible to see her features clearly. She looked so beautiful that it was difficult to keep his mind on his thoughts.

"Well?" she prompted.

"You use way too much salt on your food." He was teasing, wanting her to react.

"Now that's really astute of you. An in-depth study of the psyche of Amanda Kirk." She wondered what he'd say if she told him she'd been using an assumed name, living a lie for over a year. Would he think less of her if he knew she'd left her family and had never told them where she was? Now that she was beginning to know him better she sensed he wouldn't judge her, and that fact made her want to be open with him. Sometime during this trip, when the time was right, she'd tell him her story.

"Okay, what else do you know?" When he didn't speak, she started to stand. Now she didn't want to be analyzed. "It's okay. We should be going back."

Mark's hand on her arm stopped her. "Oh, no, you're not going to get off the hook that easily. You wanted an in-depth study and you're going to get one." He cleared his throat, stared up at the stars, then returned his gaze to Amanda. "Something doesn't quite add up about you. There are inconsistencies I can't figure out. You put on a good show, especially when you're dealing cards. You act sophisticated and pretend to enjoy what you're doing, but I think you've got doubts about your chosen occupation." He poured them both some champagne and watched as Amanda nearly emptied her glass. "I sense you were uncomfortable when the players, including myself, looked admiringly at you in that revealing dress. Am I right so far?"

Amanda turned her head and stared down at the water. The moon had turned the river into a sparkling streak of silver. "I've learned to accept the men and their stares. The way I look and dress is part of the reason the men want to play with me. I don't like it, but I've become immune."

"Okay, I'll go along with that." He paused, thinking. "I know you were worried about being here with me, and I can understand why. You've never done this kind of thing before. To tell you the truth, when you asked me to meet you, I was astonished. And then when I found out you'd planned a two-day trip, I just couldn't believe my luck. But why did you ask me? What are you trying to prove?"

Amanda set her empty glass aside. "I guess I wanted a chance to be with someone I liked, in a normal social situation, not a stranger across a poker table whom I'd never see again. You came along just when I was feeling closed in by everything—Cal and the games and being with men like Evan Rawlings."

Mark nodded. "But there's more. It's almost as if there's a battle going on inside you, yet I can't determine what it is. You're like someone who's carrying around a big secret that's becoming too heavy. Has it got something to do with Cal? Is there anything I can do to help?"

"No, it doesn't have anything to do with Cal." How could she explain her actions a year ago? She was ashamed at how stupidly she'd acted. It was going to be difficult to confess. Right now she wasn't sure she could. "When we know each other better," she said softly, "I promise to tell you all about it."

"I'm not sure what role I'm supposed to be playing," Mark said.

She reached up and erased the frown that had formed between his brows. "Let's start with friend, then see where we go from there."

Mark stood and helped her to her feet. Taking her hand in his, he said, "Hello, friend," and kissed her, not as passionately as before, but with a promise to deepen the friendship as quickly as possible.

AT THE INN Mark let Amanda precede him into the entryway, then carefully shut the door, trying not to make any noise.

"We don't have to worry about being quiet," Amanda said. "We're alone. Mrs. Wilde sleeps in a cottage down the road."

"How *nice* for us."

His mockingly suggestive tone made her smile. "If you had a mustache, you'd be twirling it. But remember, we're just friends."

"I'm sure you'll keep reminding me." After he switched off the outside lights, he asked, "How about a nightcap?"

"I don't like Scotch, and the champagne's gone."

"I only used that phrase because that's what men say to women when they don't want the evening to end. I don't need a drink. Not when you're near me." He took Amanda's hand and began to lead her into the sitting room, ignoring her weak protests. "It's too early to go to bed," he explained as they sat beside each other on the sofa facing the pond. A ribbon of light from the moon illuminated the water.

As he put his arm around her, he said, "Let's start deepening that friendship."

He kissed her until she was weak with passion. He seemed to know instinctively how best to excite her. And then, just as her resolve not to let him make love to her was again weakening, he stopped, leaned back and stared at her for a long time. Finally he said, "Come on. We're going upstairs."

Unsure exactly what his intentions were, she followed him up the creaking steps. At her bedroom door he lightly kissed her lips, then each of her eyelids. "Go to sleep, friend. I'll see you in the morning."

He turned and walked down the hall to his room. Just as she was reaching for the metal ring that opened the rough-hewn oak door, she heard a sound that made her cringe—Mark's head hitting solid wood.

"Damn!" he shouted, obviously not caring if Mrs. Wilde down the road heard him.

Before she could offer any words of commiseration he slammed his door with a force that shook the old building to its foundations. She didn't dare go to check on his head, not in the excited state she was in. She'd get a report on his condition in the morning.

"THIS IS A TYPICAL English breakfast?" Mark whispered as he stared down at his two fried sunnyside-up eggs, fried bacon as thick as a slice of ham, fried mushrooms and fried tomatoes. The toast sat upright in a silver-plated rack. Clay pots contained homemade jams and the most yellow butter he'd ever seen. In the middle of the table was a vase of fresh daisies and roses. "And that tea Mrs. Wilde served us yesterday afternoon. Scones made out of butter. And you're supposed to put more butter on it before you top it with jam and—what did she call it—clotted cream? It was so thick you had to use a knife to spread it. Hasn't any-body over here heard about cholesterol?''

"Hush or Mrs. Wilde will hear. Just eat the food. We don't want to hurt her feelings.''

Now there were two bruises on Mark's forehead, one just above the other. When they met earlier that morn-ing and went for a walk around the gardens, he'd asked her to promise she'd always remind him of the low door *before* he walked through, not after.

"Mrs. Wilde already thinks we're weird,'' Mark said. "Two adults, who obviously like each other, come to a romantic inn and don't share the same bedroom. I bet she's beginning to wonder about the American male.''

Amanda spread butter on her already cold toast. "She told me she thought you were extremely hand-some. She's a widow. Perhaps she'd be interested in...''

Mark held his hand up. "Don't say it.'' He again looked down at the high-calorie food on his plate and lowered his voice. "I bet I know how her husband died.''

Amanda put her hand over her mouth to stifle her giggle.

"And how are we doing?'' Mrs. Wilde asked, swing-ing open the kitchen door and entering the small, bright, sunlit dining room. "Need more toast? Cof-fee?''

"We're fine, Mrs. Wilde.'' Mark took a big bite of his eggs and, with determination, chewed and swallowed. "Everything's delicious.''

"Just call if you need me.'' She bustled out.

"What do you want to do today?'' Amanda asked.

"If you're really leaving it up to me...''

Mark glanced up at the ceiling, letting her know where he'd like to spend at least part of the day. He was teasing, trying to get a rise out of her. "*That* activity, my friend, is not on this tour leader's list." Amanda nibbled a piece of bacon, meat that tasted nothing like the bacon in America. "What would you like to see?"

"You're the guide and you know the territory. You decide." He finished his breakfast, even though he didn't care for fried eggs. The toast, made from home-made bread, was excellent. He grabbed and ate the last piece before Amanda got it.

She placed her folded napkin beside her plate. "Then we'll start at the beginning and go to the end."

"Is that supposed to make sense?" Mark asked as he rose to his feet. He held Amanda's chair as he rose.

"Just follow my lead, friend, and you'll see."

AMANDA AND MARK were the last to leave Warwick Castle, politely encouraged to hurry along the path by one of the uniformed attendants. Before heading toward the main gateway, they turned to have a last look at the castle with its turrets, battlements and towers. The stone buildings were set on a hill beside the Avon River. From the uppermost ramparts the view of the rolling countryside was spectacular.

Trotting toward them across the green courtyard was a barrel-chested horse on which rode a heavyset, muscular man, wearing the full regalia of a knight, including a chain mail suit, a steel helmet and a lance held upright. His mount was also arrayed in armor. Both man and horse were heading toward the stable. Peacocks, with their bright blue tails fanned out, unconcernedly sauntered out of the way of the huge Clydesdale's feet.

Amanda and Mark were again encouraged to leave. They slowly headed down the path past the glass conservatory toward the parking lot. They had to walk around defiant peacocks that screeched their protest at being disturbed. Rhododendrons, taller than a house, formed a thick barrier on each side of the path. The pink clusters were a haven for noisy bees.

Mark carried a stack of pamphlets from the book and souvenir shop. Amanda seemed to have a passion for collecting guide books, information brochures, postcards and maps of the historical sights, items Mark never bought because he knew he'd toss them out as soon as he got home.

"Why do you want all of this stuff?"

"Someday, when I'm old and gray, I'll look at the color photos and remember my whirlwind trip through the Cotswolds. I can see myself now, sitting in my rocking chair, thinking about that nice young man who went with me...uh, what was his name again? Bart Manning? Or was it Brat Manfred?"

"Very funny," Mark said. He took a particularly thick guidebook on Shakespeare and tried to swat her on the rear. She laughed and jumped out of the way.

"Isn't it time for something to eat?" he asked as they got to the car. "That 'high tea,' even with all those calories and cholesterol, didn't last me long."

"Food's next on the agenda," she said, hurrying toward the car.

THEIR DINNER WAS even more perfect than the night before. Amanda had chosen a different inn, this one an ancient manor house with a view of the Avon River. The room was full of genuine antique furniture. Sterling and silver gilt serving pieces sat on Irish damask linen cloths. The napkins were nearly two feet square and as smooth as silk. The museum-quality oil paintings above the ornate fireplaces depicted scenes similar to the ones they'd seen while driving around the countryside. There were few other diners, which was surprising because the restaurant was near Stratford—one of the most popular tourist attractions in all of England.

Amanda stared out the window. The river was no longer visible. Candles ensconced inside hurricane lamps were reflected in the glass, looking like fireflies caught in midflight. She could also see Mark's image, his profile strong and handsome. She turned to look directly at him. "I've been meaning to ask you. How did you get your nose broken?"

He rubbed the slightly twisted bridge. "Ugly, isn't it? Like a boxer who forgot to duck."

"It's not ugly. It adds character to your face, a certain rakish rogue look that's really very appealing. I can see why you made such a perfect pirate at the ship's costume party."

Mark laughed. "I wasn't so perfect. I nearly tripped over my sword. My mother accused me of being drunk." He held his hand up to stop Amanda's next question. "But I wasn't."

"How did you break your nose?"

"My stepbrother did it when I was fifteen. When his father married my mother, Rob moved into our house. He's four years older than I am. I never knew if our fight was over territory or just two males testing each other's strength. Either way I lost. So that we wouldn't get into trouble, we lied to my mother—told her we'd been wrestling. That secret was the only thing Rob and I ever shared.''

''He's the one who taught you how to play poker?'' Amanda sipped the excellent port the waiter had just served.

''Much to my expense. When I knew as much as he did, he got smart and refused to play with me.'' Mark leaned over and took Amanda's hand. ''But if he hadn't taught me, I wouldn't have been able to play poker with you.''

Amanda shut her eyes for a moment, remembering the stateroom, the men, the cards flying across the green baize. She again looked at Mark. ''Doesn't that game seem like a long time ago?''

''In a different life. Eventually I'll forget the game, but the sight of you in that swimsuit, with the sun shining through the windows illuminating your hair and body, is forever burned in my memory. I'll never forget how beautiful you looked.'' He reached over to touch her cheek with his fingertips, running his thumb over her lips.

''Mark Banning, I do believe you're a romantic.''

''You're the first woman who's ever called me a romantic.'' He poured more of the ruby-red port into their glasses.

''What do other women call you?''

''There's a whole list—hard-hearted, unfeeling, obsessed, blindly devoted to my work, interested only in myself.'' And he didn't blame the women for their opinions. Sometimes he would remember to call and break a date, but other times he would get busy on a project and simply forget to show up. Then he would have to listen to accusations about his character delivered by irate females who vowed they never wanted to see him again. Surprisingly he hadn't cared very much....

"I don't think you're hard-hearted or unfeeling. I don't know if you're blindly devoted to your work, but you could never be interested only in yourself." Amanda realized that during the time they'd spent together, their relationship had changed. She was beginning to know more about him. They were already forming a stronger bond. Now was the time for total honesty. She had to tell him about her past.

"Thank you for those kind words," Mark said, tipping his glass toward her in a silent toast, feeling a strange elation that had nothing to do with the alcohol he'd consumed.

After a long silence, Amanda sighed, trying to find the courage to speak the truth.

"That was a mournful sound." He'd been staring at her, wondering where her thoughts were leading. "Want to tell me about it?"

As if a dam had burst, she related the events that had occurred in her mother's house a year ago. He didn't interrupt to ask questions, but just let her talk. By the time she'd finished, nearly all the other diners had left. She inhaled deeply, threw her head back and closed her eyes, feeling relieved and cleansed. The only part she'd left out was her real name.

"How much of this does Cal know?" Mark asked. He purposely kept his tone neutral, not wanting to sound judgmental in any way.

"When we first met, all I wanted was to forget what had happened. I just pretended that was the first day of my life. We never asked each other about our pasts."

"Strange way to form a business partnership."

She shrugged. "Perhaps the only way."

"Why did you tell me?"

She'd been afraid he'd ask that. But she couldn't lie, not when they were growing closer, learning to know each other better each minute. "I wanted to be honest with you, to let you know what I'd done." She wanted to ask if he felt any different about her now that he knew, but she didn't dare.

"Thank you for telling me," he said just as the waiter discreetly set the silver tray on the table. Before Amanda could move her hand toward the little leather folder, Mark grabbed it. "This is my treat."

"No way. I said Rawlings's money was paying, and I meant it!" Damn, she thought. That had just slipped out.

Mark's brow rose in surprise. "Your bonus money was from Evan Rawlings?"

"He tipped for the privilege of playing cards with me," she retorted. "The reason I want to spend it on the two of us is because it came from him."

"That isn't a valid reason. You could be buying yourself something with the money. It's only fair I pay my share." Mark reached into his pocket for his credit card.

By the time he'd finished speaking, Amanda had the money out of her wallet. Moving so fast that her hand was just a blur, she grabbed the folder, signaled the waiter and handed everything to him.

"You can pay the tip," she said to Mark with a self-satisfied smile.

"Since you're faster than I am, I concede. But for the sake of my pride I'm going to buy you a special gift. So you'd better find me a place, either around here or in London, where I can."

Amanda smiled as she remembered the sign she'd seen nailed to a lamppost. It advertised a gigantic antique sale and flea market in Builth Wells, not far across the Welsh border. She'd been there once before on an antique buying trip and knew the way. The market was on Saturday, the next day. But it was a long way from London. Getting back to the city by tomorrow night would be difficult. She hadn't told Cal when she'd return. The flight to the States was to leave late Sunday evening. She and Mark could go to the market tomorrow, return to Mrs. Wilde's, then, early Sunday, drive into London. She could pack and be ready to leave England that night. And this way she could spend that much more time with Mark.

"What are you grinning about?" Mark asked as he set the pound notes on the tray.

"I've got tomorrow all worked out." Then it occurred to her that he might have thought they were going back on Saturday and had made his own plans for the weekend. Fearing his answer, she asked, "Can you stay and get back to London Sunday afternoon?"

"Yes. Mother and I aren't leaving for the States until later in the week."

Amanda smiled her relief. "We'd better get back to the inn. We've got to get up very early."

"But why? What are we going to do?" He followed her as she headed toward the massive oak doors that led outside.

"Just wait. It's a surprise."

CHAPTER SEVEN

"WHAT KIND OF A PLACE is this?" Mark asked as he stared at the white-painted structures that resembled huge barns. Amanda followed a parking attendant's directions, pulled off the road and parked beside a string of cars lined up on a grass-covered hill.

"They hold agricultural shows here and sales of sheep and cattle, probably horses and pigs, too."

"My God, Amanda, have you gone bonkers? You can't want me to buy you any kind of livestock."

She laughed. "Haven't you been reading the signs? We're in Builth Wells, Wales, at a flea market and antique show. Over a thousand dealers are here."

"Wales? I knew we were heading west, but I didn't know we'd gone that far. I didn't see a border sign."

"I've never seen any, so I guess they don't use them." She slipped on a sweater. They had left early, before the sun was up. The air was still chilly.

Mark got out of the car and put a sport jacket on over his cotton polo shirt. He rubbed his palms together and shivered. "It's cold."

"When dealers and buyers get together, the atmosphere soon gets heated up." Amanda locked the car. "Let's go. And remember to watch your step."

"Oh, great," Mark said, observing his handmade loafers. He should have brought his Nikes.

They walked down the straw-covered path. Inside the barns, along the walks and in the large fenced fields were groups of milling people, wandering around tables of merchandise. Some of the goods looked like piles of junk. "How did you even know about this?"

"I saw a sign in Banbury at the street market we went to." She'd been glad they had arrived during one of the weekly market days held in the town square. Mark had been fascinated by the variety of goods sold in the outdoor stalls—everything from baby clothes to men's suits, fresh vegetables and fruits to picture frames and lamps. He hadn't objected to wandering around the crowded square. Amanda hoped he'd like the flea market even better.

"Look," she said, pointing inside one of the barns.

Mark glanced through the tall double doors. Stalls for the animals were along the exterior walls. A huge four-poster bed and three delicate wooden chairs similar to his grandmother's sat in the cemented section in the middle. The incongruous sight of fine furniture and crystal chandeliers displayed where farm animals had recently roamed was more than he could comprehend. "But why would you even want to come here?"

"Remember? I told you I was an antique dealer in California. This is like old home week. I can feel the excitement brewing inside me right this minute. The challenge of bargaining against a tough dealer is as exhilarating as ... as ..."

"As exhilarating as last night by the river or when we were in the sitting room?"

"As arguing with you," she finished unconvincingly.

"If you find bargaining exhilarating," Mark said, "I guess I'll just have to work harder at arousing your senses."

"You did enough of that last night." She took his arm and pulled him toward a brightly painted wagon. "Isn't this just like a fair right out of the Renaissance? All we need are musicians, jugglers and a Punch and Judy show."

As they stepped closer, Mark saw what she was talking about. On a rotating spit was a whole pig roasting over a bed of coals. Already the skin was turning brown and crispy. The savory aroma filled the air.

"It's sliced and served on a bun. We can have it later, if you want. Or there are all different kinds of food—Chinese, Japanese, curry, hot dogs, hamburgers." Amanda led Mark down the road toward a huge cinder-block building. "Wait until you see what's inside here."

The vast room was filled with tables piled high with merchandise. Old half-filled medicine bottles sat beside art nouveau vases and stained-glass windows showing ecclesiastical themes. Well-loved teddy bears and pull toys, Victorian clothes, table linens and frilly parasols were lined up on the tables. Stacked precariously on makeshift shelves were complete sets of gold-embellished bone china, silver epergnes and candlesticks. There was little order to any of the displays.

"What do you think?" she asked. Mark was frowning in a perplexed way. She wondered if she'd made a mistake by bringing him here. He seemed out of his element.

"My mother would love this," he said, scanning the crowded hall. "But I'm never going to tell her about it.

She's got enough furniture and gimcracks to fill two houses."

"If she and I ever meet, I'll tell her what treasures she can find over here. Antique lovers have to stick together."

Mark put his arm around Amanda's shoulders and pulled her against him. "What about other kinds of lovers?"

"That depends."

Mark bent down and planted a kiss on her forehead, nose, then on her smiling mouth. "I'll explore that statement later." He stepped away. "If we drove all this way just so I can find something to buy for you, then we'd better get started. What do you want to see first?"

"That's the fun. We just pick a point and go from there, hitting every stall."

He looked around the vast hall. "We've got our work cut out for us."

As they headed toward one of the dealers, she said, "Oh, I forgot to tell you. Since you know me so well, *you* have to do the choosing without any help from me."

Mark stopped walking and turned toward her. "Now wait a min—" He was interrupted by a sharp pain between his shoulder blades. Behind him was a man carrying a tall metal lamp stand shaped like a spear. Ten inches down from the point protruded three empty light sockets. In his other hand were the frayed cord and a pink satin shade with a matching beaded fringe. It was one of the ugliest lighting fixtures Mark had ever seen. After checking that no damage was done either to his jacket or his body, the man begged Mark's pardon and hurried on.

"Besides watching where you walk, you have to be careful where you stand."

"Thanks a lot. Your warnings always seem to come just a little too late to do me any good."

They stepped up to the table and peered down into a glass case filled with ornate jewelry of every description. Multicolored stones sparkled like tiny rainbows.

"Help you, ma'am?" the man asked after setting his meat pasty aside and wiping his mouth.

Before Mark could answer Amanda said, "We're just looking, thanks."

"Don't you want to take something out of the case?" Mark asked.

"Not yet." She wandered to the next dealer. For three more hours she followed the same pattern, examining some of the merchandise carefully, asking knowledgeable questions, then moving on. So far she hadn't bought anything except a small brass lock and key, handmade in the mid-nineteenth century. She assured him she'd find a useful purpose, then laughed when he looked doubtful.

Mark followed along, finding he was becoming fascinated with everything he saw. He came to the conclusion that if something was junk when it was made a long time ago, it was still just junk now. And some of the prices for this junk appalled him. But he did see many items that he liked. The jewelry particularly fascinated him. He marveled that so much work and ingenuity, so much precious metal and so many gemstones could go into making a single item that had no purpose other than decoration. And not just the women had fancy useless items available to them. Men had their share, too. The one Mark particularly liked was a gentleman's gold toothpick that retracted into a gold case like a miniature switchblade.

At first Mark was tempted to buy Amanda a ring or perhaps earrings, then changed his mind. They just didn't seem right.

He started to ask if she'd help him, but she was busy talking to a dealer about the history of an English china company. "I'll be right back," he whispered. "Meet me here." She nodded and continued her discussion.

He remembered an item that had caught his eye when they entered this aisle and returned to the dealer. The pleasant, older man said he was willing to show Mark anything he wanted.

"That," Mark said, pointing to a black box about nine inches square on the counter of the back of the stall. The way the man lifted the container proved just how heavy it was. On the top was an intricate inlaid design of colored stones, set in yellow metal, smoothed to a satin finish.

"The wood is ebony. See the fine grain, like satin. The casket—that's what a small box or chest is called, I'm afraid—was made in Florence, Italy, probably during the sixteenth century. The pattern on top is semiprecious stones—jasper, agate, lapis lazuli and coral, and gold and silver. It's called *pietra dura,* which means hard stone."

"There's a table at Warwick Castle that has that kind of top," Mark said.

"Yes, I've seen it. Both pieces could very well have been done by the same craftsman, but on this there's no signature. Perhaps an apprentice made the box before attempting to tackle a more ambitious project." The man inserted a tiny gold key with a silk tassel into the lock and twisted it twice. "Wait until I show you what's inside." He opened the lid with a dramatic flourish.

The box had sectioned partitions, holding stacks of square tokens made of creamy jade. Engraved on one side was the letter *R* in Old English script. Mark was disappointed the letter wasn't a *K* for Kirk. The reverse side of the chips was marked with numbers denoting their value in hundreds, five hundreds and thousands.

"The game tokens and the inserts to hold them in stacks were later additions, I'm sure. You can see by the numbers that they were used for some kind of betting game. Perhaps, uh, what do you call it in America? Stud poker?"

Mark nodded, then held one of the tokens up to the light. They were white, translucent and so smooth that it was a pleasure just to rub his fingers over the cool surface.

"That particular color of jade is called mutton-fat. I've never seen any other game tokens made of stone. They're usually ivory or clay. The intaglio letters prove these were specially ordered, probably in China, where most of the old jade was carved." The dealer pulled out the wooden sections. "As you can see, everything is in perfect condition. All the chips are here. But wait, there's more." He closed the lid and touched the side of the lock. A hidden drawer on the bottom snapped open. Inside were two decks of playing cards in red leather cases. "They're Italian, but they aren't as old as the box. More like mid-seventeenth century. They're also complete."

"How much for everything?" Mark asked, preparing himself for the worst.

"Well, I must admit I've had the box for a long time. I bought it on impulse and paid dearly for it. Not many people want something like this, so I'm only asking five thousand pounds. And that's a bargain," he quickly added.

Mark calculated the cost versus his winnings at poker. The eight thousand dollars had been a windfall. If he hadn't met Amanda, he wouldn't have the money. He almost said he'd take it, but he'd watched Amanda bargain with the dealers. "I'd prefer four thousand pounds."

"Forty-eight hundred."

"Forty-five." Mark folded his arms and took a half a step backward, signals Amanda had said meant no more haggling. "All I've got is cash, American dollars. You could wait to turn the money in when the exchange rate is high." Mark felt certain he wasn't being overcharged. He might not know much about antiques, but he could recognize excellence. When he first saw the box, he'd thought it would cost much more. Still, Amanda must never learn what price he'd paid. She would refuse to accept the gift.

"Forty-five?" Mark asked again.

"Agreed," the man said, then smiled, obviously pleased with his sale.

After they calculated the amount he owed, Mark counted out the money, occasionally glancing down the aisle. Amanda was still at the same place, oblivious to anything except the vase she held in her hand. To the man, Mark said, "Wrap the box so it can be unwrapped, but would you give me some extra packing material? It has to go back to the United States."

"Of course. And you'll need a receipt for customs, won't you?"

Mark had forgotten about that little item. It would probably cost another seven hundred dollars. He shrugged. Easy come, easy go.

"Do you think you could hold it for me until I'm ready to leave?"

"Of course. I'll be here all day. Is this a gift for yourself?"

"It's for someone special," Mark said, only now realizing just how much he meant it.

AFTER THEY PLACED their orders at a hamburger wagon, Amanda again studied the bulky package Mark held under his arm. "What did you buy?" When Mark refused to answer, she set her own bag of purchases on the ground. "Let me try to guess." He handed the parcel to her. "My word, this is heavy. It's full of gold sovereigns—a pirate's buried treasure. You took that costume seriously, didn't you?"

Remembering the cost, he said ruefully, "You're almost right about the gold." He retrieved the package.

"No. It's not gold. Gold costs too much. I know. Brass door knockers!" He shook his head. "Ceramic tiles from the floor of a train station? Stones from an ancient abbey closed during Henry VIII's reign?"

"Do you really think I'm going to tell you?"

"But, Mark, that's not fair."

"Life isn't fair. You'll just have to wait." He took his thumb and rubbed it along her jawline to the lobe of her ear. She wore heavy gold hoops that caught the light and flashed it back to him. "I just remembered," he said. "I want to go back to the big building so you can help me buy gifts for my mother and sister. Diane's an art student in Paris, and I never know what to get her."

"I'd be glad to help. I just love to buy presents for other people, especially when I don't have to pay for them."

"Are you going to buy something for Cal?" Mark asked, watching her reaction.

Amanda's smile proved his question didn't bother her. "I already did. He's getting a pair of antique cuff links. He lost one on the last trip we took."

"Sounds like a nice gift," Mark said, then turned to accept the tray filled with their food from the waitress. They found a tent with tables and chairs inside. Mark carefully set Amanda's present on the table, just out of reach.

"Can I open it when I get to the car?" She poured mustard on her hot dog. "I'll let you see what I bought you."

"You're worse than a kid. I think I'll make you wait until we get back to London." That was the wrong thing to say. They both knew what returning to the city meant. To cover his mistake he quickly added, "If you'll keep quiet about it, *perhaps* you can open your present at Mrs. Wilde's."

Amanda took a huge bite of her hot dog. Talking around the food, she mumbled, "Then let's hurry and get there."

Mark laughed. He set his hamburger down and wiped his mouth and fingers. "I should have known you'd be the impatient type. I bet you inspected every Christmas package. Or did you find a way to see what was inside before they were wrapped?"

"I never had a chance. My mother kept them at our next-door neighbor's house." Amanda hadn't thought about Margo Buchanan for months. Margo would know what was going on with her mother or if her father had found a way to return home. Amanda could rely on Margo's discretion. Yes, as soon as she could, she'd contact Margo.

"Remembering Christmas past?" Mark asked. He'd seen the way Amanda's expression changed when she mentioned her mother. Without even being told, he knew deserting her family still bothered her conscience. Someday she would have to go back and make amends.

When she didn't respond to his question, he asked, "What are you thinking about?"

"My father. More than any man I've ever met he loved holidays, birthdays, Christmas, anniversaries— any chance to give or receive presents. I learned why by accident. In an old book I found a poem he'd written when he was ten. It was about a mother who had died, how there wasn't enough food in the house, and about the brutal father who never came home sober. I knew my dad had written it about himself. In all the time I've known him he never once referred to his childhood."

Mark reached over and placed his hand on hers. Before he could ask any questions, she smiled an apology, grabbed her soft drink and drank until it was nearly gone. She glanced down at Mark's half-eaten sandwich. "Hurry up. We've got a long way to go."

A long way to go, Mark thought, realizing just how well that phrase described their relationship. And they had so little time.

AFTER A DINNER of fish and chips at a noisy, crowded pub, they returned to the Black Swan Inn. Amanda had been quiet for most of the evening, letting Mark carry the conversation alone. She couldn't seem to shake the odd mood she'd been in since they'd returned from Wales. Tears always seemed about ready to form. She felt that if she didn't keep strict control over her emotions, she'd actually cry. Even without thinking too much about her strange feeling, she knew the cause. This was her final night with Mark. Tomorrow morning they'd drive to London, and that would be the last she'd ever see of him. She'd had her taste of independence, but all she'd accomplished was to add to her confusion.

"Let's go to the sitting room," Mark said as he closed the door behind them. "And I'll let you open your present."

Amanda almost said she was tired and would rather go up to her room, but that wasn't fair to Mark. She'd made such a big deal about opening her gift that she couldn't just ignore it. Besides, she was anxious to see what he'd gotten her and to give him his present.

"I'm going up to my room for a minute," Amanda said, heading toward the stairs. She intended to take an aspirin to see if she could get rid of the headache that had lingered just behind her eyes all evening.

"We'll need glasses for our brandy." Mark held up a paper-wrapped bottle. "I guess we'll have to use the ones with our toothbrushes in them."

Amanda laughed. "I'll bring the goblets we used for the champagne."

"Hurry back," Mark said as he entered the dimly lit room. He didn't switch on any more lamps, liking the ambience of the muted light. He retrieved Amanda's box from the cupboard by the fireplace where he'd put it before they left for dinner. After pulling the drapes aside so that they could see the moonlight on the water, he opened one of the side windows to let the floral-scented air drift in. When Amanda walked into the room, he had the brandy bottle opened and his coat off. He sat on the sofa, his arm along the back.

She had changed into slacks and a soft sweater. Instead of high heels she now wore loafers. With her hair pulled back from her face she gave the impression of being much younger than the sophisticated woman he'd taken to dinner.

"It's a little dark in here, isn't it?" Amanda asked as she put the glasses on the table. Beside it she placed a package wrapped in tissue paper. It was the size and thickness of a large book. "We won't be able to see what we bought each other."

"We'll use the braille system." Mark took Amanda's arm and guided her to sit beside him.

For a long moment he stared into her eyes. The only sound in the room was the ticking of the grandfather clock out in the hall, but Amanda was positive she could hear Mark's heart beating a rapid rhythm. She felt her own pulse quicken, causing her to catch her breath in her throat.

Mark broke the spell by kissing her lightly on the lips. "You've been patient long enough," he said, reaching for the heavy box and setting it on her lap. "You can go first."

Amanda slowly loosened the tape, again astounded by the weight of the package. She felt a need to lighten the mood. "I know, you've bought cut-up sections of the iron rails used by the first locomotives in England."

"Good guess," Mark said, setting aside the brown wrapping paper.

When the top of the box was revealed, Amanda gasped in surprise. "It's...it's like the table at Warwick Castle. *Pietra dura* set in ebony."

"I couldn't find a pirate's treasure chest. This was the closest I could come."

Amanda's eyes were bright as she turned the key and opened the lid. She said nothing more as she lifted one of the pieces of jade and rubbed her thumb over the smooth surface. She reached over and turned on a small lamp, then held one of the tokens up so that the light shone through. "There's writing on it," she said. "It's a one and three zeros. One thousand?"

"They're gambling tokens," Mark explained. "On the other side is the letter *R*. I wish it had been a *K*."

Amanda just shook her head, unable to voice her amazement. The coincidence of the letters on the chips matching her real last name was utterly astounding.

Mark closed the lid and pushed the button on the lock. The bottom drawer slid open to reveal the playing cards. With shaky hands Amanda lifted one of the decks and pulled it out of its soft leather case. The cards were in excellent condition, considering their age. The colors had been hand-painted and were faded, but the figures were still clearly visible.

"Look," Amanda said, "this is the nine of swords and here's the five of cups. This suit is the coins and this is the baton. I've only read about the early Italian cards. I never thought I'd see any." At that moment she realized what Mark had done. "How much did you pay for all of this?"

"Didn't your mother teach you not to ask questions like that?"

"Mark! I'm not kidding."

"I'm not going to tell you," he said, reaching for the package Amanda had bought for him. "My turn."

She touched his arm. "Please tell me, Mark. I need to know."

"Why? What difference does it make?"

Amanda sighed. She had no right to ask. "No difference, I guess." She closed the lid and ran her fingers over the smooth surface. The stones had been fitted together so perfectly that it was impossible to discern by touch alone where the lapis met the coral, the agate touched the jasper.

Mark lifted her chin with his finger. "I wanted to give you a gift, and I found the perfect one. Don't spoil it for me."

"It's wonderful, and I'll treasure it always. Thank you." She still felt shaken by the knowledge of what the box must have cost. No dealer would have sold the ebony casket, the jade chips and the cards for under twenty thousand dollars, and even at that price he would have cheated himself. At a Sotheby's auction the bidding could have been three or four times that amount. She remembered reading about a perfectly preserved and hand-painted fifteenth-century Flemish pack of cards that had sold at Sotheby's in 1983 for ninety thousand pounds—nearly a hundred and fifty thousand dollars.

"Okay?" Mark asked. "Can I open my present now?"

Amanda glanced up. "Yes. But don't get your hopes up. If I'd known you were going to get so carried away, I'd have bought that vase you *so* admired." She slipped her shoes off.

"Sarcasm, my dear, is the last resort of the loser in an argument." He poured brandy into the two glasses and handed one to her. They touched the goblets together in a silent toast.

Mark sipped his brandy, but Amanda only inhaled the heady fumes, then set her glass down. She didn't need the intoxication of liquor tonight. The excitement Mark generated in her was more than she could handle. "Open your present."

When Mark finally revealed what was in the cardboard box, he was too surprised even to speak. Finally he glanced up and smiled. "You knew exactly what I'd like." Using the tips of his fingers on the edge of the thick cream paper, he carefully lifted an original three-view drawing of a Sopwith Camel. The lines were sharp and clear, as if they'd just been completed. On the bottom was the date, 1915, and the signature of the artist. "Thank you. This is the best present I've ever received."

"I wish I'd been able to get it framed," Amanda said. "I could get it done and mail it to you in Philadelphia." Her words echoed in the silent room, reminding both of them that soon he had to return to his duties, she to hers.

"Yes, I suppose you could." If she took the picture, then he'd know for sure they'd be in contact. He placed the drawing back in the carton and moved it, the ebony box and the wrappings to the table. His actions were slow and leisurely, as if he had all the time in the world.

But in truth he was barely able to contain his impatience.

"Come here," he whispered to Amanda, drawing her toward him. She offered no resistance as he lifted her arms and wrapped them around his neck.

After a long kiss, Amanda nestled her head against his shoulder and sighed. She again felt tears sting her eyes, but she had no idea if they were tears of happiness or regret that their time together would soon be over. All she knew for sure was that she wanted to be in Mark's arms. What happened tomorrow didn't matter. She'd face that when she had to.

"Amanda?" Mark murmured with his mouth against her hair. He stroked her back.

"Hmmm?"

He reached up with one hand and loosened her hair from its clasp, which he tossed onto the table. "What are you thinking?"

"My mind's stopped working." She placed her hand on the side of his neck, feeling the heat of his flesh.

"I want to take you upstairs . . ."

Surprised, she started to sit up, but he held her in place. "Mark, I—"

"Hush. Just listen. I want you to know exactly what I plan to do. When we get to my room, I'm going to close the drapes, but I'll keep the light on. Then I'll pull this sweater over your head and toss it aside." He slipped his hand under the knitted material and let his fingers lightly trace random patterns on her back. Her skin felt as smooth as the ebony of the box, yet warm and yielding.

"Then what are you going to do?" The sensations that washed over her kept her from protesting when he unfastened the back of her bra.

"When you're naked from the waist up, I'm going to touch your breasts...."

Her breath caught in her throat as his palm glided over her nipples.

"Then I'll kiss you like this." His lips found hers, causing her head to swim.

When the kiss ended, he said, "I intend to loosen the button and zipper of your slacks. When they fall to the floor, I'll step back so I can see your beauty. Are you visualizing the scene?"

"Yes." She spoke the whispered word without thinking. Mark's descriptions and the actions of his fingers were creating vivid images in her mind that she couldn't control, nor did she want to.

"Then it can be your turn." He placed her hand on the buttons of his shirt. "You can start to undress me."

She did as he directed. When his shirt was open to the waist, she ran her fingertips over his naked skin. His breathing deepened, matching her own. He no longer acted as cool and detached as he had when he was describing his planned scenario.

"What'll you do next, Amanda?"

"I thought you were the type of man who liked prac—Mark!" she gasped as he again ran his hand over her breasts.

"You were saying?" His tone was formal and serious, as if he had no idea why she'd reacted that way.

She grabbed his hand. "I thought you liked practice better than theory." She finished the sentence with laughter in her voice.

"I do. But before we go up those stairs I need to ask you something."

She gazed quizzically at him. "Yes," she responded, already knowing he was giving her a way to end his seduction. "You're going to ask if we know each other well enough to be doing this."

"I don't want you to have any doubts or regrets."

It only took her a few seconds to decide. "At the pool, when I asked you to meet me in London, I thought of us as two friends, planning to spend time together. But from the moment I decided to ask you to come here with me, I suspected we'd make love. Subconsciously I guess I've been planning it all along but wasn't brave enough to admit it."

"And you haven't changed your mind?"

She smiled, feeling totally free of all restraints. "No. Have you?"

Mark didn't answer. He stood, grabbed her hand, then hurried out of the room and up the narrow, winding stairs.

"Don't forget to duck," Amanda said just as he opened the door to his room.

"Thanks," he said, pulling her in after him.

From that moment on they followed the stage directions that Mark had described. When Amanda stood naked before him, she felt no embarrassment, only excitement as she watched the admiration in his eyes change to desire. Every place he touched became a pleasure point, deepening the throbbing ache inside her.

When it was her turn to undress Mark, she didn't hesitate. As she let her fingers explore his chest and back, his long thighs and legs, she realized she'd never been this bold, this uninhibited. There was no question in her mind what effect her actions were having on Mark.

"Amanda, I—" He had to stop and take a deep breath. When he gained some degree of control, he pulled her into his arms and pressed her body against his, lifting her off her feet and carrying her toward the bed. Mrs. Wilde had closed the drapes, turned down the blankets and replaced yesterday's flowers with lilacs and roses. Their scent filled the room.

With his lips lightly touching Amanda's, he murmured, "You're beautiful," and placed her on the bed, taking the opportunity to touch her golden-red hair spread out on the pillow. She had removed her earrings.

"You're not so bad yourself," she answered.

Mark's laughter was a joyous sound, making her smile in response.

"Move over," he ordered.

She slid to the middle of the double bed, lifting her arms toward him.

He lay beside her. "If we don't know each other well enough now, just wait." He shifted his weight, pulling her under him. "I'm going to show you what I meant by an act of sharing."

Never before had she known what heights of passion her body could reach. Each place he touched, every time he kissed her, she felt her passion building... intensifying...inundating her until she could no longer think, until all she could do was feel. Where a few moments before they'd been two people, now they became one. And for the first time in her life she understood that the act of love could be a true sharing.

CHAPTER EIGHT

AMANDA AWAKENED at a little past five. At that hour she was usually just going to sleep. The room was chilly, but she felt warm and protected lying next to Mark. His arm lay over her stomach, as if he were afraid she'd try to escape. Sometime after she'd fallen asleep he must have covered them both with the sheet and blanket.

Trying not to disturb him, she shifted so she could see his face in the dim light that filtered through the closed drapes. In repose he looked younger and more vulnerable than when he was awake. The two small bruises on his forehead enhanced the image. But all of his strength of character, intelligence and handsomeness were also visible. She placed her head against his shoulder, breathing in his unique scent. She recalled last night's events. The memories brought a blush to her cheeks, not of shame but of remembered passion. She felt no regrets, only a deep satisfaction that they'd been able to give and receive so much pleasure.

But now reality had to be faced. In just a few more hours she'd be in London. Late in the afternoon she and Cal were to fly to San Francisco, where they would rent a car and drive to Lake Tahoe. A year ago, when she met Cal there, she'd made choices that had changed the direction of her life. Returning to Tahoe might offer her an opportunity to change direction again. She was older and a little wiser than she'd been the night she'd arrived at the lake. This time she'd be in control of her destiny.

But would her future include Mark Banning? Was it possible she was falling in love with him?

She had no answers. Just because they'd made love didn't mean they were committed to anything permanent. She had obligations she couldn't ignore. Her time with Mark might have to be relegated to memory, a period in her life that she would never forget. Because of the uncertainty of her future, that was the only attitude she could take right now.

Mark turned in her direction, startling her. "Amanda?" He sounded sleepy.

"I'm still here," she said. At that moment she remembered her gift. She had carelessly left the box downstairs. She sat up and started to slip out of bed. "I've got to get—"

Mark grabbed her around the waist and pulled her on top of him.

"Where do you think you're going?"

"My box. I want to—"

"Nothing's going to happen to it. We're alone in the house."

"But—" Her words of protest were cut off by his lips. When the kiss ended, she again tried to tell him she wanted to go downstairs, but her argument was soon forgotten as Mark began to arouse her passion.

"Oh, Mark..." she murmured, giving in to the sensations that swept through her. There was magic in Mark's fingers that made it impossible for her to think straight. The night before he'd discovered how to make her weak with pleasure. But that was nothing compared to this morning.

When the heat of their passion had cooled, Mark sighed in utter contentment. "Come to Philadelphia with me. We can leave today and—"

Amanda had placed her fingers over his mouth. "Don't spoil what we've shared, please. You know as well as I do that I have to go back. Not to would be dishonorable, and neither of us wants that." By being here with Mark she'd already been less than honorable to Cal. She couldn't just keep compounding her errors.

"But we could work something out."

"Mark, I refuse to listen." She sat up, slipped out of bed and grabbed the first piece of clothing she could find—Mark's shirt. She pulled it around her naked body and held the front closed with her shaky fingers. With the other hand she brushed her hair back from her face. As much as she hated to, she had to put on a show of anger. She knew if she let him continue with his persuasive talk, he would convince her to go with him.

"I'm going to take a shower." She gathered her clothes from the floor and headed for the door. "The car is leaving for London in one hour. If you want a ride, be ready."

Mark lay back down and shoved the pillow behind his neck. "Damn." He should have known there was no way he could persuade her to leave Cal in the lurch, at least not in such an underhanded way. When was he going to learn that her loyalty to Cal ran deep, perhaps so deep she'd never be able to get out of the relationship? No, he'd find a way to get her to come to Philadelphia.

The next question that formed in his mind made him sit straight up in bed. What kind of commitment was he willing to make? Marriage? "Yes, by damn." He again spoke out loud, the words echoing in the still room. He was in love with her, and unless he'd received the wrong signals, and he knew he hadn't, she was learning to love him, too. Before they got to London he would get her to make some plans for a reunion in the not-too-distant future.

And what about Orion? he asked himself as he slipped out of bed. He could juggle both priorities. He would arrange it so that Amanda was with him while he learned the company's secrets.

AMANDA SILENTLY CURSED the London traffic. Today was even worse than the day they'd left. A truck and a double-decker bus had collided a few blocks from Mark's hotel. Now she and Mark were caught in a gridlock, which didn't make the situation in the car any more pleasant. Since they'd left the Black Swan Inn, they'd only spoken in brief questions and answers, making decisions about where to stop for lunch, or whether to visit Oxford or continue on. Amanda had purposely tried to maintain a neutral stance, friendly yet reserved. Mark hadn't objected to the long silences.

She knew their making love had totally changed the relationship. But why should it? They were two consenting adults. Neither had done anything that could cause them to regret their actions. And yet thoughts of Cal kept creeping in, especially now that she would be seeing him in a short time.

She again asked herself the question that had haunted her for hours. Was what she felt for Mark love, or was it merely infatuation? Whatever she'd experienced with him was totally different from anything she'd experienced before with any man. As far as her feelings for Cal, she was so confused that she couldn't form a logical thought. Was it possible to be in love with both Cal and Mark? Love, she had just realized, could assume many different guises. She was just having difficulty recognizing them.

"It looks like we'll be here for a while," Mark said, startling her out of her thoughts. "I could get out and walk to the hotel."

"No! That's not necessary," Amanda quickly added in a softer tone. She put the car in neutral and turned toward him. "I'm sorry for the way I acted this morning."

"There's no need to apologize. We were both on an emotional high. And we knew your time for fraternization was over."

"Mark, that was uncalled for."

He took her hand in his. "I know it was. But, damn it, I don't want to lose you. This weekend has meant too much to me just to kiss you a fond adieu and go back home. I want some assurances—"

"You said you were willing to accept only what I was prepared to give. Now it's time for us to get back to the real world. I have a job to do. I can't make any promises. Until I can...well, until I see what my future holds, you'll just have to be patient."

"Are you going to talk to your parents?"

"Yes. As soon as I can." She'd start out by using Margo Buchanan as an intermediary.

"How long will I have to be patient?"

"I don't know." Mark wasn't making this easy. There was no way she could judge what was going to happen with the partnership between her and Cal. The main problem was she didn't know how she felt toward Cal or what direction to take. She wished she had someone in whom she could confide, a nonjudgmental friend who could advise her. But the only friends she had were Cal . . . and Mark.

"Make some kind of commitment," he said. "Don't just leave me dangling."

"Okay. In the next few days I'll talk to Cal about the partnership. I haven't said anything to him, but I think he suspects I've been feeling a need to make some changes. He mentioned how much pressure we've been under lately. When I've got everything worked out, I'll contact you in Philadelphia." She smiled. With the tips of her fingers she rubbed away the frown that had formed on his brow. "I promise to get everything done as quickly as I can."

"I'm going to make reservations at the Black Swan Inn for one month from today. We'll meet there."

"Mark, don't do that. I'm not sure—"

"Anything you have to do can be done in thirty days."

"I'll try, Mark. That's all I can promise."

He sighed, knowing she'd made as much of a commitment as she could.

A horn honking made them realize the traffic had moved ahead of them. When she pulled in front of his hotel, he bent forward and kissed her, a long, leisurely kiss that was meant to be remembered. Then he reached behind him, grabbed his bag and Amanda's wrapped box and opened the door. "Don't forget to get my sketch framed." He stood on the curb and bent down to look inside the car.

"I won't forget." Seeing her gift in his hands, she was reminded of how he had insisted he take it back to the States and pay the customs fee on it. No amount of arguing had changed his mind. "Hang on to my box until I contact you. I'll tell you where to mail it."

"Oh, no, you don't. The gifts will be exchanged, in person, one month from today. At the Black Swan Inn."

His intense frown made her laugh.

"Do you agree?" he growled.

"I'll try."

"Be there!" He slammed the door, stood back and waved as she drove off.

FOR THE HUNDREDTH TIME since she'd walked into her hotel room to find Evan Rawlings waiting for her, she wished she'd gone to Cal's room first. But, coward that she was, she'd felt she needed time to gather her thoughts before confronting him. And now she had to face Evan alone, without knowing what was going on. He'd refused to let her talk to Cal. Rawlings said *he* was in charge now. His motto seemed to be divide and conquer.

They sat opposite each other in the sitting room, she in a wing chair, he on the couch. He poured vodka over ice and handed her the glass. She accepted it but didn't drink. While she'd been with Mark, many important, possibly disastrous, events had taken place. Another straw had just been added to her already heavy load of guilt.

Evan settled back in the sofa, acting totally at home. Amanda kept her spine stiff, offering nothing that would encourage him.

"So you know my real name is Susan Ross. If you think that's going to change my mind about refusing to have you as a partner, you're wrong."

"Oh, I'll be your partner, all right. In more ways than one."

"You're bluffing."

He shook his head, amusement creating wrinkles at the corners of his eyes. "I only bluff at cards. Besides your name, I learned all about your father and the phony plane crash. I knew he won a lot of money from a man named Septimus Garland and just how much Septimus wants to get his hands on Craig Ross."

This time Amanda gasped. The full realization of what Evan was saying finally dawned on her. Unless she cooperated he would tell Garland that her father wasn't dead. Who knew what a man like Garland might do then?

Evan began to talk about Craig and the business troubles that had plagued him before his disappearance, information which she already knew. She sat with her hands in her lap, hoping she looked calm and fearless. But her heart was pounding in her chest; her throat was so dry that she couldn't swallow. She couldn't seem to keep her mind on what Evan was saying. All she could think about was how to get herself and Cal out of this predicament. Suddenly something Evan said caught her attention. She sat up, now listening intently.

"He thought he could win the money he needed. Your father was a cocky bastard, wasn't he?" When Amanda offered no response, Evan continued. "He,

Garland and a group of businessmen organized a game. Everything clicked for Craig that night. He won a huge amount of money. Garland wanted to recoup his losses, so he and Craig played double or nothing on the winnings, just on the turn of a single card. Garland claimed Craig won only because he cheated. I don't know how your father got away, but he kept his money, which proves what a resourceful man he is. He escaped and disappeared before Garland could do anything."

"Did my father cheat?" Knowing the truth was important to her. She wanted to find some way to begin loving him again.

"No," Evan said, "I don't think so. I don't see how he could have. Craig liked to gamble, but card tricks weren't his strong point. That's the trouble with playing with men like Garland. They don't like to lose. I'd have paid a thousand grand to see him when he heard about the plane crash." Evan laughed quietly, then rubbed his knee, acting as if he were lost in thought for a moment.

Finally he looked over at Amanda. "Garland even tried to make a claim against the estate. Felicia's lawyer, Bill Delaplane, told Garland that money lost at gambling wasn't a legitimate claim. A threat of a court injunction kept him from bothering your mother again." Evan looked at Amanda. "You see, a court injunction might have resulted in an investigation into Garland's affairs."

"Go on," she said, wishing she hadn't returned to the hotel. She could be with Mark....

"By faking his death your father saved himself and his company. Felicia used the money to get the business out of the hole. She's a clever woman. I guess Ross Computers is doing very well."

"I don't see what any of this has to do with me," Amanda said. Even though she was feeling nauseated and shaky, she held herself steady, refusing to reveal the physical manifestations of her fear. "It's all in the past. Better forgotten."

Evan didn't speak for a long moment. His expression was without his usual mocking humor. "Garland's got a long memory and far-reaching resources." He again rubbed his knee. On his face was a momentary expression of pain. "If he ever found out Craig wasn't dead, he'd get his revenge, even if he never got his money back. Garland would kill your father... slowly and painfully."

For the first time in her life Amanda felt true terror. She quickly stood. "I... I'm going to the bathroom."

"You'd better start getting ready. Our plane is scheduled to leave in about three hours."

"*Our* plane? You're going with us?"

"Yes, I am. I'm the new partner, remember?"

She didn't make the comment that came to mind. Instead she hurried across the room, entered the bedroom and leaned against the shut door, gasping for breath. She shivered uncontrollably.

For a moment she couldn't think. Then it occurred to her to wonder how Rawlings had discovered that Craig wasn't dead. And why had he investigated the matter so thoroughly? What connection was there between Rawlings, her father and Garland? And what about Cal? Had he meekly acquiesced to Evan? No. That was impossible. There had to be some other reason why he'd allowed Evan to take over.

After she finished getting packed and dressed, she reentered the sitting room and asked the question that had kept repeating in her mind.

"I wondered when you'd think to ask that." He stood and poured himself a drink. She refused his suggestion to take one. When they were both reseated, he said, "A gambler friend of mine happened to see Craig in the Dallas airport. You haven't seen him lately, so you wouldn't know he's changed his appearance with cosmetic surgery. But he still has that habit of rolling a thick gold coin back and forth across the tops of his fingers."

In an instant Amanda could visualize her father. As far back as she could remember, he had constantly played with the good-luck talisman, a Spanish doubloon he'd won a long time ago. He had let her hold it as a child, promising that someday the gold coin would be hers.

"The coin was a sure giveaway," Evan said. "When I found out Craig was alive, I decided to investigate why he needed to disappear. I learned about his connection with Garland and the three-million-dollar gambling session."

Amanda's head spun. Rawlings knew everything.

"I was amazed when I learned he'd won that much. I guess it was just one of those nights when everyone at the table went a little crazy. It can happen."

She looked over at Evan. He had nearly finished his drink. "How did you get on my trail?"

Evan smiled, looking smug. "When I heard Craig's daughter had disappeared, I wanted to see whether there was a connection with Garland. But I reached a dead end. Your mother's expensive private detectives couldn't find you, and neither could I."

"But how—?"

He held his hand up. "I don't want to give away all my secrets. We're going to have a lot of time for true confessions, so just relax."

Amanda stood. "I'm going to talk to Cal."

Before she could take one step Evan was beside her. "You're not doing anything until I say you can."

"What gives you the right—?"

"This."

In front of her face was the gold doubloon. Craig's! She'd seen it often enough to know. She felt her knees begin to buckle, but Evan was holding her arm. His fingers dug in, hurting her. She couldn't break loose.

"My men have got Ross tucked away in a nice, safe place. But don't worry. After I accomplish what I want, you can be reunited with your father. Then all of the interested parties can go their separate ways."

Amanda realized she was trapped. Everything hinged on her total submission to Evan's will, or he'd reveal Craig's whereabouts to Garland. Her only hope was that she and Cal could find a way to counter Rawlings's threats and escape.

She thought about Mark and was glad he was going back to Philadelphia and wouldn't be in harm's way.

"Seen anything of Mark Banning?"

Hearing Evan say the name startled her. It was as if he'd read her mind.

"He hasn't been at his hotel since Friday. Did you go away with him?"

So he'd checked up on Mark's whereabouts. It was important to his safety that Rawlings not know her relationship with Mark. "No. I went alone." She yanked her arm out of his grasp and stepped back. Lifting her head, she stared straight into his eyes. He relaxed, seeming to accept her answer.

"Good," he said, and reached for his glass, draining it. He shook his head, as if his next thought amazed him. "On the ship, when I realized who the fifth player was, I couldn't believe my bad luck. I thought everything was going to get screwed up."

Amanda frowned, confused by his words. She tried to think back to the poker game and the conversation between him and Mark. Evan had gambled with Mark's stepbrother. But why was Mark's presence on the ship bad luck? "What do you mean?"

"Rob Quintero's been given a part to play in the little production I'm putting together."

If Rob was involved, it had to be because of his passion for gambling, and Rob's connection with Rawlings might somehow present problems for Mark. How could she warn him? Something in her expression must have triggered Evan's anger because he stepped closer to her, forcing her to look at him.

"You're the linchpin of this whole setup, which means you are *not* to have any contact with Banning. No one can learn what we're doing, especially not that man. He could mess everything up." His eyes narrowed, becoming even more threatening. "If I get the tiniest hint you've talked to him, I can goddamn guarantee he'll be killed. You've graduated to the big time now, and there's no way out."

Rawlings seemed to shake off his ugly mood and began to act more agreeable. He smiled and said, "I've got to get packed." His abrupt change of subject disconcerted her. "Since you and Cal were on your way to Tahoe, that's where we'll base our operations. After we get there, I'll reveal the next step in my plan."

CHAPTER NINE

WHEN AMANDA DROVE OFF, leaving Mark standing in front of the hotel, he'd never felt more alone. As soon as he got to his room, he walked to the phone to call her, then changed his mind. There was no point in making her confrontation with Cal any more complicated.

When he entered the hotel, the front desk clerk had handed him a stack of messages from his mother in Paris. He knew he'd better call his sister's apartment immediately. When Diane answered the phone, he said, "I'm surprised you're home. Did the stores close early?"

"Very funny."

"What does mother want?"

"I'm fine, thank you, dear brother."

He grinned, remembering the teasing sessions with his sister that had infuriated his mother. "Sorry, dear sister. How are you? How are the art classes coming? Does Andrew Wyeth have anything to worry about yet?"

"I'm well. The classes are super. Andy had better pack up his easel and retire."

"Send me a picture for my birthday," he ordered. "It's next week, remember?"

"I've got one all ready. It's a nude, so I hope it'll pass customs."

"Nude male or female?"

"I prefer working with male models, for obvious reasons. But for you, old confirmed bachelor, I've painted a female. Just so you can get the idea. I'd like to have some nieces and nephews before I get too old to enjoy them."

Mark thought about Amanda and smiled. Instead of reporting that he'd found a woman he was particularly interested in, which would only result in endless questions, he said, "You could have some kids of your own."

"Bite your tongue! I'm having too much fun." She paused. "I'll send the painting back with Mom. Here, you can talk to her."

"See you later, pest."

"Not if I can help it, brat."

After a moment, Connie came on the line. "Where have you been?" she asked accusingly.

"I went out to see the English countryside."

"You could have let me know."

She was right, of course. He hadn't bothered to call and tell her he was leaving the hotel. "Sorry. It was a last-minute change of plans. What did you want?"

"I'm not going back with you. I've decided to stay here. You can come to Paris or go back home whenever you want."

Mark smiled. Give his mother a slice of freedom from her domineering husband and she takes the whole loaf, he thought. "What'll Edward say?"

"I've talked to him. He said he had no objections to my staying. Before we left he was busy on a big project and hardly ever came home, so I doubt he'll miss me."

That statement summed up their seventeen years of marriage.

"I'm glad you'll be with Diane. You two have a good time. Call if you want me to pick you up at the airport."

"Yes, I will. Bye."

Mark set the phone down and sighed. The temptation to phone Amanda had become too great to ignore. No matter the consequences, he had to talk to her. The hotel operator connected him. The phone rang for a long time. With each passing moment his fears grew. Had she already gone to Heathrow? He couldn't have missed her! He had to talk to her before she left.

Just as he was about ready to put the receiver down, she answered. Her voice sounded breathless, as if she'd been running.

"Hi, my darling," he said. "Where—?"

"Mark!"

He couldn't believe what he'd heard in the single whispered word—something akin to fear, with a little anger mixed in. "What's the matter?"

After a moment she said, "Nothing. I was on my way out the door. I've got a plane to catch. What is it you want?"

"Just to say goodbye and to tell you how much I enjoyed our time together." He gave a short laugh. "That's the understatement of the year. I'm not sure I recognize all the signs, but I could swear I'm falling in—"

"Mark, please. Don't say anything you might regret." She continued to keep her voice low, as if she didn't want to be overheard.

"But I don't understand. What do you mean?"

"While I was with you I had a wonderful time, too. But let's not lose our sense of proportion."

"If that's a brush-off, you're sure beating around the bush about it." He didn't like his choice of clichés, but right at that moment his anger had disturbed his thinking processes.

"It isn't a brush-off. I told you. I have a job to do. I'll meet you in England in a month. Or else I'll call you in Philadelphia. Other than that I can't make any promises. Now I've got to go. Goodbye, Mark. I—I'm sorry...."

The line went dead. When he tried her room again, there was no answer. His next call was to the registration desk at the Berkeley. Miss Kirk's bill had been paid earlier that day. He asked if the receptionist could check to see if she was still in the hotel. In a moment the woman was back on the line. Miss Kirk had just left, accompanied by two men. The doorman said they ordered the taxi to take them to Heathrow.

Mark slowly returned the receiver to its proper place. Two men! Who the hell...? Rawlings? She'd said that Rawlings wanted to become a partner in their gambling operation. But Mark had gotten the distinct impression they were going to turn him down. Rawlings could have stayed at the Berkeley, planning to try again to convince them to let him join their operation. Perhaps he'd succeeded. No. Amanda disliked the man too much. He would have been turned down. It was possible he was leaving London at the same time and had hitched a ride to the airport. Sure, that was it.

But why had she been so cold and distant on the phone? Had Cal learned that she hadn't been alone on her little vacation and had been giving her a hard time? If that was true, Mark knew he deserved to share in the blame.

But there was nothing he could do to help now. When he got back to Philadelphia, he might try to contact her, to see if she needed any help. But where had she and Cal said they were going to visit when they left England? Right at that moment Mark couldn't remember. It would come to him—he hoped.

He again reached for the phone, changing his plane reservations. He could leave at nine that night. As soon as he got to Philadelphia, he'd go to the plant to start looking into Rob's affairs. He only had a month before he'd be meeting Amanda.

"WHAT DO YOU THINK?" Cal asked Amanda as she walked into the living room of the luxurious house.

Through the floor-to-ceiling windows she could see the sparkling blue waters of Lake Tahoe. "I'm all turned around. Are we in California or Nevada?"

"Nevada," Rawlings said, following her into the room. "Sort of on the northeast side." He, too, surveyed the room, acting pleased with what he saw. "The rent was steep, but I decided we might as well be comfortable. It's got a dock on the lake, and we can use the speedboat if it ever gets warm enough." He turned toward Amanda. "Do you like it?" he asked, as if her opinion were important to him.

"Yes, it's very nice." She lifted the smallest of her suitcases.

Cal grabbed the rest of her luggage and said, "Your room's down here." Amanda followed him. He opened a bedroom door for her, entered and set her luggage on the bed. "You take this room."

Amanda watched as he carefully placed Mark's paper-wrapped print on the pillows, out of the way. He hadn't asked her about it, and she hadn't volunteered any information. There hadn't been an opportunity to give him his gift.

"It's got a view of the lake." Cal smiled at her, the first emotion he'd shown since they'd left London. "I'll be right across the hall."

Amanda knew he'd thought out the room assignments when the agent showed him the house. Rawlings had told Cal he was to be the contact person with the real estate agent. Only Cal's name was on the rental agreement. Rawlings was playing it safe. Whatever his plan was, he intended to be as anonymous as possible.

"And where'll I be?" Rawlings asked, peeking his head around the door.

"I'll show you. It's at the opposite end of the house, but you'll have your own bathroom and a lake view." Cal's message was clear. Evan was to be as far away from Amanda as possible. Surprisingly he didn't object, but just followed Cal across the living room to the west wing.

Amanda walked to the window, but the spectacular view didn't register on her brain. She wasn't sure what ached worse—her head or her back. The flight had been crowded. All night people had wandered up and down the aisles like restless cattle, except that cows would have been less noisy. She had felt so tense that she couldn't sleep. And Rawlings had insisted she sit next to him, so she hadn't had a chance to talk to Cal.

After their arrival in San Francisco, she'd waited in the airport while Cal had phoned Tahoe agents requesting a house to rent. After driving four and a half hours, while Amanda had tried unsuccessfully to keep her mind off Mark and her memories, they had gotten to the agent's office. Amanda had refused to participate in deciding what house they'd rent. She'd said she didn't care and she'd meant it. What difference did it make where she spent her prison term? In fact, prison would have been preferable to being with Evan.

After what seemed like hours of driving around the lake, Cal had finally made a decision about the house, choosing a place built in the 1960s—a private estate once owned by a millionaire attorney in San Francisco.

Now, in the privacy of her room, she could try to unwind. She glanced at her watch. It was nearly five, but she didn't feel hungry. Since there was no food in the house, they would have to go out to eat their dinner. Before they left she'd take a shower and then she'd sleep, just for a little while....

THE MORNING LIGHT awakened her. Despite the sun streaming through the windows, the room was cool. She wore the robe she'd put on after her shower and was covered with a soft white blanket—undoubtedly Cal's contribution to her comfort. She'd slept as if she'd been doped. Yet she didn't feel truly rested. As soon as she opened her eyes, she remembered Rawlings and his threats. All her fears, doubts and questions returned to haunt her.

Why had Cal agreed to Rawlings's terms? Had Rawlings told him about her father and what would happen if they didn't cooperate? Or did Rawlings have something on Cal, a secret he didn't want revealed? As soon as she could, she'd get Cal alone and find out what was going on.

She smelled bacon and coffee, and her stomach growled, reminding her it had been nearly twenty-four hours since she'd last eaten. No wonder her head ached.

Within minutes she'd pulled her hair back and tied it with a scarf and had dressed in jeans, a long-sleeved plaid shirt and loafers, one of the few casual outfits she had with her. If they were going to be here for any length of time, which she desperately hoped not, she'd have to find a store and buy more clothes.

When she entered the kitchen, Rawlings sat at the table, reading the paper. Cal was frying bacon. When he heard her, he turned and said, "Well, good morning. You slept over fifteen hours. You must be starved." His chipper tone didn't match the expression in his eyes. He stared at her for a long moment, as if trying to convey a message. Then he shrugged and turned back to his task.

"Sit down, Amanda," Rawlings said. "Have some orange juice. You look a little dragged out."

"Thanks for the kind words," she said, sitting as far away from him as she could. She didn't look in his direction, knowing that if she did, she'd say something that could only make matters worse. The juice was fresh and tasted like ambrosia. "Did you go to the grocery store, Cal?" She knew Rawlings wasn't the type to do anything domestic.

"Yes. I've been up since about six. Couldn't sleep. It's going to take us a while to get used to the altitude and the jet lag." He wiped his hands on the towel he'd inserted in the waistband of his slacks. "How do you want your eggs?"

"Scrambled." In that instant, thoughts of Mark filled her mind. She could see him sitting in that sunny little room at the Black Swan Inn, looking at his fried eggs and the rest of the high-cholesterol breakfast with amazement. She smiled when she remembered his comment on knowing how Mr. Wilde had died.

"What's so funny?" Rawlings asked.

She realized he'd been staring at her. "Nothing." She grabbed the *San Francisco Chronicle* and lifted the front page so Rawlings could no longer see her face. She'd better be careful. Since she'd found him in her hotel room, he'd kept close watch on her, commenting on her moods, trying to draw her out. So far she'd been able to cut him off.

She wished she could be alone with Cal. She glanced up at him, watching him as he worked at the stove. It never ceased to amaze her how a man as large and strong as he was could be so graceful and gentle.

Cal set her breakfast in front of her. With his back to Rawlings he winked, his signal that was supposed to mean all was well. But she knew everything had gone wrong. Her whole life, and his, too, was in a mess, and all because of her father and Evan Rawlings.

When Cal stepped away, she glared at Rawlings, an unmistakable message of animosity. But he merely smiled at her and buttered a piece of toast.

When they finished their nearly silent meal, Rawlings stood and stretched. "Guess I'll check out the action at the clubs. Want to join me, Amanda?"

"Walking on hot coals sounds like more fun. I'm going to sit in the sun."

Cal also declined, saying he had to clean up the kitchen. Amanda didn't think Rawlings would give her and Cal an opportunity to communicate. But after warning them not to do anything stupid, he left the house, acting happy to be on his way to a casino. As soon as he'd gone, the tension in the room lessened appreciably.

Cal sat at the table opposite her. "I didn't *just* accept Rawlings's proposition. I wouldn't have done that without asking you first. But I...I, well, that is..." Cal shook his head, unable to continue.

"You don't need to explain anything. I know Rawlings can be persuasive." Cal nodded and stood to fill their coffee cups. He got the milk from the refrigerator and busied himself with pouring it into a small cream pitcher.

How could he tell her what he'd done thirteen years ago? He knew she'd always looked up to him as her teacher and her friend. He didn't want her to know that he was a coward, a man who hadn't been able to accept responsibility for his actions. Keeping Amanda from learning the truth was more important than the possibility of being caught by the police.

Cal sat at the table but didn't speak, letting his thoughts jump from one subject to another. Since he'd met her, he'd been able to forget his past, at least whenever she was with him. She had such a power over him that he'd do anything for her...except tell the truth. Coward! he said to himself.

He remembered when they were first introduced at Harrah's Casino by his friend Tim Upland. Cal knew right then that he'd found the beautiful and skilled female business partner he'd been trying to find for years. In the next second he'd fallen in love. When she agreed to be his partner, he'd thought everything was going to be perfect. Given time she would come to love him. In the past two months he'd been positive her feelings for him were changing. She'd acted as if she'd been willing to deepen the relationship. But he'd waited too long. Rawlings had stepped into their lives, changing everything.

Cal realized that Rawlings's interference wasn't the only thing that had thrown a wrench into his relationship with Amanda. Something else had happened to her. Since her return from her trip to the Cotswolds, she'd acted differently. But he didn't know why.

"Cal?" Amanda said, placing her hand on his clenched fist, which lay on top of the table. He looked up and nodded. "We've got to decide what we're going to do about Rawlings."

"Got any ideas?" He ran his fingers through his auburn hair. "I sure as hell don't."

"He's got us just where he wants us," Amanda said. "I wish I knew what he was planning." Cal nodded again. His expression was one of total misery. She knew just how he felt. "I guess Rawlings has already told you my secret and that you went along with him just to protect me and my family. I thank you for that." Before he could speak she continued. "No matter what he said about my father I want to give my version of the story."

In relating the facts as she knew them, she again saw just how stupid and unfair she'd been the night she'd left home. She told Cal everything except the part about how she'd treated her parents, judging them without even bothering to learn all the facts.

When she finished the long, convoluted story, she leaned back in her chair and sighed. As she had when she told Mark the story, she felt better.

"Your father played in a poker game with Septimus Garland and won?" Cal's voice sounded incredulous. "And then managed to escape with all his winnings? By God, that's something to write home about."

"Do you know Garland?"

"Just by reputation, which isn't good." Cal laughed. "Craig Ross is the luckiest man I've ever heard about. He wins against Garland, gets away with his money and then survives a plane crash in the Atlantic."

"I don't call that lucky. He wouldn't have gotten into all this trouble if he'd simply weathered out the storm at his company and not tried to solve his problems by gambling."

"Yeah, but he won. The money saved Ross Computers."

When Amanda thought about the turmoil her father had caused in her own life and what pain her mother had suffered, she knew no company was worth the cost. "Sometimes winning isn't everything," she said in a low voice.

Cal grinned. "No, but it comes a close second."

Amanda laughed, glad to see his sense of humor return. "Spoken like a true gambler." She stood, lightly kissed his cheek and said, "I want to get outside before the sun gets too hot, if that's possible at this altitude. I've been indoors too much lately. Meet me on the patio in ten minutes, and we'll decide what to do with Rawlings. My suggestion is cyanide in his cereal."

"That's going to the top of my how-to-do-in-Rawlings list," he called out as she hurried down the hall to her room.

As Amanda slipped on a pair of shorts and halter top, she realized that Cal was again becoming her anchor.

During the past two days, Rawlings's threat, his mysterious plan, his manipulations, had changed her and her feelings toward Cal in a subtle way she couldn't explain. She visualized the two of them as survivors in a shipwreck. All they had was each other. To win the battle of wits against their adversary she must rely on Cal. The two of them would have to work closely together, forming a bond even stronger than the one that had existed before.

She left her bedroom and found Cal waiting on the patio, sitting in one of the two chairs that faced the lake. After she joined him, he handed her a glass of lemonade.

"Thanks." She said nothing more, content for the moment to stare across the lake, remembering the fun parties Cal had organized when they lived at South Shore. He'd always managed to invite a variety of interesting people, some local business owners, singers and dancers from the clubs, even a casino executive who had told fascinating stories about the inside operation of a gambling house....

"I wish we'd never gone on that trip to England," Cal suddenly said.

Amanda couldn't make that same claim. "How do you suppose Rawlings learned about my father? I asked, but he wouldn't tell me."

"Before deciding to join our operation he investigated us. He must have found out you've got a phony name."

"One thing about him, he's resourceful."

Cal smiled and nodded. "Besides cyanide in Evan's breakfast, got any other bright ideas on what we can do?"

She put on her sunglasses to cut down on the glare bouncing off the water. Holding her cold glass against her forehead momentarily soothed the headache that seemed to linger just behind her eyes. She felt as if she could sleep for a week, but she knew that was impossible. She and Cal might not be offered too many opportunities to speak alone.

"Right now I can't think of any way to get out of the hole we're in. I guess we can't do much until we hear what his plan is." She sipped the cold liquid.

"I know men like Rawlings," Cal said. "If we don't cooperate, we can be sure he'll carry out his threat against your father."

"What do you think he's going to have us do?" Amanda wasn't sure she wanted to hear Cal's theories.

"I think he's lining up an illegal poker game for you. Have you noticed how he's been keeping a low profile in this operation? We're back in the U.S. now where it's against the law to play poker for money without a Gaming Commission permit. If everything comes tumbling down, I'll be the one caught in the spotlight."

"So that's why he's been using you as the front man."

"I played it safe with the rental agent. I paid cash for the rent and gave a phony name. That way we've got a little protection."

"Do you think you'll be the contact with the other players?"

"I'm sure that's Rawlings's plan. You're the reason they'll come. But guess who keeps the profit from the games."

"If he's too successful, we could be in for a long-term partnership. Or do you think he's going for one big...?" She couldn't think of the word she wanted.

"One big killing? Yeah, I think that's more Rawlings's style. Then he'll clear out, leaving us behind to face the consequences."

Amanda sat up and stared at Cal. She slipped off her glasses so that she could see him more clearly. "You mean, he's going to have me *cheat?*"

Cal shrugged and sipped his lemonade. "It's a possibility."

Amanda leaned back in her chair and crossed her arms. "I won't do it. I just won't. It's too dangerous. And it's...it's—"

"Against everything you've ever been taught?"

She shut her eyes for a long moment and said nothing.

"Amanda, I'd never let you do that, so stop worrying. The two of us will handle Rawlings."

She didn't know if Cal was putting on a brave front or if he really believed his own words. Either way she was reassured. The bonds of her affection for Cal had suddenly become stronger.

Her thoughts turned to Mark. Such thoughts had been a constant distraction since she'd left him in front of his hotel. But until she knew what direction these next few days would take she would have to learn how to ignore the errant memories that flitted through her brain like wisps of smoke. What she'd experienced with him was a roller coaster ride. The trip was exhilarating, but there came a time when it was necessary to get back to solid ground. Mark was her experiment in freedom, her onetime fraternization. Perhaps given the right circumstances and enough time, she would have allowed herself to fall in love. But events had occurred that now made it impossible to continue the relationship.

"When Rawlings gets back," Cal said, "we'll find out what he's planning." He turned to look at her. "But remember this, Amanda. He needs us. We know he's afraid to have his own name connected with his scheme. Maybe he's got bad gambling debts, or maybe he's been caught cheating. Either way he knows that without me he doesn't have a front to cover for him. Without you there's no game. His ace in the hole is your father. I don't mean to minimize the danger he's in, but Evan's not stupid. He knows he's got one chance to pull this off. If it's a straight poker game, we can handle that. Even if he plans a scam, we can outwit him. Once you sit down at that poker table, you're in charge. There's not much he can do to you then."

"What's going to happen to us... or to my father after the game?"

"I don't know. We're just going to have to play it as it comes." He took her hand in his. "I'll always be here for you." He stared deeply into her eyes. "Don't forget that."

She nodded. There was nothing to fear. Cal would protect her.

CHAPTER TEN

"WHAT DO YOU MEAN I'm not *allowed* to look at those files?" Mark's voice echoed in his small office. He noticed the stricken expression on his young secretary's face. She'd been assigned to him while he was on the cruise—without his knowledge or approval, of course. Even though he'd been back to work for three days, she continued to act half-afraid of him. In softer tones he said, "I'm sorry, Andrea. Now please tell me what you know."

Andrea cleared her throat. "I was refused access to the classified material you wanted, so I went to Harold Perrine—he's head of security."

Harold, who had known the Quintero family for years, had been appointed chief of security, replacing Philo Webster, an old friend of Mark's father. Philo had set up the entire security system at Orion, but had just recently been forced to retire, ostensibly for failing health. The association with Mark and his father had led to Philo's being asked to leave the company.

Mark glanced up at the silent Andrea. "Please go on."

"Mr. Perrine said that you haven't been cleared for top-secret material. I haven't either. When I—"

Mark held up his hand. "Wait a minute. When I first started working here, I was issued a clearance."

"The files you want are a code ten. That's Orion's designation for top secret, military. Perrine's secretary and I walk after lunch in the park, so I asked her." Andrea paused, as if waiting for a response. When none came, she continued. "She said the papers haven't even been submitted to the FBI, and she didn't know why. Without a code ten clearance you can't have the documents you want. There are areas of the plant that are now off-limits to you. That happened while you were gone. To get in you have to have a special card that inserts into a computer box. To get the card you have to have a code ten clearance."

Mark's feelings of frustration were building. "Okay, Andrea. You did fine. Thanks."

She offered a tentative smile and hurried to the door. Before she could leave, Mark said, "See if you can find out anything more, please."

"I'd be glad to. I don't have enough work to keep me busy, er, I mean . . ."

"I know what you mean. I don't, either." He stood. "I'm going to talk to Harold Perrine right now." He walked across the floor of his insultingly small office. "But I won't mention where I got my information, so stop looking so worried."

Her smile revealed how young she was. He felt ancient in her presence. At that moment Amanda's face formed in his mind, and he again experienced the same catch in his breath, the same longing that had been a constant ache since they'd parted. The only way he'd been able to function since he'd arrived home was to keep his memories in a separate compartment, bringing them out only when he was alone. He'd never dreamed he could miss anyone as much as he missed

Amanda. She'd become a part of his life; no one could ever replace her.

He walked through the halls of the ultramodern, multistoried office building, built since Edward Quintero had taken over Orion. Russell Banning would never have approved this ugly, functional structure. The new headquarters of Orion emanated a cold and stark ambience. It had no soul... just like the Quinteros, Mark thought with a grim smile.

How he hated those two men, especially his stepbrother. Without his mother acting as a buffer between Mark and Robert, their rivalry and hatred had grown more fierce. Since Mark's return, they'd only seen each other twice, once at an uncomfortable dinner with Ed and another time at a meeting to discuss hiring new engineers and other personnel. The Quinteros had wanted to replace the older men, who'd been with the company for years, with younger, less experienced men who would come in with low salaries. Mark had quietly informed the committee that if that happened he would help the older employees file an age-discrimination suit against Orion. The suggestion was shelved for further discussion, but Mark knew the battle had just begun.

Right now, though, his main dilemma was getting a top clearance. Without that it was impossible to learn what projects Orion was working on. Even general, nonclassified information about plant operations had become difficult to obtain. With Edward fading from the picture Rob was accountable to no one. As far as Mark knew, the younger Quintero could be systematically stealing the company's assets to cover his gambling debts.

Mark's imagination leaped to another possibility. Rob could be involved in a deal with unscrupulous subcontractors. Mark knew well what could happen to a jet going faster than the speed of sound when an engine part suffered metal fatigue.

He forced his mind away from a scenario that was too horrifying to contemplate and entered Harold's office, which was a good deal larger than his own and furnished with much better furniture.

"Mr. Banning," Perrine said, rising to shake Mark's hand. "How did you enjoy your vacation?" The man was shaped like a pear.

Mark sat in the chair placed in front of the large desk. "One thing I learned while I was gone was never to take any time off."

"Oh?" Perrine leaned back in his chair, making it squeak in protest. "Why's that?"

"There's always the chance that something might not get done...such as my code ten clearance." Mark watched Harold's eyes, which reflected his inner thoughts. Harold wouldn't make a good poker player, Mark decided. "I want to know what's happened to my clearance."

Perrine held up his pudgy hand, a gesture that was meant to placate but only served to make Mark more angry. "I'm not sure I know what you mean," he said soothingly.

"Show me the paperwork that proves it was sent to the FBI." From the look on Perrine's face Mark knew that Andrea's information had been right. Nothing had been done. "Get the forms now." Mark's voice was quiet but forceful.

Perrine got to his feet. "I don't have to do anything for you. I take my orders directly from Robert Quintero." He said the name with respect, even a touch of awe.

Mark also rose. "And Rob's orders were to find some way to keep the clearance from going through. Right?"

As soon as the implication of Mark's comment registered on Perrine's mind, he reddened, making him look like a puffed-up toad. "Now, see here," he blustered. "You have no authority to talk to me like that."

"Save it, Harold. I may be the new kid on the block, but I'm not without some power and rights. And I'm warning you, get that application sent to the FBI before five this afternoon, or there'll really be hell to pay." With that threat echoing in the room, Mark left, shutting the door behind him. Harold's secretary still hadn't returned, so he was alone in the outer office. After waiting a few moments, he reopened the door and saw Perrine with the phone receiver pressed against his ear.

"Robert Quintero," Perrine said frantically. "It's an emergency."

"You bet it is, Harold," Mark said, again closing the door.

He returned to his office and called Philo Webster, Orion's former head of security. After leaving a message on the answering machine, Mark felt a little better about the day. At last he was taking some positive action.

ON THE THIRD MORNING at Tahoe, Cal stood alone at the kitchen stove, preparing breakfast. He thoughtfully stirred the pancake batter, again spending his free time trying to understand what was different about

Amanda. She was more confident and self-assured than she'd been before. More independent. She had become a stronger person.

Cal was aware that she'd had a confrontation with Rawlings. Even though Amanda hadn't told him any details, Cal knew she'd handled the situation. For the rest of the day Rawlings had acted subdued and had only spoken once—to offer a surly comment about Amanda's poker playing.

Cal stared out the window at the shimmering lake, lost in thought. He still couldn't figure out what was happening to the relationship between himself and Amanda. Whenever Rawlings was present she was especially attentive to Cal, as if to prove where her loyalties lay. Even when he was alone with her, she was more open than she'd ever been before. He felt her drawing close. Maybe there was a chance of winning her. What concerned him were the reasons behind her different behavior. Was it only because she feared Rawlings and what he could do to her father? Was she using Cal as a shield? Had something happened while she was in England that had changed her attitude toward him? Could she at last be falling in love with him? Or was that just wishful thinking?

"Cal?" Amanda called from the living room. "Are you in the kitchen?"

"Yes. Pancakes are almost ready."

"I got the latest *Chronicle*," she said, entering the room. Her hair was in fiery disarray from the wind. With cheeks red and glowing she looked about sixteen. Seeing her standing there, in her sweatshirt and pants, he felt almost dizzy with love. If he ever lost her, he wasn't sure what he'd do. . . .

After they sat down to eat, Amanda said, "I guess we have to spend another day playing poker." She sighed. "I'm sick to death of Rawlings's constant nitpicking about the way I deal, the cards I keep or throw away, the sloppy habits I've gotten into playing with amateurs. I can't seem to do anything right."

"You've been very patient." Cal smiled. "At least Rawlings hasn't asked you to practice cheating."

"I think he knows how we feel about that. What galls me the most is that he's given me some good pointers."

"I agree, but I sure hate to admit it."

"Cal, has he said anything about his plans?"

"He said that tomorrow I'm to make contact with the two main players, but he didn't give any names. When that's all set, he'll give us the next chapter in the little play he's producing."

Amanda ran her hand through her hair. "I feel so frustrated. We're at the man's mercy and all because of my father's stupid behavior."

"Don't blame your dad too much, Amanda. He did what he thought was necessary at the time. When you're panicked, that's when the instinct to survive kicks in."

"I didn't mean to sound so bitter," Amanda said. "It's always easier to pass judgment rather than try to learn someone's true motivation." For the first time since she'd arrived in Tahoe, Amanda remembered she hadn't yet called Margo Buchanan. Now she wasn't sure if contacting her mother's friend was such a good idea. Until she knew what Rawlings's plans were perhaps it would be better to wait.

After they finished cleaning up the kitchen, they went to the patio and looked out over the lake. Cal could hear Rawlings in the kitchen. Even though it was nearly nine, Rawlings complained loudly that no one had waited breakfast for him. Both Amanda and Cal smiled, glad they hadn't had to share another meal with the man. Amanda's smile turned into a sigh. Cal knew she didn't want to play poker.

"We need a change," he said. "I'm going to ask the warden if he'll let us drive down to South Shore today, just to see if any of the old gang is there."

"I'd like that." She felt a sudden excitement. She'd called information in Pennsylvania and gotten the number of Orion Aeronautical Company. After memorizing it, she'd destroyed the paper. Right now she desperately wanted to call that number. He'd be at work now. It was only noon in Philadelphia. He'd be going to lunch soon. Did he eat with the other employees, or in the executive dining room? He would probably forget to eat at all, but would work on a project without stopping.

She didn't want to think of him with other people, interacting with them, communicating his ideas, laughing, enjoying their company, having a good time. She hoped he was as miserable with loneliness as she was.

She remembered the night they made love. In her mind's eye she could see herself, standing naked in that small, moonlit room, slowly removing his clothes. He had kindly not commented on her shaky hands and fumbling fingers, silently letting her explore his body, learning the places that excited him. She hadn't known the act of love could be accomplished with such a feeling of freedom, without a sense of shame or embarrassment. The experience was as vivid in her mind as if it had just happened. She felt the same excitement, the same anticipation that even now made her breathless. She knew by letting her thoughts run free that she was only torturing herself, but the enjoyment far outweighed the misery....

"Amanda?" Cal said, breaking into her reverie. "Let's go inside. I'll try to talk Rawlings into letting us go into town."

TWO HOURS LATER they entered Harrah's Casino, where Cal had met Amanda nearly thirteen months ago. They both smiled, remembering the moment they'd decided to become partners.

Rawlings had come with them. "We'll meet at the hotel reservation desk at six-thirty. Be there."

"Don't worry," Cal said. "We know the rules by now. You've drummed them in our ears often enough."

Rawlings seemed to relax. "See you later," he said, and limped off.

"Let's find Tim. I'll bet you a dollar he's still a pit boss, standing on his flat feet behind the blackjack dealers."

Tim Upland was an old friend of Cal's. When she and Cal went on the road, Amanda had left her car—a red Porsche—in Tim's care. It was a good deal for Tim. He got to drive the car. Amanda paid the upkeep.

"You win," she said to Cal. "There he is." Amanda recognized Tim Upland's emaciated body. He still wore the bored expression that was as much a part of him as his black trousers and white shirt. But now he was a little balder and skinnier.

Fifteen minutes later Tim was allowed to take his break. When they were seated in the coffee shop, he asked, "Where are you two staying? Is this R and R or work?"

Cal looked at Amanda, then replied, "This is a break for us. We're staying at Incline, just relaxing."

"How's the Porsche?" Amanda asked.

"Fine. I don't get much of a chance to use it, but I keep it in good condition. The checks you send pay for first-class treatment. Want the car back?"

"Not yet," Amanda said, looking at Cal. "Perhaps in a few months." She wondered what he was thinking. His face revealed nothing of his thoughts or reactions.

Tim's conversation turned to other people in the Tahoe area, many of whom Amanda didn't know. When it was time for him to leave, she said, "Thanks for being caretaker. We're staying near Incline Village. If I can, I'll come down and take the car out. See if I remember how to drive it."

"I don't think you'll have any trouble," Cal said. "Once learned, never forgotten."

"Like playing poker." Tim bid them goodbye and headed back to his post.

As Amanda and Cal walked across the crowded floor, past the banks of slot machines that contributed to the noise level, she sighed. All she wanted to do was to get in her little red car and take off, heading east...toward Pennsylvania.

But she knew that until she was finished with Rawlings it was too dangerous even to phone Mark. And really, why should she want to? They'd only spent a few days together. She couldn't really be in love with him, could she?

No, her infatuation with Mark Banning could be no more than a schoolgirl's dream—a dream of love and security. And she only yearned for that dream to be true so much because she had no security at all in her life right now. All she had was danger.

CHAPTER ELEVEN

DURING THE FIVE DAYS Mark had been back to work, whenever he wasn't thinking about Rob and Orion, he spent hours trying to remember where Amanda had said they were going to take their break between gambling junkets. As he sat at his desk, which was totally devoid of any papers, confirming he had nothing to do, he reviewed the many conversations he and Amanda had shared. Only after a long, enjoyable process of remembering everything she'd ever said in his presence did he at last recall that she'd met Cal at South Lake Tahoe, and they were returning there when they left England...unless they'd changed their minds and had stayed in London. No, he felt confident they'd gone to Nevada.

Now that he'd remembered, what could he do? The Tahoe region was spread over a large area with many tourists and residents. Trying to find her there could be a lesson in futility.

He again surveyed the top of his desk. It should be piled high with schematic drawings and plans for a big project ordered by the air force. The phones should be ringing as he conferred with the design department, the tool and die supervisors, the buyers of steel. Instead, his office life was as quiet and dull as his personal life.

He stood, knowing he had to do something active or go stark raving mad. Just as he was walking around the desk, planning to head for the coffee machine down the hall, Andrea knocked and came in. In her hand was a piece of paper.

"This just came from on high from Mr. R. Quintero." She held the paper toward Mark.

He noticed that Rob hadn't bothered to write the personal note in longhand. It had gone through his secretary, even though it would have been easier to call. Since the contents of the note would probably affect Andrea, Mark read it out loud.

"Because of the mix-up in your clearance I know you can't get much done. I am authorizing a week-long paid vacation for you, beginning today.

"Now that the last big contract has been fulfilled and accepted by the powers that be at the Pentagon, and we are still waiting for word on the next proposal, Orion hasn't got much going on right now."

Mark glanced up. "Seems an odd way to do business. There shouldn't be any lag time between projects."

Andrea nodded but said nothing. Mark continued reading Rob's words.

"I'm taking a few days off, too. You aren't the only one who can take vacations. In fact, I'm nearly out the door. I promise we'll have a nice long talk when we get back in a week—perhaps with Dad at the house. Connie should be back by then.

Robert Q."

Mark glanced up at Andrea, waiting for her reaction.

"Mr. Banning," she said, "you might as well take some time off. There isn't anything you can do until that clearance comes through. My, uh, friend in security said she made sure it was correct. But it will take some time—at least two weeks, if not more."

Mark nodded, not really listening as Andrea made some suggestions where he could spend his free time. He knew exactly where he'd be the next seven days. But first he had to call a private investigator named Maynard Butler. According to his attorney, if anyone knew how to track a missing person, even in the wilds of Nevada, Butler would.

"BOTH QUINTERO and Garland agreed to come?" Amanda asked Cal. "They didn't suspect a thing?"

"We've got a good reputation," Cal said, pouring himself a drink. The sun was low in the sky, making the shadows long. He held up a half-full bottle of rye. "Want one?" he asked Amanda.

She shook her head no. She and Cal were alone. When Rawlings heard Cal's report that everything was arranged for the game, he had gone back to his bedroom to make some phone calls.

Cal kept his back to Amanda as he spoke. "I was surprised about Robert Quintero being asked. Didn't Mark Banning mention they were stepbrothers?"

Amanda should have known Cal would remember that bit of conversation from the poker game on the ship. "Yes, I think you're right." She hoped she had put the right emphasis on her words—as if she'd just been reminded of that fact.

"Strange coincidence, isn't it?" Cal returned to sit beside her.

"Those things happen," Amanda said. "Did the players go along with all of Rawlings's terms?"

"Yes. They even agreed to the million-dollar stake, which has to be in cash. When I mentioned that Jesse Hite and Orson Adler were the other players, Garland didn't hesitate for a minute. He's never met them, he said, but he knows their reputations. Quintero seemed equally enthusiastic. It's all set for five days."

"Where's it going to be? Here?"

Cal shook his head. "I don't think so. I had to tell all four of the invitees that they'd be informed of the exact location of the game by telegram." He had lowered his voice. "Rawlings insisted on that little detail. This way nobody can set us up."

Amanda felt chilled and wrapped a large cashmere scarf around her shoulders. Blowing rain dashed against the windows, obscuring the view. Pine trees waved frantically, as if trying to signal her to flee, to run away. But there was no escape.

Cal sat down on the sofa that faced the lake. She joined him, sitting close. He didn't touch her, even though she knew he wanted to.

"Amanda..." He stopped, unsure of what to say. Whenever he thought about declaring his love for her, he remembered that he had no right to even contemplate getting involved with a woman and especially someone he loved as desperately as he did Amanda. It wouldn't be fair to her... and yet he couldn't resist any longer. He knew if he didn't make his bid, he might lose her. But first he had to reveal his past.

He set his drink on the side table, but kept his gaze straight ahead. "You weren't the only one Rawlings investigated. He learned my secrets, as well. It's time I told you the truth."

"Cal, you don't have to tell me anything. Whatever happened in your past doesn't make any difference to me."

"No, I want you to know—now. I think Rawlings will be putting you through the paces these next few days, honing your skills. He's got to make sure nothing goes wrong. After Garland and the others get here, we won't have a chance to talk."

Amanda nodded and again pulled her shawl around her shoulders. She wished they'd built a fire, but she didn't want to interrupt. "Okay, go ahead." She feared what he would say. But there was no way she could stop him.

"My real name is William Bainbridge. I changed it to Caleb Norton."

Amanda glanced over at him. "So that's how you knew how to do it."

He nodded.

"Can I still call you Cal? It's going to take me a while to get adjusted to Bill."

"You'll always be Amanda to me," he said with a crooked smile.

"Susan Ross is another person, someone who lived another life...a long time ago." Cal's silence continued until she said, "Please go on."

He inhaled deeply and began. "When I was eighteen, I was almost the size I am now. We lived in Cheyenne, Wyoming. I was great at sports, but shy around girls, didn't have many of the social graces.''

''I find that a little hard to believe,'' Amanda said, surprised by his revelation.

''You should have known me when I was eighteen. All I wanted to do was play basketball and football. I thought a lot about girls, but I never knew what to talk to them about, so I avoided them whenever possible. For graduation night a bunch of my friends talked me into asking a girl to the prom. I was absolutely stunned when she accepted. Well, anyway, after the dance we went to a kid's house, down to the basement den. All evening there'd been drinking, mostly beer, a little pot. Cassy, my date, didn't take anything. I didn't, either. I really enjoyed being with a pretty girl. She made it so easy to talk.''

Cal paused, remembering the night that had changed his life in so many ways. It had started out so well, and had ended so tragically.

''There was one kid named Gene Reginald...'' Just saying the name made Cal feel sick to his stomach. He became lost in his memories, no longer aware of Amanda or his surroundings. Finally he began to speak again. ''Even as a little kid Gene was a bully. As a teenager, he became a tormentor. Gene showed up at the party just drunk enough to be dangerous. He made an insulting remark to Cassy. Then everything happened so fast that I've never been able to reconstruct the exact sequence of events. All I know is that I lashed out to try to hit Gene but missed him. He stepped back and fell, cracking his temple on a corner of a coffee table. If it had been one inch farther away, just one inch, he wouldn't have hit it. But he did hit it, and he died. Just like that. Without giving any thought to what I was doing I began to run.''

"And you never stopped and you never went back."

Cal shook his head. "My mother was a widow. I was her hope for the future. I killed her—"

"No, that couldn't be true."

"I might as well have. Before I could contact her and tell her what really happened she was dead. I'm sure it was the shock of what I'd done that killed her."

"Oh, Cal. I'm so sorry." Amanda laid her head against his shoulder. She understood why he'd agreed to Rawlings's plan. If he hadn't, her father would be killed and the authorities in Wyoming would be notified of Cal's whereabouts.

"Now you know. There aren't any more secrets between us. You said you had to go back and make peace with your past. I don't know if I can."

"But if it was an accident . . . ?"

"If I'd stayed, I probably could have proved that. There were plenty of witnesses. But I ran. That makes it a felony, just as if I had accidently hit him with a car and left the scene." Cal grabbed his glass and drank deeply. "I wish I knew why I ran. That's what's always puzzled me. I had physical strength, enough for two. But when I needed to be morally strong, I failed."

Cal got to his feet and walked over to fix himself another drink. When he returned to the sofa, he again sat beside her, leaving his drink untouched on the coffee table.

After a long silence, Cal took her hand. "Amanda, I love you." There, he'd said it. Not very eloquently, but at last he'd spoken the words he'd kept buried deep inside for over a year. "I love you," he repeated.

"Yes, Cal, I know." She slipped her hand from his. "And I love you, too. But..." She let her voice trail off, hoping he caught her meaning.

"But you're not *in* love with me." He grabbed his glass and drank.

Amanda used silence as her answer. Cal had always been uncannily astute about her. It was as if he could read her mind. When she looked over at him, only the side of his face was visible. Even from that angle she could see his pain. She inhaled deeply and spoke. "Cal, I don't mean to hurt you. And I swear that nothing you've told me makes one bit of difference. It's just that I'm so mixed up now that I don't know what to do. I'm worried about my father and what's going to happen when I have to play against Garland. I'm almost sick with fear. Rawlings has all the power, and we don't even know what he's planning."

She took Cal's glass from his hand and sipped the chilled whiskey, then handed his drink back to him. "I've never been in a situation like this. The whole time we've been on the circuit we never once had to face real danger." She held up her hand to stop him from speaking. "I know you shielded me from some of the more unsavory characters we had to deal with. You always managed to make everything run so smoothly that I forgot parasites like Evan Rawlings existed."

"Do you regret this past year, Amanda?" Cal's voice was so low that she barely heard him.

"No, I don't regret a thing we've done. But now it's time I went home and became a part of my family again. I've got to make some sense out of my life."

"And when you've done that, what will you do?"

She thought of Mark and realized again that what had happened to her in England was a dream. Perhaps the most exciting experience in her life, but still just a dream. And all dreams eventually faded. What she had with Caleb Norton was reality. She owed him so much that she could never repay her debts. And if any man needed her love and understanding, it was Cal.

"After I've made peace with my parents, then we'll start thinking about you and me."

"Promise?"

"Yes, I promise."

Cal bent over and kissed her lips, a tentative, poignant, questioning kind of kiss that left her feeling sad and hollow.

"WHAT'S THE MATTER with you?" Evan asked Amanda as she came into the kitchen.

Cal was standing at the stove, wiping the frying pan clean. He turned and looked at Amanda, then set his spatula down and walked toward her, pulling out a chair. Her cheeks were pale, almost matching the cream color of her heavy velvet robe. She had on slippers, which didn't offer much warmth to her cold feet.

"Are you all right?" Cal asked her, noticing how shaky her hands were.

The morning sun shining through the windows nearly blinded her. She turned so that the light wasn't in her eyes. "I have a roaring headache." She smiled up at Cal. "Too much excitement going on around here, I guess."

"What can I do?" In all the time he'd known Amanda she'd never once been sick. "Want some coffee? Juice? Eggs?"

Amanda shook her head, then regretted it. Her stomach had felt queasy for hours. She hadn't slept much. "Don't mention food, please. Aspirins, ice water and soda crackers, if you've got them. Or plain toast. Then I'm going back to bed."

"Damn!" Rawlings shouted. "You can't get sick. I've got plans for you and me to go to L.A. this afternoon."

Both Amanda and Cal looked at him with surprise. Rawlings hadn't mentioned it the night before when they played poker.

"Change your plans, Rawlings. I'm not going anywhere today except back to my room."

Rawlings continued to scowl at her, but kept quiet while Cal prepared the toast. While she nibbled at the food and sipped the water Cal stood behind her, holding her shoulder with his large hand. "As long as we're speaking of plans, Rawlings, I think it's time you told us what you're doing."

After a long silence, Rawlings nodded and said, "Okay. I guess you're ready to hear the next act."

"You aren't setting us up to play a crooked game, are you?" Amanda asked, sucking a piece of ice.

Rawlings laughed. "Hell, no. You can win without any flimflamming. And considering the men you'll be playing with, cheating could be suicide."

Amanda nearly choked. When she could speak, she asked, "Why did you pick those men for the big game?"

Rawlings leaned back in his chair. He wore neat slacks and a starched white shirt, left unbuttoned partway down, revealing a tanned, hairy chest. His gold

chain glinted in the sun. For the first time she saw where
he kept her father's doubloon.

"I've got a score to settle with Garland and Quintero," Rawlings said. "I had to use Cal as a front man
because my name's too well known. If any of the players knew I had anything to do with this operation, they
wouldn't show."

"Why?" Amanda asked.

"About three years ago I played in a marathon poker
session with Quintero, Garland and two other players.
That game lasted for three days and nights. I won close
to five hundred thousand. Before I could get out of
town I was attacked by Garland's gang. All my winnings were taken." He looked over at Cal and Amanda,
hate filling his eyes. "But taking my dough wasn't
enough. They beat me." He seemed to shudder, then
inhaled and continued. "It took me months of operations and physical therapy to be able to walk again.
You've seen me limp. I'm in constant pain, but I don't
take anything for it. I use the pain as a way to remember Garland."

"What happens if I win?" Amanda asked. "Won't
they try to do the same thing to me and Cal?"

"That's why we're doing this on our turf. Our four
invited players know Kirk and Norton are clean. They
wouldn't have agreed to play if they had any doubts.
And Garland won't be coming in with his hired guns.
Besides, I've got certain safeguards that you and Cal
don't need to know about."

"But what if she loses?" Cal asked.

"I know all the players' strengths and weaknesses.
I've been teaching them to you for days. Amanda,

you're the best poker player I've ever met. But because you're a woman they won't credit you with the degree of skill you have. Your reputation has spread, but they still won't accept that a mere woman can be a better poker player than they are.''

"There really is going to be a game?" Cal asked. "You aren't just bringing Garland and Quintero here so that you can get your revenge?''

Rawlings smiled. "Oh, there'll be a game, all right. I want to watch Garland and Quintero squirm when they see Amanda take their money hand after hand. But even if she should lose, I still win. Either way I'm walking away with the proceeds.''

"Leaving us to face the consequences," Cal said softly.

"After thirteen years, isn't it about time you learned how to do that, *William?*''

The implication hung in the air, like thick, acrid smoke.

Amanda stood. "What about my father? We've done everything you wanted. Now I demand to know where he is.''

Rawlings stood, too. "Look, you're not in any position to demand anything. I swear Craig's all right. He's my ace in the hole, so I'm taking very good care of him." He started to walk around the table toward her. "Now get packed. You and I are going to L.A.''

Amanda straightened her shoulders. "No, I'm not. I'm going to bed." She ran out of the kitchen, the pain in her head worse than she'd ever felt before.

"Amanda?" Cal spoke softly through the door.

She looked out the window. The sun was more than halfway across the sky. She had slept for hours. "Come in, Cal." She brushed her hair from her face.

"How do you feel?" He looked worried.

"Better, but don't tell Rawlings. I am *not* going with him."

"No, but I am."

She sat up. "Oh, I thought he'd—"

"He wanted one of us as security so the other wouldn't try to escape. I'm glad you've got a good excuse. I'd rather go than have you be alone with that bastard."

Cal rarely swore, so the impact of the word was more meaningful.

"When are you coming back?"

"I don't know." He sat on the edge of the bed. "Rawlings wouldn't say. Will you be all right here alone?"

"Of course." It occurred to her that since she'd left her parents' house in Beverly Hills, she'd never once been totally on her own. Cal had always been in the next hotel room, within calling distance.

He reached into his pocket. "Here. I want you to keep this with you."

Amanda looked at the small gun lying in the palm of his hand. The slate-colored steel gleamed in the light. The sight of it made her shiver. "Where did you get it?" She knew he wouldn't have taken it on the plane.

"I told Rawlings I was going to the grocery store the other day. I hitched a ride into Carson City and bought the gun and the ammo at a pawnshop. I tried it out, so I know it works."

"But I don't know how—"

"See this? Push the release up and it's locked. Down, it'll fire. The range is short, so it's not much good if the target's any distance away."

"But, Cal, I'm not going to have a target. No one even knows I'm here."

"Rawlings does. And he has henchmen who might come and check on you. The gun is in case something goes wrong. You'll be alone here. If anything happened...well, you know what I mean. This is just so I'm not leaving you totally unprotected."

Amanda nodded and mumbled her appreciation. She knew that as soon as Cal left she'd put the gun in a drawer. It wouldn't be needed. No one would be coming to the house.

"When do you leave?"

"In a few minutes. We're driving to the airport at South Shore, so you won't have a car. I've laid in supplies for you. And if you need something, you can walk to the grocery store."

"Don't worry about me. I'll be fine. I'll read and get some sun." Cal stood. She reached for his hand. "Please be careful."

He bent down and lightly kissed her lips. "I'll be back."

"Promise?"

He smiled. "Promise."

MARK LOOKED across Harrah's crowded casino floor, realizing the immensity of his task. He'd made the rounds of all the clubs, large and small, including Harrah's, asking for Cal Norton and Amanda Kirk. Everywhere he'd gone he'd been offered blank stares and denials. He couldn't tell if he was being lied to.

He sat at a padded chair in front of a quarter slot machine, but he didn't play. Before leaving Philadelphia he'd called Maynard Butler, a private investigator. Butler had told Mark that if Amanda or Cal had worked at the clubs, he should start his search there, making sure to check the crews that worked the different shifts.

Besides inquiring at the casinos, Mark had asked around at the property and car rental agencies in the area, but nothing showed up on the computer screens under Norton, Kirk or Rawlings. He finally admitted he'd reached a dead end.

"Hey, I've been looking for you." A thin, almost emaciated man sat next to Mark.

"Why?" Mark asked.

"'Cause I heard you were looking for Norton. You a friend?"

Mark sat up, smiled his most friendly smile and said, "I sure am. I met him and Amanda Kirk on a cruise going to England. They said they were coming to South Lake Tahoe. I had to come out this way, anyway, and thought I'd look them up." Mark stuck out his hand, hoping he was projecting sincerity. "I'm Mark Banning."

"Tim Upland. Cal and Amanda are up at Incline Village, but I don't know where exactly. They came down a couple of days ago, but I forgot to ask how to reach them."

"Where's Incline?"

"On the north shore just past King's Beach." The man stood. "Got to get back to my shift. If you see them, tell them to be sure and stop by to see me again. Amanda can take the Porsche out anytime she wants.''

Before Mark could ask what Tim meant, the man was gone.

Mark got his rental car, learned from the parking attendant that going on the Nevada side of the lake was the fastest way to get to Incline Village, then took off at a speed just a little above illegal. He knew it was stupid to get his hopes up, but he couldn't help it. Amanda was close. Now all he had to do was find her.

''I'M SORRY, SIR, I can't find any house or apartment rentals made out to Rawlings, Norton or Kirk. In fact, rentals have been a little slow this month.''

Mark sighed. This was the last real estate agency on the north shore of the lake. He hated to give up, especially since he had nowhere else to look. The agent had been particularly patient, but now he knew he was pushing his luck. It was nearly closing time. The conversation had been repeated so often that he knew the words by heart. But he might as well finish the routine. He described Amanda, then Evan and finally Cal.

The woman shook her head. ''Sorry. I've never seen any of those people.''

A woman sitting at a desk next to them hung up the phone. ''I've been listening. I saw a man who looked like that in the grocery store. I thought he was a movie star. Gad, he was good-looking.''

''Yeah, I guess he is,'' Mark unwillingly admitted. He'd never thought of Cal in those terms.

''He had dark hair, right?'' the woman asked eagerly. ''And brown eyes and long, thick eyelashes? And a tight, uh, a good-looking rear end?''

Mark smiled. "I can't say I noticed that particular feature, but the rest seems to fit. Where did you see him?"

"At Raley's Shopping Center on Highway 28. It's on your left as you're heading east. You can't miss it. Is he somebody famous?"

"He's going to be," Mark said, wanting to give the woman a thrill. "I'm a movie producer, and I'm here to offer him a contract."

"Gosh, that's great. What movie—?"

"Thanks for your help." Mark stood and quickly walked out of the small office.

Within minutes he was at the grocery store, which was large and well lit. Mark realized that Cal was so distinctive-looking that he was sure to be remembered, especially by women. The second clerk he spoke to had waited on him a number of times. She also recalled that one of the bag boys had helped him carry some packages to his house and received a large tip.

Just as Mark was beginning to think he'd never get the information he needed, the store manager found the employee's address. Within half an hour the young man had told Mark what he wanted to hear and had accepted a generous tip with a blush and stammered appreciation.

A few minutes later Mark reached his goal as a clap of thunder rolled across the night sky. Heavy rain fell in slanting sheets, as it had most of the afternoon. Around the secluded house was a tall stone wall and a locked gate. He parked the car off the highway. Instead of carrying his luggage he brought only Amanda's box, now wrapped as a gift.

As soon as he had assessed the formidable barrier around the property, he wished he'd left the box in the car. But rather than go back he'd try to find a way in without anyone hearing him. Just in case Amanda hadn't told Cal all the details of the trip to Cotswolds, he wanted to make contact with her without Cal's knowledge. But if worse came to worst, Mark would just have to confront Cal and see what happened.

CHAPTER TWELVE

AMANDA CLEANED UP her dinner dishes. The meals she'd fixed during the past two days were nothing to compare with Cal's. She missed him. The house was too quiet, too empty without him. Rawlings had said he'd call and let her know when they'd be back, but she'd heard nothing from either man. Before they'd left the house, Rawlings had reiterated this threat of what would happen to Cal and her father if she didn't behave. She hadn't bothered to reply to his threat, but she knew he meant every word.

Being alone had presented another problem. She had too much time to think. Most of her thoughts had been about Mark, even though she'd tried to control her memories. Everything she did conjured up images of their time together: the cove in front of the house reminded her of the pond with its black swans; seeing the small shops in the area brought back memories of the flea market and the expression on Mark's face when he first saw the masses of merchandise; waking up in the morning evoked a view of the sun-filled room at the inn with Mark lying beside her in the four-poster bed....

She sighed, forcing herself to think about something besides Mark. As soon as Cal and Rawlings returned, she would again have to concentrate on practicing her poker game. She couldn't let her attention be diverted by anything. Her father's life might be at stake.

After drying her hands, she returned to the living room with her wineglass and added logs to the embers. She couldn't seem to keep warm, not with the wind blowing a gale strong enough to shake the house.

She looked out the window and shivered. Hearing the wind moaning through the pine trees only added to her chill. Perhaps what she was feeling was fear. Every sound seemed magnified. She could swear she heard someone walking around outside, but that was impossible. The property was protected by a high wall. When she took a walk after Cal and Rawlings left, she'd made sure the gate was locked. She was alone, and she might as well stop being so silly. Music would help, she decided, and chose a tape of popular piano renditions, loud enough to drown out the noises of the night.

She wrapped a wool lap robe around herself, snuggled down in the recliner chair and found her place in a book she'd taken off a shelf. It was a story of a mass murderer who preyed on women, not the most appropriate subject, considering her mood and the circumstances, but she'd started it that afternoon and had to find out how they caught the man. She quickly became engrossed in the story, forgetting her fears.

A loud, crashing sound from outside, at the front of the house, made her gasp and jump, tearing a page in her book. Then a scream of pain filled her ears. Was it an animal or a human? Her heart pounded against her chest so hard that it ached, making it difficult to take a deep breath. She tried to climb out of the chair without releasing the lock, but her legs became entangled in the footrest and her lap robe. She was concentrating so intently on the simple act of standing that she had no idea whether the noises outside had been repeated. She calmed down by convincing herself that the commotion on the deck had been a branch loaded with huge pinecones falling off the tall trees that surrounded the house.

Or... it could be one of Rawlings's men, coming to check on her. She'd put the gun Cal had given her in the drawer where she kept her lingerie, clear across the house from where she was. Now she could hear the rain pounding on the roof. Perhaps she'd heard thunder and not—

"Amanda!"

A man's voice registered on her brain, but all it did was to add to her fear.

"Amanda!"

She stood, ran toward the locked sliding glass door and peeked out. On the deck at the front of the house she saw a man crouched on his hands and knees. She switched on the floodlight.

"Mark!" She was too stunned to say anything more.

He turned his head in her direction and looked plaintively at her. One of his feet was stuck in the empty bucket that Cal had used to wash the rental car. Sitting beside Mark, looking incongruous and bedraggled in brightly colored paper and a big, drooping bow, was a gift about the size of the box he'd given her in England.

She didn't know whether to be angry or ecstatically happy to see him. She'd decide later. Right now she had to get his foot out of the bucket and let him come in out of the downpour.

She quickly unlatched the triple locks on the doors and hurried toward him. "Are you all right?" she asked, wiping rain from her face.

"Not exactly," Mark growled. "I'm in one piece, but my manly pride is in shambles."

She noticed his pant knees weren't in very good shape, either. "Pride is the least of your problems," she said, and grabbed the bucket, pulling, then twisting, trying to release his foot. His yelp of pain stopped her rescue efforts. "Is your ankle broken?"

"I don't think so," he said through gritted teeth. "But it hurts like hell, so stop whatever torture you're doing and help me get into the house."

With surprising agility he stood, leaned his arm across her shoulders and hopped on one foot through the door, keeping the bucket in the air behind him. He leaned against the wall while she went to the deck, grabbed the heavy box and returned, shutting out the driving rain.

"Mark, what are you doing here?" she asked, helping him maneuver into the living room.

"Is Cal here?"

"No. He went to Los Angeles." She pulled off her dripping socks and threw them onto the tile at the front entryway. Running into the kitchen, she grabbed an armful of dish towels. She paused for a moment, smiling at the thought of her struggle to get out of the chair and Mark's attempt to free himself from the bucket. She was glad no one had witnessed their clumsy ballet.

She returned to the living room. Mark sat on the floor, pulling off a wet windbreaker. She threw some towels in his direction, sat beside him and began to dry her face and arms. "Stop ignoring my question," she ordered. "I thought we'd arranged to meet in England. I told you my conditions."

"I'm glad you're so pleased to see me."

"Sarcasm won't work, Mark. I'm not glad to see you." She couldn't even tell him why. If Rawlings found out that Mark was here... but how could he? He was five hundred miles away. She felt almost positive he had left no one to watch her. She and Mark were alone. The thought boggled her mind, conjuring up all sorts of images.

"Amanda? Could you stop drying your hair and help me? I think my ankle's swelling."

She crawled over to him. "What do you want me to do?"

Before she could reach the bucket Mark grabbed her. His kiss was infinitely better than what she'd experienced in her imagination. Relying on remembrances of past passion was frustrating and totally unsatisfactory. This was so much better, she thought, intensifying the kiss.

When their lips parted, Amanda sighed his name. Her response to his kiss proved just how glad she was to see him, even if his presence compounded her problems.

"I guess suggesting we go to bed right now is out of the question." Mark lifted the bucket and gently dropped it back onto the carpet, then winced in pain.

"You haven't changed." She examined the situation. The heel of his loafer was lodged against one side of the plastic pail. The toe was caught on an indentation that circled the bucket. Well, it shouldn't be too hard to free him....

But in the struggle to free his foot she broke one of her fingernails and uttered a few choice swear words. Mark teasingly chastised her until she threatened to stop helping him.

When he was at last free, he tentatively moved the ankle around. It was still painful, but there was no real damage.

"Want an ice pack?" Amanda asked, getting to her feet.

He shook his head as she helped him to stand. He didn't put much pressure on the ankle as he walked over to the sofa. But after looking at his wet pants, he didn't sit down. He was shivering.

"Where's your luggage?" she asked. She ran over to put more logs on the dying fire.

"In the car. It's clear out on the highway, though."

Mark obviously couldn't walk, and she didn't want to go out in the pounding rain. "I'll get changed and see if I can find something of Cal's." She quickly left, heading for her bedroom. Rawlings had left most of his clothes, and they would certainly fit Mark better than Cal's, but she wasn't yet ready to tell him anything about Rawlings or the stranglehold he had on her and Cal.

She partially dried her hair, then put on wool slacks and a warm sweater. She found the plaid Pendleton wool bathrobe she'd given Cal for Christmas last year, some socks and underwear.

While Mark dressed in the living room, she made coffee and got out a bottle of brandy. When she returned, carrying the tray, she had to stop and stare at Mark wearing Cal's oversize robe. She bit her lip to keep from laughing.

"Please don't say it," Mark warned, sitting on the sofa and closing the robe around his bare legs. "Put that tray down and come here."

"I see you've got your manly pride back." She sat on the couch, but out of his reach. They had to talk. Mark could make her forget everything except the passion he aroused in her. She poured coffee, added brandy and handed him a cup, keeping a safe distance.

Mark sighed and leaned back in the sofa, knowing he wasn't going to get anywhere with her, not until she decided the time was right.

Before she sat down she retrieved the soaked package. "I can't imagine what it is." She tore off the sodden paper. Inside was her ebony box, looking polished and shiny. She dried it with one of the towels. "It's still the best present I've ever been given." She rubbed her hand over the smooth surface, remembering what had happened the night they'd exchanged gifts. She glanced up. "I haven't got yours ready," she explained. "I couldn't find any place to have it framed."

"We'll get it done in England."

Amanda didn't reply. She sipped her coffee and watched Mark, feeling joy that he was here and panicked over what would happen if Rawlings found out. She would just have to convince Mark to go back to Philadelphia before the men returned.

"You broke your word to me," she said, deciding a frontal attack was the best. "We were to meet at the inn in a month. I was making arrangements to—"

"I want to know what you and Cal are doing here and what role Evan Rawlings has in all of this."

"How did you know Rawlings is involved?"

Mark sat up straighter and set his cup down. "So he is part of the action."

Damn. If she'd been thinking more clearly, he never would have tricked her. Now the battery of questions would begin, and she couldn't give him any answers.

"Is Rawlings in L.A. with Cal?"

She nodded. "Please, Mark, I don't want to talk about them. Tell me how your work's going at Orion."

"Later. Are you and Rawlings planning a poker game here on U.S. soil? Pushing the legality of your livelihood a bit far, aren't you?"

"There's no game," she said, hating to lie.

"I don't believe you. Rawlings wouldn't waste his time enjoying the scenic delights of Lake Tahoe. He's too much of a hustler. Is he your new partner?"

Amanda stiffened her spine. "Yes, he is, not that it's any of your business." She stood. "I think we'd better end this right now. I'll go out to your car and get your suitcase. You can dress, then leave."

Before she could step away from her chair, Mark was standing. With his hand in hers he led her back to the sofa and continued to hold her. "I'm sorry."

His words didn't sound totally sincere, but Amanda didn't comment.

"I agree that your arrangement with Cal and Rawlings is none of my business...up to a point. But you've got to understand. I'm in love with you, and anything that affects you affects me. I want you to leave here and go to Philadelphia with me." He paused, then looked intently at her face. "I want to marry you."

His words frightened her. Too much was happening too fast. "You've made quite a quantum leap from spending one weekend with me to declaring your love and proposing."

"I'm a fast worker."

"Well, I'm not. You're putting too much importance on...on what happened between us at the inn. You said yourself that we were spending the weekend together so that we could become better acquainted."

"I think we became very well acquainted." Mark's smile implied more than his words.

"Our making love doesn't necessarily mean we've made a lifetime commitment. You just can't barge in here and ask me to leave Cal and go off with you. We're practically strangers except in a—"

"Except in a very fundamental, essential, important way. But let's forget that for a moment. I want to know what kind of game Rawlings has planned. And until I'm satisfied that you'll be safe I'm not leaving."

"Mark, I—"

The ringing of the phone made them both jump. Mark reached over to the end table beside him and handed her the receiver.

"Hello?"

"Amanda, it's Evan."

The sound of his voice chilled her. She said nothing, waiting for him to continue.

"You okay? Is anything wrong?"

She glanced at Mark. He was staring at her, frowning. "Is that Rawlings?" he asked, mouthing the words rather than saying them out loud.

She nodded.

"What's wrong?" Rawlings repeated in her ear.

"Everything's just fine." The lie stuck in her throat. "When are you coming back?"

"We're at LAX now, but the flight's been delayed. I guess you're having a storm up there, right?"

"Yes, it's raining hard . . . with terrible winds."

"We might try to get routed to San Fran or Sacramento and rent a car. So I can't give you an exact time. Probably early morning, anyway. Don't wait up for us."

"Don't worry. I won't." Her mind was in a whirl. It was ten now. The flight from L.A. to San Francisco or Sacramento probably took about two hours. Considering time to rent a car and the three or four hours to drive to the lake, they could conceivably be here by four-thirty. What could she do with Mark?

She cleared her throat. "How's Cal?" She wanted to ask if Rawlings had seen her father but didn't dare. Any bit of information Mark learned would only result in more questions she couldn't answer.

"Cal's in his room, but he said to tell you hello. I don't know how you've lived with him all those months. He's been moping around here like a sick cat. Definitely not a fun date."

That was the first bit of humor she'd ever heard Rawlings utter. He sounded excited, as if he'd just been dealt a royal flush in a high-stakes game.

"Everything's going great, darlin'." He said the term of endearment in a lowered tone, which made it sound all the more intimate.

When she saw the look on Mark's face, she knew he suspected that Rawlings was overstepping his bounds.

"I miss you," Rawlings continued, speaking to her like a husband or lover. She felt nauseated, now realizing that her own and Cal's warnings about Rawlings leaving her alone had done no good. He considered her his property. He was only biding his time before he made another move.

"When I get back, we'll take some time alone and—"

"Look, Rawlings, I've got to go. The teakettle's blowing its top."

Without waiting another second she reached past Mark and replaced the receiver.

"Were you talking about me or yourself?"

It took her a moment to realize he was referring to the teakettle. Her anger at Rawlings was boiling over, but she couldn't let Mark know how much the call had disturbed her.

"What did Rawlings say?"

Amanda quickly stood, hoping to change the direction of the conversation. "He and Cal should be here about two," she said, lying to give herself a margin of error. "That's *this morning*. So you've got to go. They can't find you here."

"Why not?"

She had many reasons, but the main one was Rawlings's direct order not to have any contact with Mark. And for his own safety Mark must not learn about Rob Quintero's involvement with Rawlings and Garland, nor about her father's situation. Mark might try to do something to help her, which would only make matters worse.

Mark repeated the question. She sighed and said, "Because Rawlings ordered me not to have anything to do with you. I think he suspects we were together in England. And he doesn't like you. Why, I can't imagine." She began to gather up the coffee cups, trying to keep her thoughts focused on how to convince Mark he had to leave. "You've got to see all of this from my point of view. I'm caught in the middle in a no-win situation."

"I'll tell you one way to win. Come with me tonight before Cal and Rawlings get back."

"You know I can't do that." Amanda walked into the kitchen with her tray and unplugged the coffeepot.

Mark followed her, bringing his wet clothes and the towels they'd used. "Where's the dryer?" he asked.

She pointed to an alcove at the end of the kitchen, but said nothing as he limped across the room. She knew his ankle hurt. As she placed the cups in the dishwasher, she said, "How did you find us?"

"With great difficulty." He detailed how he'd gone about discovering their location.

When he finished, Amanda said, "You mean, if we hadn't gone down to see Tim Upland at Harrah's, you probably wouldn't have found us?"

"Well, his information helped. Without him it might have taken me longer. But I wouldn't have given up."

Amanda shook her head in disbelief. Visiting an old friend had resulted in bringing Mark back into her life...at the worst possible time.

She dried her hands on a towel. Before she could move out of the kitchen Mark grabbed her and turned her around to face him, applying pressure with his body until her back was against the counter. "Tell me Rawlings's plan. Who's going to play? When and where?"

She tried to get away, but he wouldn't release her. He repeated his question.

"Rawlings hasn't told us," she said, hoping she could offer enough information to satisfy Mark. "All I know is four men are coming here in a few days. Rawlings has been very secretive about the whole thing."

"Why did he involve you and Cal? Couldn't he arrange it himself?"

Amanda knew she'd have to give Mark more facts. She wished he weren't holding her like this. Having him near disrupted her thought processes. She again tried to squirm out from his embrace, but he merely tightened his hold.

"Tell me or we'll stand like this all night."

"Rawlings said his own name was too well-known. Cal has been the front. I'm to be dealer and to play."

"Are the proceeds to be divided three ways?"

"I don't know. We haven't discussed that." The minute the words were out she knew she'd made a mistake.

Mark stepped back to get a better look at her face. "Now I know something's not right. You and Cal would have ironed out all those details long before you made this deal. The only other explanation is that Rawlings has got something on one of you, perhaps both. He's forcing you to take part in the game, or you'd never have agreed."

"That's not true." She had to think fast. "I meant Cal and I haven't discussed the deal. He made it. I wasn't interested enough to care." She managed to slip out of Mark's grasp and hurried into the living room. She couldn't concentrate on both his demanding questions and the sensations she felt when he was so near.

He followed her but kept his distance. She knew he was watching as she piled more wood on the fire. She sat down near the hearth, pulled her knees up and wrapped her arms around them. She kept her face turned toward the flames to avoid looking at him. Why should she be so unnerved by Mark's presence? Was it because, during the past few days, she had almost succeeded in convincing herself that he was no longer a part of her life? The time they'd spent together in the Cotswolds, even their making love, had been just memories, no longer influencing her every waking moment.

But now she again had to contend with the very real Mark, who was showing no inclination to leave her alone. She wasn't in love with him, she argued. If she loved anyone, she loved Caleb Norton, a man who had done so much for her in the past, a man whom she was relying on to help her deal with Rawlings. She realized how self-serving that sounded, but it was the truth.

Mark was only making everything so much more complicated....

"Amanda?" He sat beside her, wrapping the voluminous robe around his legs. "What's going on between you and Rawlings? And don't tell me any more lies. I know he isn't your new partner. Cal wouldn't have allowed a man like Rawlings to have close contact with you." Mark smiled. "Cal reminds me of a mother bear, protecting her cub. He sure as hell is the right size, anyway."

Amanda smiled but said nothing, nor did she look at him. Somehow she had to find a way to get Mark to leave. But how? What could she say that would convince him of just how much danger he was in? But if he knew there was danger, he'd try to do something to protect her.

"Let me see if I can guess what's going on," Mark said in a low voice. "Rawlings approaches you two with a plan, but you won't do business with him. Then he uses threats, a little blackmail. Do what he says or else. Am I close?''

Amanda turned to look at Mark. ''You're making too much out of all this. Both Cal and I are in it for the money. After this one time, Rawlings will be out.''

''Who's in the game?''

''Some high rollers, but I don't know their names. Rawlings has it all figured out. Cal's the front man. The players have heard about us and know Cal conducts an honest game, which this one will be, I swear.'' She paused to make sure Mark believed her. When he nodded his acceptance of her words, she continued. ''Rawlings says these men want to play against Amanda Kirk, the legendary woman poker player. They want the challenge of beating me. It's practically a sure thing that I'll win. I'm better than they are. But because I'm a woman they won't credit me with the degree of skill I have.''

''The logic of that seems a little shaky. What if you lose?''

Amanda straightened her shoulders. ''I won't.''

Mark shook his head in amazement. ''Those words are said by every gambler in the world.''

Amanda started to stand, but Mark stopped her. ''You aren't going to tell me any more, are you?''

''That's all there is to tell. There are no threats or blackmail or coercion of any kind. We're just three people involved in a business deal.'' Seeing the doubt in Mark's face, she quickly changed the subject. ''I thought you were supposed to be working at Orion.'' She paused, then added, ''But since you're the son of the founder, I guess you can be as free as a bird.''

"That's about it. I can do what I want. And more than anything I wanted to find you."

Before Amanda could respond she was pulled against him. Next she was lying on the floor, with Mark hovering over her.

"We've got until two. I don't think we should waste any more time."

"Mark, I am *not* going to bed with you." Her words were muffled as he kissed her. When the kiss ended, she repeated her order.

"Why?" he asked as he let his lips wander down her neck.

For a moment she couldn't think of any good excuse. But then her common sense took control. "Because you're leaving here—now!" She tried to wriggle out from under him, but it was impossible. "If Rawlings got a flight directly to Tahoe, he could be here in less than three hours." She wasn't sure of her facts, but the timing was close enough to make her feel panicked.

Mark surprised her by standing. He banked the fire, then bent down to take her hand and help her to stand. Without saying a word he led her across the living room floor, heading toward the end of the house where her bedroom was.

"It's cold in here," he said. "You've been shivering since I arrived. We're going to bed, dear Amanda. We can make love, if you want. If you don't, we can lie there without touching. Or we can simply hold each other, offering warmth and comfort. Any of the three possibilities is okay with me. It's up to you."

Amanda knew it would be pointless to argue. Besides, they did have some time, and she *was* cold. What better way to get warm than in Mark's arms?

CHAPTER THIRTEEN

"Amanda, I've dreamed about this since you left me in London. I haven't been able to concentrate on anything except thinking of you."

Mark's whispered words set Amanda's heart racing. He lay on his side, facing her, his head propped up by his hand. The bedside light was off, so she couldn't see his face clearly. Before climbing in beside him she'd undressed and put on a gown. He'd slipped off Cal's robe and now wore his own dry shorts. He continued to make no attempt to touch her. She lay still, listening to his quiet breathing, inhaling his unique scent.

"Amanda?" She didn't answer. He waited a moment for her to look at him. When she didn't respond, he again spoke. "I want to tell you what's been happening in my life since I got back from England. Okay?"

"Yes." Her answer was barely audible.

Mark told her about his clearance and how he'd been prevented from doing any work at Orion. He explained about Rob's gambling and his elevated position in the company. All Mark's frustration was evident in his voice. "I can't do what I've spent years training for. I haven't had a chance to find out where Rob's getting his gambling money. And worse than that, I've got a terrible feeling something's not right at Orion. I can't even explain why I feel that way. I may have waited too long. The company my father worked so hard to establish could be in jeopardy right now, and I've got my hands tied.''

Amanda pulled herself up until she was leaning against the headboard. ''Are they trying to get you so angry that you'll quit?''

''I think that's the plan.''

''Shouldn't you be at the plant, especially when Rob's not there?''

''Yes.''

His simple answer told her a great deal. To be with her he was willing to ignore a perfect opportunity to learn something about Rob and Orion. He was making a sacrifice, one that could have far-reaching, possibly disastrous effects.

They continued to lie next to each other, but there was no physical contact. True to his word he was letting her set the pace, deciding what they were going to do.

At that moment she realized just how frightened she'd been, how the past few days with Rawlings and Cal had taken their toll on her strength and confidence. She'd been existing on nervous energy, fueled by her fear. She had selfishly relied on Cal, and now she was falling into the same pattern with Mark. But there was a parallel here that made her feel better. Although both men had different reasons, they needed her just as much as she needed them. She would do anything to help Cal face the consequences of what he'd done as an eighteen-year-old, but there was nothing she could do until Rawlings got out of their lives.

Right now, though, she could help Mark forget his problems, at least temporarily. Without allowing herself any more time to think of what she was doing, she said, "Please, Mark, hold me. I'm so cold."

He pulled her toward him, enfolding her in his arms, wrapping his legs around her. Their bodies fitted together, a perfect match. His heat felt so good. At last the core of ice deep inside her was beginning to melt.

"Are you glad I came?" he asked with his lips against her temple.

"No," she lied in a teasing voice. "But you are serving a useful purpose."

"What's that?"

"Raising my body temperature."

"I know even better ways." He began to run the palm of his hand across her back, fast at first, then slower as he focused his attention on her lips.

When she could speak, she asked, "Do you promise to leave before midnight?"

"That sounds like a warning from Cinderella's fairy godmother."

"I mean it, Mark. You've got to go before Cal and Rawlings get here."

"Are you afraid Cal will learn about us? Or is it Rawlings you're so worried about?"

"Why do you ask so many questions? We only have a little time before you have to leave."

Mark drew her closer, again touching the sensitive spots along her spine, her breasts, her abdomen, lingering for a moment, then moving on. It was difficult to differentiate between her smooth satin skin and the silk of her gown. "I'll leave the house," he said, "but not the area."

"You've got to go back to Philadelphia... tomorrow morning at the latest. We can't take the chance of Rawlings seeing you."

Mark pulled his head back so that he could see Amanda's expression in the dim light. "So it is Rawlings you're afraid of. What's he got on you?"

"Nothing! He's jealous, that's all. He tried to find you at your hotel in London and learned you weren't staying in your room. He suspected you were with me."

Mark had stopped touching her back. He placed one of his hands on the side of her face and tried to read her expression. "He certainly has a proprietary attitude toward you. You haven't given him any encouragement, have you?"

Amanda shuddered uncontrollably. "How could you even ask something like that?" she demanded. Her voice was loud and slightly shrill. "I find him utterly detestable." She tried to escape Mark's embrace, but his lips touched hers, calming her.

"I believe you," he said. "I'm sorry. I just had to be sure." Mark began his campaign to arouse her, instantly recalling all the sensitive areas that had elicited an excited response from her.

Amanda sighed and relaxed, letting her mind become free of her worries and fears. For a little while longer she was safe. Time lost all meaning. Mark hadn't forgotten how to make her respond in a way that gave them both pleasure. Her body had been like the dry earth, waiting for the rain. Only Mark could fill the emptiness she'd been feeling. But what would she do when he went away? Without him and his strength she wondered how she could survive for the months it would take her to get her life in order.

Mark began to make love to her, inundating her with sensations and emotions that she'd never experienced before. Their bodies rediscovered the rhythm of love. Her senses soared to new heights, and her thoughts evaporated—all except one—Mark.

"IT'S MIDNIGHT," Amanda whispered, hating to say the words. Now that her heart was no longer racing and her breathing was somewhat back to normal she could again think clearly. She realized the temptation to leave with him might prove impossible to overcome. "You've got to go."

"I know," Mark said in a low, rumbling voice. Amanda's head was lying in the crook of his arm. He shifted his elbow to relieve the pressure.

"Where will you stay?"

"I rented a motel when I got up here. Do you think it's still raining?"

She listened for a moment. "No, it's stopped. The rest of your clothes should be dry by now." She asked herself why they were talking about such inconsequential matters when all she wanted to hear was how much he loved her. He'd whispered the words in her ear as he'd brought her to the peak of excitement, and she knew he'd been speaking the truth. She had wanted to echo his chant, to feel the joy of freely declaring her love. But she had forced herself to keep still. If he knew how she felt, he'd have one more hold over her, and he wouldn't leave. The only way she could protect him was to get him away from Tahoe.

"What are you thinking?"

His voice startled her. "You've got to promise me you'll drive to South Shore or Reno and catch the first plane out."

"I'm not promising anything. You said the poker game wasn't for a few more days. We can meet—"

"No." She sat up, turned on the lamp and faced Mark. They both blinked until their eyes had adjusted to the strong light. Amanda didn't cover her naked breasts, didn't even feel the cool air chilling her. "Listen to me. Rawlings has a lot riding on this game. The money he's hoping to win is only part of it. He's planning revenge against a man who hurt him."

"For his knee?"

"Yes." She hesitated, then added, "The man's name is Septimus Garland." In a few brief sentences Amanda told Mark what Rawlings had said. But she made no mention of Robert Quintero.

"My God, Amanda," Mark shouted as he sat up. "Septimus Garland! Even *I've* heard of him. Does Rawlings think he can really win against a man like that?"

"Yes, he does."

"Garland's got a reputation for double-dealing that makes the Mafia look like a Boy Scout troop." Mark leaned against the backboard. The sheet was around his waist, leaving his chest bare.

Amanda pulled her hair away from her face and cleared her throat. "I think you're exaggerating. Rawlings says Garland's coming alone, which means he's got complete trust in Norton and Kirk."

"I don't know who's more naive, you or Cal. You both seem to think this is a perfect world where you can trust everybody. But let me tell you—"

Amanda slipped out of bed and pulled on her robe. "You're going to have to tell me some other time," she said. "You've got to get away from here now. I'll get your clothes."

Before he could argue she was out of the bedroom, leaving him alone. He was positive there was more to Amanda's determination to get him to leave than just fear that Rawlings might be jealous.

Knowing a man like Garland was involved in the up-coming game worried Mark. No government or state law-enforcement agencies had been able to pin anything on the man. But anytime large-scale corruption, vice or crime were mentioned in New Jersey, New York or Washington, D.C., Garland was mentioned, too. He'd become famous for telling every reporter who interviewed him that he was a simple businessman devoted to his family and friends.

Amanda entered, carrying Mark's clothes. "They're still a little damp, but you can go straight to your motel to change."

As Mark dressed, he asked, "Who else is playing in the game?"

"I . . . I may have heard, but I didn't pay any attention. I remembered Garland's name because Cal said much the same thing you did." Seeing the expression on Mark's face, she quickly added, "But Cal said there isn't anything to worry about. He and Rawlings can handle any trouble."

"Sure they can."

Mark had said the words in a biting, sarcastic way. She now knew that all her talking had done no good. Mark was here, and here he'd stay. He had set himself up as her protector, even though his presence only added to her danger.

She had to try one more time to encourage him to go back home. But what she planned was going to be one of the most difficult things she'd ever done.

"Mark, you know why I want you to leave, don't you? I'm afraid of Rawlings and what he'd do to you and to me if he found out you were here."

"Yes, I understand that. But it doesn't make any difference. I'll just make sure he doesn't suspect a thing."

She tightened her fists so hard that her fingernails dug into the palms. The pain helped her focus her thoughts. "What just happened... our making love, having sex or whatever you call it... well, it was beautiful and incredibly exciting. But I was wrong to let it happen." She rubbed her temple, then ran her hand through her hair. "I don't mean to denigrate the experience, but I shouldn't have..." She shook her head as if to clear it. "I want you to know that Cal has told me he's in love with me."

Mark silently bent down and slipped on his squishy loafers that would have to be thrown away. He straightened, looking at Amanda's face. He knew what she would say next.

"I'm going to stay with Cal." Mark said nothing, just continued to stare at her without expression. She felt frantic that he wasn't responding. Perhaps he didn't understand what she was trying to tell him. "Cal and I are going to continue our gambling partnership. We'll probably end up getting married, but he hasn't mentioned it... yet."

"Oh?" Mark said, adjusting the collar of his shirt. "That's interesting."

Mark's calmly spoken words stunned her. Why wasn't he arguing with her, trying to talk her out of her decision? Then she understood. He didn't believe her. She hadn't said she loved him, but he knew. Her actions had proved the depth of her feeling. The sexual act had communicated a message of love that erased any doubt he might have had. No matter what she said or how ignoble she acted, she would never be able to convince Mark that she didn't love him.

And she'd made a tactical error. She hadn't said she couldn't love Mark because she was in love with Cal.

She turned and ran into the living room, where she stood by the windows facing the lake. All she could see was her own reflection. Her hair was tangled, but she didn't bother touching it.

When Mark entered the room, she didn't turn around. He walked up beside her. "When I leave here, I'll scout around the area and find someplace for us to meet." He thought for a moment. "Outside the wall near the front gate is a large flowerpot filled with pansies. I'll leave a message in it, telling you where to go."

"Damn it, Mark, don't you understand what I've been telling you? We can't meet."

"I know you can arrange it. You're not a prisoner here. Rawlings needs you, remember that. His whole plan is built around you."

Amanda reminded herself that Mark was operating without knowing that Rawlings held her father prisoner. That one factor tilted the balance in Rawlings's favor.

"I'll make sure we won't be seen," Mark said, smoothing her hair back from her face. "I'll pick a place to meet you that you can walk to from here. You'll be perfectly safe."

His nonchalant attitude was driving her crazy. He was the most stubborn, the most persistent man she'd ever met. "You should be in Philadelphia, trying to save your company."

"True. I'll go back in a few days, after the game, when you can come with me."

He kissed her, more like a brother than a lover. "I'll see you tomorrow. Go to bed. You look a little tired."

And then he was gone, leaving her to sort out her confused thoughts.

"WAS EVERYTHING OKAY while we were gone?" Rawlings asked, studying Amanda's face as if memorizing its features. "Did you see anybody?"

The morning sun shone brightly through the window behind him, casting his face in shadow. Amanda gathered the newspaper off the sofa and sat down, thinking about the flowerpot outside the gate. Right now it was impossible to look for a message.

"I didn't leave the house, if that's what you mean."

Rawlings and Cal had gotten home about two, but she'd pretended to be asleep. She wished she could talk to Cal, to find out what they'd done in Los Angeles.

"The weather wasn't too cooperative, huh?" Rawlings said, grinning in a way that chilled her. He sat in a chair opposite her. "Not much sun to get a tan."

"I read and listened to music. It was nice being alone." The statement was directed at Rawlings. Cal winked at her, letting her know he understood.

"Where'd you get the fancy box?" Rawlings asked, looking at the coffee table where Mark's gift now sat.

She'd forgotten to hide it the night before. Rawlings's question sounded innocent enough, but she had felt all morning that he suspected something had gone on while he and Cal were away.

Rawlings raised the lid, lifted one of the jade chips and held it up to the light. "The letter *R*. How appropriate."

Cal turned around to face Amanda, studying her. She knew he was curious, too. "I got the chest while I was in England at an antique fair. I brought it out last night so I could polish it."

"How did you get it through customs?" Cal asked. "You didn't declare it."

Now the lies had to start. "Well, I, that is, I just took a chance. I'm not very proud to admit that I didn't want to have to pay the fees. I hid it in the large suitcase, and no one asked to open my luggage."

"No wonder that case weighed so much," Cal said, and returned to the window to stare across the lake. "But next time don't take a chance on getting caught. It's better to pay the customs."

"I know. I'm sorry." Amanda's mouth was dry, but no amount of coffee helped. At last she gave up trying to drink. Setting the cup down, she focused her attention on Rawlings. With her shoulders pulled back and her spine stiff she asked the question that had been burning in her mind for hours. "Did you see my father?"

Rawlings quickly glanced over at Cal, as if judging whether he should answer or not.

"Amanda told me all about her father," Cal said.

"Did you see him?" Amanda asked again.

"Yes."

Rawlings's curt reply was a warning not to pursue the matter, but she had to continue. "How is he? Did he say anything about me?"

"He's okay. Going a bit stir-crazy, but it'll soon be over. He doesn't know you're part of this deal. When everything's finished, you two can have a happy reunion."

"Are you holding him just so I'll do what you want?"

"Yeah, a kind of insurance so you and Cal won't do anything stupid."

"And there's no other reason?"

Rawlings kept his gaze directed at Amanda. His cold blue eyes seemed to penetrate her thoughts. He lit a cigarette, which proved his agitated state. He'd made it a practice to always smoke outside whenever she was in a room.

"You're not in a position to ask questions." Any trace of his earlier good humor had vanished. Then he shrugged, changed his expression and said, "After the game I'll tell you where he is. I promise. Everything's going to be okay." He got up and walked toward the door, dragging his bad leg. Before leaving the room he said, "I've made arrangements to rent another house where we'll be playing. This place is too public and too far away from Reno." He looked at Amanda. "Later, I want to talk to you . . . alone."

She started to speak, to tell him he couldn't just order her around, but Cal's hand on her shoulder stopped her. "I'll see you later," she said through gritted teeth.

"Right."

After Rawlings went out on the deck, she looked up at Cal. He was still behind her but no longer touching her shoulder.

"What's Reno got to do with the game?" she asked.

Cal shrugged and sat on the sofa next to her. "The players must be flying in there. It's got a bigger airport than South Lake Tahoe."

"Makes sense," she said. Her mind turned to wondering what Rawlings wanted to talk to her about.

Cal played with a crystal ashtray, twirling it around on the coffee table. "What I'd like to know is where we're going to be playing. I wish he'd let me find the place."

"There's nothing you can do about it now. We just have to do what he wants."

Cal looked over at her. "I want you to know I did try to see your father, but I never got a chance. I'm sorry."

"What happened in L.A.?"

"I was ordered to stay in the hotel room with one of Rawlings's 'friends.' Not the most intellectual man I've ever met. I tried to teach him gin rummy, but even old maid and go fish were more than he could handle."

Amanda's smile elicited a response in Cal that stunned her. His expression was a bold statement of his love. Tears stung her eyes, and she turned away. She thought about Mark, and the love she felt for him that she could no longer deny. What could she do to keep from hurting Cal? Right then she could think of no way out of her dilemma.

Cal reached over and took her hand. "We're in Nevada, remember?"

She looked at him blankly.

"Nevada's known for its easy marriages. We could take the car, get married and be back here before Rawlings even knew we were gone."

Amanda was utterly amazed. She could think of nothing to say.

"Rawlings is getting ready to make his move on you. To his way of thinking he's been patient long enough. But if we were married, he'd leave you alone. I would have already staked my claim. He wouldn't try anything. But that's not the only reason. I love you."

"Oh, Cal, I can't—"

Before she could finish, Cal released her hand and said, "Yes, you're right." His disappointment was visible in his face, audible in his voice. "I was thoughtless. We can't do anything that would jeopardize your father's safety. We'll talk about it later—when Rawlings isn't controlling our lives."

Amanda knew she should tell him the truth, that they'd never be married. She wasn't being fair to let him continue believing he had a chance. And yet what harm was there in waiting until all of this was behind them? Then they could get their business partnership and their personal lives in order. Also, given more time, she might be able to find a way to reveal the truth without hurting him.

She stood. "Thank you for...everything." She kissed his cheek, turned and headed for the door. "I'm going to take a walk, uh, over to the grocery store. I want to get a new book and some hand lotion. The air here is so dry." She paused, then smiled. "Do I need permission from our lord and master before I go?"

"I'll handle Rawlings," Cal said, standing and heading toward the kitchen. "But don't push it. Get back in time for your little chat and the afternoon poker game.''

''We aren't playing again today, are we?''

''That's what the boss ordered.''

''Damn.'' The word hung in the air as she hurried out of the room.

MARK LAY in his motel room bed, thinking about the events of the night before. After leaving Amanda, he'd stayed in his car until he'd seen Cal and Rawlings arrive at two. He'd driven around until he found a good rendezvous place—the parking lot at Raley's, the store where he'd finally learned how to find Amanda. He'd been able to leave his message in the flowerpot without being seen. Now all he had to do was wait until noon when he could meet her.

Right now he'd call Diane to find out when their mother would be leaving Paris. He reached for the phone, dialed and surprisingly got straight through.

''*Allô?*'' Diane sounded a little out of breath.

''*Allô* to you, too.''

''Mark? Is that you?''

''*Oui, ma soeur. Avez-vous un crayon bleu, s'il vous plaît?*''

''Your accent's terrible, and what do you want a blue pencil for, anyway?''

Her laughter made him smile. ''Just trying out the only French I know, *ma soeur.*''

''Thanks for the opal ring, Mark. I love it and it just fits. Where did you find anything so unusual?''

''In Wales,'' Mark said, remembering Amanda helping him to choose the gifts at the flea market. ''Does mother like her present?''

"She wore the earrings on the plane."

"Has she gone back home?"

"Left this morning. I just got back from Orly." Diane paused, as if hesitating to say what was on her mind.

"What's wrong?" he asked.

"She left because Ed has a proposition for her, and for you and me, too. He needed to talk to mother about it."

"What kind of proposition?" All of Mark's warning signals were going off.

"Ed wants to buy our interest in Orion." Before Mark could respond she hurried on. "He's paying top price, anticipating the company's growth over the next twenty years. And the trust funds that Dad left us wouldn't be affected. We'd get our share now rather than after mother di— Er, that is later."

Mark was stunned by what he'd heard. He should have expected a move like this from the Quinteros, but it just never occurred to him that they could be so underhanded. Yet he had to admit their plan was ingenious. By buying out the heirs' interest they were getting rid of the one man who could cause them trouble.

"Mark? Are you still on the line?"

"I'm here," he said, trying to keep his voice calm.

"Mother said this way you'd have enough money to start your own design company, a new beginning. And the, uh, the rivalry and hate between you and Rob would be ended."

Mark knew those were his mother's words. "It sounds like you're in favor of the idea."

"Well, you know me. I don't understand high finance. But I could use all that money. I want to start an art school for children here in Paris. It could be a real gold mine. Rich, indulgent parents are just begging to spend money on their kids."

"Diane, listen to me. When does mother have to make a decision?"

"Ed and Rob want to get started on the negotiations as soon as possible."

"Rob said he was going on a little vacation," Mark said, his mind in a whirl. "Do you know where he is?"

"Ed told Mother that Rob was going to be in northern California or Nevada, somewhere like that. I heard you've gone out of town, too. Where are you?"

Mark didn't want to tell her the truth, just in case she might mention anything to Ed. "I'm in New York. But I'll be back home tonight. I want to talk to Mother about all of this." He paused, then quickly added, "Don't make any kind of commitment to Ed or Rob until I can talk to you again, okay?"

"Sure. I know it'll take awhile to get everything settled, so I won't make any plans to spend the money. Besides, I've still got three more quarters to finish at school."

"Graduating should be what you're concentrating on right now and not all that money. You'll have plenty of time to spend it."

"You're right, big brother, as usual."

"I've got to go. Love ya."

"Ditto," she said, and hung up.

Mark sat with his head down, trying to sort out what he'd just learned. He knew now he had better hurry before his mother signed the agreement. Ed Quintero had always had a strong influence over his weak wife. In a shockingly short amount of time after her husband's death, Connie had married Ed, and he'd taken over the running of the company. During the next seventeen years, his power had become stronger, especially after Mark's mother discovered the magic of martinis. Ed could convince her to do anything. Right at this minute she might be signing away her children's birthright. Mark had to get back to Philadelphia.

But what about Amanda? There were only a few days before the game. He couldn't leave her... and yet he knew he had to.

He found his wallet, called a number in Philadelphia and learned that for an exorbitant fee Maynard Butler, Private Investigator, would be glad to come to Tahoe to protect Amanda Kirk, as unobtrusively as was possible, of course.

Next Mark got reservations out of Reno. He'd have to change planes three times before getting to Philadelphia, which meant he'd arrive in the early morning. But the timing was right to put into action the plan that had been forming in the back of his mind for days. He packed and got ready to meet Amanda.

As AMANDA WALKED across the parking lot toward the grocery store, she saw Mark standing by a gray sedan. The rear license plates indicated the car was rented. When he noticed her, he waved but didn't smile.

"Get in," he ordered as he opened the door for her. "We haven't got much time."

"What's wrong?"

To keep from having to drive in front of the house, just in case Cal or Rawlings was standing in front, Mark headed east along the two-lane highway that followed the curves of the lake.

When he finished relating what he'd learned from his sister, Amanda realized Mark's stepfather had solved one of her problems. Her sense of elation was quickly tempered by concern for Mark. "You've got to go back to talk to your mother as soon as possible."

"I know." He pulled into a parking area that provided a view of the blue water and shut off the engine.

"I hate to leave you, but..." He stared across the lake.

"Mark, Orion's more important than what I'm doing. I'll be perfectly safe, I know."

Yes, she would be with Maynard Butler keeping watch on her and the house twenty-four hours a day. Mark moved his hand to the back of her neck, pulling her closer. "God, I'm going to miss you. When we get everything settled, I'll never let you out of my sight."

"That should prove interesting," she said, kissing him on the bridge of his broken nose.

But Mark wasn't satisfied with such an innocent display of affection and began kissing her deeply, leaving them both breathless.

Finally reality returned. Mark glanced at his watch. "I've got to go."

"Drop me off at the grocery store. I need to buy a book and hand lotion."

Mark reluctantly started the car and headed west.

"What are you going to do at Orion?" Amanda wanted to ask if he would be in any danger, but she knew it would do no good. He wouldn't tell her.

"I'm going to ask a former employee of the company to help me." Philo Webster knew more about Orion's safes, its security systems and how to bypass them than any man alive. Webster hated the Quinteros so much that he'd personally escort Mark into the plant and do whatever was necessary to pin something on them.

"What do you think you'll find?" Amanda asked.

"God knows. If Rob's been dipping into the till for gambling money, well, that's something we can handle. But if the quality of Orion's products has been compromised, then we're really in trouble."

"How can you learn if the products are all right?"

"I don't know." He pulled into the grocery store parking lot, found a space that had cars on both sides and turned off the engine. He took a business card from his pocket. "Here's my home number and how to get me at work. If I'm not there, leave a message telling me how to contact you."

She nodded, wondering if she'd ever get a chance to call him or even see him again. She deliberately didn't mention that she, Cal and Rawlings would soon be leaving the lake house. Mark would only worry, which never accomplished anything. He had his own problems to contend with.

He drew her closer, kissed her, then leaned over and opened her door. "I'm going to miss my plane if I don't go now. Please stay away from Rawlings." He smiled. "That's a dumb thing to say, but you know what I mean. Remember, I love you."

With tears forming pools in her eyes she slipped out of the car, slammed the door and hurried toward the brightly lit store. "I love you, Mark Banning," she whispered. She didn't dare turn around and wave, knowing that if she did she would run back into his arms.

CHAPTER FOURTEEN

"I'M IN A NO-WIN situation," Mark said to Philo Webster. The words reminded him of what Amanda had said about her own status. They'd both been put through a wringer these past few weeks.

Philo set the sheet of paper he'd been reading on the ash-covered table beside him, stretched, then lit another cigarette. "Got any ideas about what you're going to do?"

Mark was in the only other chair in Philo's sparsely furnished apartment. It was nearly five in the morning and time they finished their task.

Since three, when he and Philo completed their inspection of Orion, they'd been reading letters and documents they'd extracted from Rob's safe. Philo's past experience as Orion's security chief had come in handy. Without him, Mark wouldn't have gotten into the off-limits area.

The furnace clicked on, the warm air stirring the smoke around the room. Philo coughed and gasped for breath, sounding asthmatic. Mark knew his bachelor friend was drinking and smoking himself to death. For thirty years he'd had one interest: working at Orion, being part of Russell Banning's team. When that was taken away by Ed Quintero, Philo had started his slow decline.

"Blowing the whistle on the Quinteros will destroy Orion," Mark said. "I might as well go back and dynamite the damn place."

"What other choice have you got except turning the bastards in?" Philo asked. "You can't let them get away with it." Philo's gravelly voice reflected his anger at the Quinteros. He drew on his cigarette. "Damn it all, Mark, we've got undeniable proof that they've been bribing military officials to get contracts for Orion. They've made campaign contributions to congressmen in exchange for advantageous legislation. We've got to do something about the Quinteros," he said forcefully.

"I know. But if I use the material, there'll be a congressional investigation. Every government agency ever created will be down on us like a posse after a bank robber."

"I don't see how you're going to avoid an investigation," Philo said. He again began reading from the papers he'd found in Rob's safe.

Mark closed his eyes. They felt gritty, as if they'd been sprinkled with sand. His thoughts were like hot popcorn kernels jumping around in his head. He couldn't seem to come to any decisions. He knew his first concern had to be saving Orion and keeping the employees from losing their jobs. But the other side of the coin, and equally important, was bringing the Quinteros to justice. Seeing father and son behind bars might be worth losing Orion.

At least he'd had one triumph since he'd returned to Philadelphia. He'd convinced his mother to wait before agreeing to Ed's plan to buy out his and Diane's share of the company.

"Mark? Are you asleep?"

Mark realized Philo had been speaking, but nothing he'd said had registered. "What?"

"I just came across a name that might interest you. If this guy's involved with the Quinteros, well, Orion's in really deep—"

"Who?" Mark asked impatiently, sitting up. "What name?"

"Septimus Garland."

Mark grabbed the letter from Philo's hand. It was written to Rob from Garland, dated two weeks before, and contained surprisingly incriminating information about an air force general who was willing to accept a cash gift in exchange for a report to the Pentagon favoring Orion's bid on jet engine parts.

"Oh, my God," Mark whispered. Everything had suddenly fallen into place: Rob's big-time gambling would have led him to a man like Garland. For years there had been suspicions about Garland's friends in high places. The next step for Rob would have been to let Garland show him the ropes of corruption in government agencies.

Mark felt sick and dizzy with his next thought. Rob could even have been a player in the game when Evan Rawlings was beaten and his money confiscated. Diane had said Rob had gone to northern California or Nevada. He could be one of the players in the game with Amanda. "No!" Mark yelled.

"What the hell's the matter?" Philo asked.

"Let me think," Mark said as he began gathering up the papers in the same order he'd found them. As he worked, his mind returned to Amanda and what could be going on at Tahoe. Then another area of his brain informed him that he was assuming too much. Just because Rob had gone out west didn't necessarily mean he was at Lake Tahoe. But Mark instantly denied that assumption. Some instinct told him that Rob was a player in the game. If his stepbrother learned that Rawlings, Amanda and Cal had met Mark Banning, there could be trouble.

Philo cleared his throat. "I hope your silence means you're coming up with a plan. What is it? Is there anything I can do to help?"

Mark thought about Philo's offer. Maynard Butler and one of his operatives were watching the Tahoe house. If Philo came along, that would make four men against an unknown number of soldiers in Rawlings's army. Philo's field of expertise might come in handy.

"Do you know how to get one of those cameras that can photograph documents?" Mark asked.

"Sure. I've got one right here." Philo spoke with pride in his voice. "It's the newest and smallest one made. The negatives are tiny, but once they're blown up they're incredibly clear." He smiled broadly. "I can even develop them."

"Let's get to work, then." As he followed Philo to the back bedroom, Mark asked, "How would you like to go to Nevada with me?"

"Just try to keep me away," Philo said with a grin.

AMANDA AWAKENED but kept her eyes closed, enjoying the warmth of the elusive sun that had chased clouds all morning. An hour before she had come out on the deck to lie in a lounge chair and eat an apple and a slice of cheese while trying to work on her suntan. The book she'd bought at the grocery store the day before lay unopened on her lap.

She hadn't meant to fall asleep, but it proved impossible to keep her eyes from closing. While she slept she'd had a brief but vivid dream of Mark arousing all her senses. As she thought about the erotic images that had formed in her unconscious mind, she smiled. Her dreams had been reenactments of their lovemaking. It had taken a long moment for her breathing to quiet, her heart to return to a normal beat.

She opened her eyes and gasped. Rawlings was sitting near her chair, staring at her with intense interest. She wished she were dressed instead of wearing the revealing bathing suit, and desperately wanted to cover her body.

"We haven't had a chance to talk," Rawlings said, keeping his gaze on her. "You seem to keep yourself just out of reach."

"Does that surprise you?" She looked around. "Where's Cal?"

"Took the car to the store. We need to stock up on supplies. Where we're going we won't find a grocery just down the road."

Amanda pulled herself up so that she was sitting more than lying. "Where is this place?"

"Up in the mountains."

Instead of commenting on his vague answer, she asked, "When are we leaving?"

"We'll go as soon as Cal gets back. The other players are coming in the morning. You don't need to know anything else." He studied her face, then his gaze drifted over her body. "We haven't got much time before we have to pack." He stood and sat on the side of Amanda's chair, moving her over to give himself room. His fingers lingered a little too long on the bare flesh of her thigh. One of her arms was pinned against her body by his leg.

She suppressed the shudder that ran down her spine. When she tried to get up, Rawlings grabbed her shoulders and kept her in place with his strong arms.

"This is the last chance we'll have to be alone."

As he spoke, his face kept moving closer. She knew he was planning on kissing her. Before she could do anything to prevent it, his lips landed on hers. She clamped her mouth together, trying to twist her head away from him. He grabbed a handful of hair and held her in place as his tongue tried to make inroads into her mouth. She felt as if she were strangling. All she could do was moan her protest, sounding like a sobbing child. She'd been concentrating so intently on evading the kiss that it took her a moment to comprehend what Rawlings was doing with his free hand. His fingers caressed the inside of her thigh, rubbing the skin roughly, then lightly. Wherever he touched she felt her flesh crawl. She thrashed her legs, hoping to knock him off the chair, but his strength defeated her.

When he at last lifted his mouth, he didn't release her. "That wasn't much of a kiss," he said with a sneer.

She reached up and rubbed her lips with her fingertips, as if to erase any trace of him. "You are the most despicable, the...the—"

He smacked her across the face with the back of his hand. The blow had been too light to bruise, but it stung enough to bring tears. The shock of being struck like that left her speechless.

"You think you're so high and mighty," Rawlings said, continuing to hold her down. "Father a big shot, lots of money. Both mother and daughter beautiful enough to twist men around their fingers. Well, let me tell you, I've met your kind before. You cover yourself in prissy respectability and a hands-off attitude, but I know you're no different from a Vegas hustler. You've given out for Cal and no doubt for countless other men, letting them win at poker, then getting them in your bed while Cal takes their dough. I bet even that bastard Mark Banning got his share.''

Amanda's initial rage became tempered by logic. She remembered the joke she'd played on Mark. He'd willingly accepted her as a call girl, had accepted her as an easy lay, until he'd learned she was a gambler. Rawlings knew she and Cal had spent the last year living together. Their unique relationship was incomprehensible to a man with his background and mentality. His accusations were based on observed facts, which she could deny forever, but he'd never believe.

"I'll have you," Rawlings said, breathing heavily. "And you'll do just what I say." His smile was diabolical. "Remember, I've still got your father." Just in case she needed a physical reminder he opened his shirt to reveal the golden doubloon that hung on the end of a chain around his neck.

"You're all bluff, Rawlings. You wouldn't dare do anything to hurt him." Her display of bravado sounded weak even to her ears. Where was Cal? He'd said he would protect her from Rawlings, but now that she needed him he wasn't here. No, that wasn't fair. He'd done everything he could, even giving her a gun, which she'd carefully placed in her underwear drawer.

She again tried to stand, but Rawlings just tightened his grip and began kissing her, his actions becoming more bold. His hands were at her breasts, freeing them from the top of her suit. She felt her panic rise, knowing she could do nothing to stop him—no, she did have a way. She had used a small paring knife to cut the apple she'd had for lunch. It was still on the deck out of Rawlings's line of vision. She relaxed, hoping he'd think she was giving in. She slowly reached down, wrapped her fingers around the handle and raised the knife toward his neck, applying just enough pressure to draw a drop of blood.

When Rawlings realized what was happening, he lifted his head a fraction of an inch. As he moved, Amanda adjusted the angle of the knife, but kept the point directly on his skin, right at the brain stem. His eyes widened in disbelief. "You bitch," he growled.

"Don't make any sudden moves. If I'm all those things you called me, then I'm capable of killing you. And I'd dearly love to," she added, meaning every word.

For a long moment they both said nothing. A tiny rivulet of blood ran across the back of his neck, around the front and dropped onto Amanda's breast. She managed to free her right hand and adjusted her bathing suit to cover herself.

She carefully drew the knife along his skin, following the red trail until the point was right under his chin. "Move back very slowly," she ordered quietly. Rawlings pulled himself away from her, and she matched his movement, keeping the knife against his neck. Like two dancers waltzing in unison, they stood.

Amanda paused a moment, listening. "Cal's here. I just heard the car in the driveway." She knew her tone reflected her relief. "If he learns what you've done, he'll kill you without thinking about the consequences."

Amanda stepped away from Rawlings, feeling safer now. "For everybody's sake, don't put him in a position where he has to kill you." She inhaled deeply, feeling on surer ground. "But if you *ever* touch me again, I'll tell Cal. Do you understand?"

Rawlings didn't respond. He used a handkerchief to wipe away the blood on his neck, then turned and walked toward the beach.

Amanda's hands began to shake so much that she dropped the knife onto the deck. It slipped between one of the cracks, landing on the ground underneath.

She made sure she looked composed and that her suit covered her properly. She used a napkin to wipe away Rawlings's blood, smoothed her hair from her face and turned to go inside. She had to tell Cal they were leaving for the second house that afternoon.

MARK AND PHILO KNOCKED on Maynard Butler's motel room at Lake Tahoe, the same one Mark had vacated only a day and a half before. After introductions were made and they found places to sit, Maynard cleared his throat, opened a small notebook and read aloud. "Norton Rawlings and Miss Kirk left the house about an hour ago."

"Damn!" Mark said. If the plane hadn't been delayed, they'd have made it in time.

Maynard frowned at the interruption. Then he continued reading. "The back seat and trunk of the rental car had grocery bags inside. Norton had to struggle to get their luggage packed in. I ascertained from their conversation that they were unsuccessful in getting all of their belongings out of the house, which means they might be returning. Or sending someone back. Miss

Kirk was carrying a black box that appeared to be heavy. She refused to let anyone touch it.''

"Do you know where they've gone?" Mark asked, fearing the answer.

"No. I had an operative follow the car. Amos just called in. He lost them in the mountains. He's going to stay in the area and look for them."

"I thought your men were trained."

Butler sat up straight and looked offended. "They are trained, but he was at a disadvantage. The man in the car knew the terrain. He couldn't have known he was being followed. Amos is too good for that. But the driver was extra cautious. He must have taken an unmarked side road that Amos didn't see. I know you're disappointed, Mr. Banning, but all I can say is that Amos is still up there looking. As I said, he's good. I have faith in his abilities." He looked steadily at Mark. "I'd have gone myself, but I decided I'd stay here so we could talk. I need to know what you want me to do."

Mark nodded, accepting Butler's explanation. "How did Amanda look? She wasn't hurt in any way, do you think?"

"She seemed fine, but she sure wasn't smiling or laughing. She didn't say anything and acted kind of serious, like she was on her way to a funeral."

"Thanks for the encouraging word," Mark mumbled sarcastically. Louder, he asked, "When do you think you'll be hearing from Amos again?"

"Can't say. Could be hours or days. The territory he has to cover is mighty wild. He'll keep searching. When he finds another phone, he'll call in."

"Seems to me all we can do is relax and wait," Philo said. He lit a cigarette, then glanced at Mark and quickly extinguished it. "We could do with some food."

"I haven't eaten, either," Butler said. "I've been waiting for you to arrive."

"You two go," Mark said, standing. "I'm going to the house. Amanda might have left a message of some kind."

"I checked the property after they left," Maynard said. "No one was anywhere around, but, of course, I didn't go inside."

Philo got to his feet. "Want me to pick the lock?" he asked Mark.

"No, I've got a key." He had taken it off Amanda's dresser, tried it on the front door, then pocketed it without telling her.

Maynard stood. "I'd better stay here in case Amos calls. Mr. Webster can take my car and bring me back something to eat."

Mark nodded. "I'll only be gone a little while. I'll meet you back here."

Soon Mark stood outside the stone wall surrounding the house. Memories of the night he'd spent with Amanda returned to him in clear detail. That time seemed so long ago, but it was only two days.

As soon as he got over the wall, he opened the front door and entered, walking partway across the room. He stopped, thinking he'd heard a noise behind him. Just as he turned, a blinding pain exploded at the back of his head. All sense of feeling faded as darkness filled his mind.

WHEN AMANDA first saw the lodge Evan had rented, she'd never felt more alone in her life. It seemed they'd driven forever around forested mountains and through deep canyons to get to this isolated spot, miles from any sign of civilization. And for the past hour of the drive Rawlings had insisted on blindfolding her and Cal. "Just in case," he'd said.

Rawlings had finally told them they could remove the blindfolds, and Amanda had stumbled out of the car, feeling disoriented. Now she surveyed granite outcroppings sharing the land with huge pine trees. The terrain was rugged; walking would be difficult on the steep slopes. If the opportunity to escape ever came, the only way out would be along the road.

Cal helped her maneuver on the uneven, rock-strewn path. She wore slacks, a sweater and boots, appropriate clothes for the topography. She'd had to leave some of her clothes at the lake house, but Rawlings had assured her he'd have someone bring them along later. She carried the ebony box, denying it was too heavy.

Neither she nor Cal spoke as they walked past Evan, who held the door to the lodge open for them. It took Amanda's eyes a moment to adjust to the dim light. Then she saw three men sitting on ugly, mismatched upholstered chairs placed around the large, high-ceilinged room. One of the men stared at her with such intensity that her gaze was drawn to him. The man hadn't shaved in a number of days. His hair was reddish-blond, slightly curly and needed to be cut. He stood and took a step forward. Something about him, the shape of his mouth, the way he held his head and body reminded her of—

"Daddy...?"

"Susan?"

"She's known as Amanda now, Mr. Ross," Rawlings interjected. "Amanda Kirk."

"Amanda Kirk?" Craig shook his head as if to clear it and took a hesitant step forward.

Cal applied pressure to Amanda's arm, urging her to move toward her father. But she held back, aware that everyone was watching the little drama unfold.

"Your mother and I...we feared you were dead," Craig whispered. Then the full implication of what had happened seemed to hit him. "You bastard!" he shouted, and headed for Rawlings. "Why did you have to drag her into this?" Before he could wrap his hands around Rawlings's throat a man nearly the size of Cal rushed over and held him back.

"I've waited to spring this little surprise. Your daughter is the famous Amanda Kirk, best woman card player in the world. She's been the bait to draw Quintero and Garland in. Tomorrow everyone'll be here. We're going to play a little poker." Rawlings smiled. "Okay, Liston, let him go."

Craig looked at Amanda as if seeking confirmation of Rawlings's statements.

"We can talk about it later," she said, feeling torn between her love for him and her anger that he'd been the cause of everything that had happened.

"Let's get the luggage and groceries in," Rawlings said cheerfully, acting like a social director on a ship. "Then we can have a nice long talk."

Amanda whirled and ran outside, needing to get away from her father, the other men and Rawlings, with his sneering amiability. She had to try to get everything in perspective. She slowed to a walk, blindly following a path toward a large level clearing surrounded by a thick stand of aspens. When she was again in the shelter of the forest, she found a small log cabin, much older than the main house. The door was open. Inside the single room she could see furniture and a lamp. She didn't enter but continued walking down the trail.

Questions buzzed in her brain like bees around flowers. What was Rawlings planning? Why had he brought her father here? After everything was finished, what fate did Rawlings have in store for his three captives? Would he kill them? What would he do with Garland and Quintero after he reaped his revenge?

Amanda sat on a log and buried her head in her hands. Thank God Mark was out of all of this. At least he was safe.

EVERYONE SAT at the long wooden table eating the dinner Amanda and Cal had prepared. Liston and O'Grady, two of Rawlings's henchmen, continued to keep a careful watch, especially on Craig and Cal. Throughout the meal, conversation was sporadic. They discussed the contents of Amanda's mysterious box, admiring the beautiful jade chips. No one discovered the hidden drawer. The chest now sat on the mantel, its simple elegance looking out of place under the mounted deer head that hung over the fireplace. After that subject was exhausted, no one seemed to know how to break the tension that filled the room like static electricity.

Amanda set her fork down, her appetite gone. Since seeing her father, she'd found it difficult to focus on anything. Disjointed thoughts would form in her mind, then disappear like smoke. He sat next to her at the table, but he'd said very little. A silent agreement existed between father and daughter to wait until they were alone to try to talk.

Now she tried to concentrate. What was he thinking? He must have questions about how she'd spent the past year. At least Rawlings had given her a little information about what had happened to her father, but he knew nothing about her. He'd said he feared she was dead. That gave her an odd feeling, as if she'd been given a second chance.

There was an ironic parallel to their situations. Now they both had experienced what it was like to think a loved one had died and then to discover that the person was alive. Father and daughter would need time to become reacquainted.

At that moment Amanda thought about her mother. She must know by now that her husband was missing and was undoubtedly frantic. She, too, had been a victim of her husband's ill-conceived plan.

Amanda tilted her head, thinking for a moment that she'd heard car tires on the gravel roadway. She listened more intently until the sound got louder, and she was sure. But no one else seemed to notice.

Suddenly Rawlings looked up, hearing the car, too. "None of you move," he said, going to the door and stepping outside.

Amanda crossed the room and sat on the sofa. She felt detached from everything. She didn't even care who had arrived. It was probably more of Rawlings's men, bringing the rest of their belongings from the lake house.

Rawlings reentered the room, then stepped aside to reveal a tall figure outlined against the light coming through the door. At first all Amanda could see was a silhouette of a man. No facial features were visible. He had his arms behind him. From the awkward way he stood she thought his hands were bound. He entered the room just as she said his name. "Mark!"

"Isn't this a real surprise?" Rawlings said, sounding pleased.

Cal stood. When he realized what Amanda had said, he stopped, as if frozen in place. All color drained from his face. He lowered himself onto his chair, calling on every reserve of strength to gain control. Mark Banning's presence reconfirmed his suspicions. Amanda must have been with him in England. Somehow she'd gotten a message to him to come to the house at the lake. But Mark had walked into a trap.

"Who is it?" Craig asked Cal.

"He's a friend of Amanda's—Mark Banning." Cal spoke in an emotionless tone. Just saying that name out loud made his heart ache. He'd lost Amanda. Nothing else mattered.

Amanda got to her feet, and on shaky legs she headed across the room.

"Hello, Amanda."

"Oh, Mark! I told you to stay away."

Mark twisted his body so that she could see his tied hands. "I really didn't have much of a choice."

Around his neck was the blindfold he'd had to wear during the ride. She saw the dried blood on it and on the skin above the shirt collar. When she realized he'd been hurt, she wanted to rush over to embrace him. But she couldn't. That would only anger Rawlings and upset Cal. She'd seen Cal's face when he recognized Mark. All the guilt she'd been feeling for days came back to haunt her. She walked to the window, keeping her back to the room.

"Rawlings, get these ropes off of me," Mark said. "I'm not going anywhere." He turned around and spotted a stranger near the table. He wasn't Garland. Probably one of the players, Mark thought as he acknowledged Cal's presence with a nod. He didn't speak to Cal, knowing what he must be feeling.

A sudden noise at the door made Mark turn. O'Grady, Liston and Frankovich, the man who'd cracked Mark's head at the rental house, entered the room, then positioned themselves along the wall like sentries.

"O'Grady, use your knife and cut Banning free," Rawlings ordered. "I don't think he's going to be much of a threat."

As O'Grady severed the rope, Mark counted the people in the room. Eight. And three or four more to come. It was turning out to be quite a party.

His gaze returned to Amanda, who remained at the window. As if sensing his scrutiny, she turned to face him. She looked pale and shaken. Her eyes were directed at the blond man sitting by Cal. She walked to the table and stood between the two men.

"Mark Banning, this is my father, Craig Ross."

"Your father?" Mark asked. The name of Ross rang a bell in his mind, but he couldn't remember why. Something about a businessman in the computer business who'd been in a plane crash in the Atlantic, but that was all he could remember. "I don't understand."

"When I . . . I came to Tahoe, I changed my name," Amanda said.

"Are you one of the players?" Mark asked Craig.

Rawlings was suddenly beside Mark. "What do you know about the game?"

Mark regretted his words. He decided the best policy was to keep silent, a technique he'd used when arguing with Rob. His lack of response had always infuriated his stepbrother and was having the same effect on Rawlings.

Rawlings repeated the question, but still Mark refused to answer. Until he knew more of the facts he'd keep quiet. Behind him he felt the presence of Frankovich. The man bent Mark's arms behind him, preparing him for Rawlings's blow.

Amanda stepped between the two men. "Leave him alone, Rawlings. You brought him up here. He's got a right to know what's going to happen."

Rawlings let out his pent-up breath and seemed to relax. He nodded to Frankovich to release Mark. "Sure, babe," Rawlings said. "Since Craig knows everything, Mark should, too. Tell him all about the big game. Let him know who's coming." He nonchalantly walked to a side table and poured vodka into a glass.

Mark took Amanda's arm and led her back to the window, one of the few places in the room where they could talk privately. He looked down at her. "When I was in Philadelphia, I learned that Rob might be part of this deal. Is he?"

She nodded.

"You knew before, didn't you?"

Amanda kept her gaze on his shirtfront, second button down. "I should have told you, but I was afraid you'd insist on staying. I was trying to protect you." She looked up and offered a weak smile, aware of how pointless her gesture had been. "You should have stayed in Philadelphia. I told you I'd be all right."

"Even if I hadn't known that Rob was going to be here, I wouldn't have stayed away. Just in case you've forgotten, I'm in love with you."

She focused her gaze on Cal and Craig. Her father's duplicity and her own decision to ask Mark to go to the Black Swan Inn had begun a cycle of events that had brought them to this impasse. And of the four accidental participants, Cal was the main victim.

"Do you love me?" Mark asked, keeping his face turned away from the other people in the room.

She shifted her gaze toward him. "You know I do, damn it all. Everything would be so much easier if I didn't."

Mark smiled and ran a finger along her chin. "What's your father doing here? Is he going to be one of the players?"

In as few words as possible she explained that Rawlings had kidnapped her father and was using him as a way to make her cooperate. Again she didn't mention Cal's crime. That was his business and had no bearing on their predicament. When she finished, she stared out the window. The sun was setting behind the mountain, plunging the world into darkness.

"No wonder you were so panicky."

"And to make matters worse you had to show up." Her words didn't carry quite the sting she'd wanted. Her love for him had clouded her good sense.

He grinned. "Just think what fun I'm going to have when Rob sees me here."

She frowned at his flippant remark. He didn't seem to be taking any of this seriously. "Do you think there's any chance we can get away?" she asked doubtfully.

"I don't know, but we've got to try." Mark remembered Butler's man, Amos, and wondered if he was still under orders to continue his search. With Mark's disappearance Butler and Philo would have notified the police and perhaps the FBI. But could the law find this remote place in time?

"What do you think Rawlings will do?" Amanda asked.

Mark shook his head. "I don't know. One thing in our favor, he's got a lot of witnesses he has to deal with. There's strength in numbers."

Amanda shivered. Before Mark could offer any more words of hope Rawlings began to issue orders.

"Okay, everybody, find a place to sit and relax. We've got a long wait. Our guests won't be here until morning. Amanda, Banning, you two have talked long enough. If you've been planning to escape, forget it." He pointed to his three men, who had continued to stand against the wall like wooden soldiers. Guns were prominently displayed in their leather shoulder holsters. "They're expert marksmen," Rawlings said, "and they've got orders to shoot to kill if they see anything they don't like."

No one in the room doubted the truth of Rawlings's threat.

CHAPTER FIFTEEN

FINDING PLACES for everyone to sit presented a problem. Sleep was going to be difficult, if not impossible. The light from the kerosene lamps made the mismatched furnishings look even uglier. Amanda thought longingly of the huge, luxurious house at the lake and regretted they'd left it.

Complaining about the temperature, O'Grady threw another log on the fire. Amanda was chilled, too, and adjusted the blanket she'd been issued, but she still felt cold.

Mark had managed to sit next to her on the sofa. Earlier she'd washed and bandaged the not-too-serious wound at the back of his head. Their conversation was hampered by the presence of Frankovich, who sat near them and watched their every move.

Liston was outside, taking his turn at patrolling the grounds. Rawlings nervously paced around the room, unable to sit still. Amanda realized he'd accepted Mark's loving attentions to her with equanimity. Was Rawlings biding his time before he tried to take some action against her or Mark? Perhaps she should have acted outraged that Mark had come. She could have put on a pretense of hating him for bothering her after she'd told him to leave her alone. But she knew she wasn't

that good an actress. Rawlings and Cal would have both
seen the truth in her eyes.

Her attention shifted to her father. He was in the upholstered chair, legs stretched out in front of him, head
on the back of the seat. His eyes were closed. His face
was so different from before that she had to keep reminding herself that he really was her father.

In a chair near him was Cal, vigilantly awake, his expression unreadable. He avoided looking at her and just
kept staring at the fire. She wished she'd had a chance
to talk to him, to explain about Mark. But since Mark's
arrival, the right time had never presented itself. Now
she regretted not telling Cal the truth after his return
from Los Angeles. The perfect opportunity had been
when he asked her to marry him, but she'd been too
much of a coward.

Mark took her hand in his and squeezed. "I know
you're thinking about Cal," he said in a low voice. "I'm
sorry he had to learn about us this way."

"There never would have been a good way to tell
him." She sighed. "I wish you could have had a chance
to know him better. He's one of those rare, special
people, the kind who it's so easy to take advantage of.
And that's what I've done. If I hadn't met you ... well,
everything would be different."

Mark felt no triumph that he, rather than Cal, had
won Amanda. He just felt extremely fortunate. He put
his arm around her shoulders and drew her closer. She
laid her head against him, at last feeling relaxed.

"It's only midnight," he said, kissing her temple,
breathing the scent of her hair and skin. He'd had no
idea he was capable of loving anyone as much as he

loved this woman. "Why don't you try to get some sleep?"

She nodded and shut her eyes, feeling protected and loved. She was glad that Mark was with her, even if his presence gave Rawlings one more hold over her.

WHEN AMANDA AWOKE, the sky was pearl gray, a forewarning that the sun was about to make its appearance. She couldn't believe she'd slept that long. Mark had his eyes closed, but she didn't think he was asleep.

"Don't move," he whispered in a barely audible tone. "Frankovich's finally dozed off."

Amanda didn't turn to look, assuming Mark was right.

"Do you know how Garland's getting here?" Mark asked with urgency in his voice. "Are they driving?"

In that moment she remembered the level clearing she'd walked through the day before. Now she could make sense out of the piece of conversation she'd overheard. She put her lips against Mark's ear. "Down by a small cabin there's a flat, cleared area that would be perfect to land a helicopter. Not an airplane, though— there isn't enough space for a runway. Rawlings mentioned the men were coming in to Reno."

"Rob's good at flying choppers," Mark said, convinced that Amanda's assessment was accurate. "In fact, I helped train him." Mark realized that having a helicopter available might be to his advantage. So far that was the only one he had.

Frankovich stirred and sat up, rubbing his eyes. He quickly glanced over at Mark, obviously making sure his charges were still there. He stood and stretched. "Make some coffee," he ordered Amanda.

"Make your own," she retorted. "I'm not the maid around here."

The sound of her voice caused Cal and Craig to sit up. O'Grady also came to attention. Rawlings wasn't in the room. Frankovich stepped closer to Amanda. "Damn it, woman, I gave you—"

"I'll get the coffee," Mark said, drawing everyone's attention to him. "Cal can help me." He stood and signaled Cal, hoping he understood that they needed to talk about what they were going to do.

Amanda said with forced brightness, "Cal makes the best coffee in the world. Mine always tastes like bilge water or weak tea." She was quoting Cal's exact words. His private smile made her feel good. Perhaps he was beginning to forgive her.

MARK STOOD beside Craig in the trees that circled the makeshift landing field. A few feet away Rawlings and Frankovich stood looking up at the sky. The four men were out of sight of the aircraft overhead. Everything had been arranged so that only Amanda and Cal were visible from the helicopter. O'Grady and Liston were at the main house and would be presented to the players as a protection team. Until after the game Rawlings, Craig, Mark and Frankovich would wait in the small cabin.

Overhead a helicopter hovered like a hummingbird. Mark was impressed at Rob's choice of craft. The Bell Jet Long Ranger was top-class.

When the noise became loud enough that the two men couldn't hear, Mark turned to Craig and whispered, "Cal and I talked in the kitchen. We've come up with a plan." After a long silence, Mark repeated his words. "Did you hear me?"

"I'm listening," Craig answered, barely moving his lips. He didn't turn his head toward Mark.

The sounds of the rotors became louder. Mark rapidly outlined what he and Cal had worked out. Craig agreed, then stared at Mark with cold gray eyes. "I don't know anything about you or Cal Norton, but I can see Susan's in love with you. I guess that means I have to trust you. No matter what else happens, make sure she's safe."

"I promise."

The draft from the landing helicopter stirred the branches above their heads. Needles fell like rain. The rotor blades slowed, then stopped. The sudden silence seemed deafening. Four men dressed in informal clothes climbed out. "Here're Rob and Garland," Rawlings said. "And Hite and Adler." When no one else appeared out of the helicopter, Rawlings said to Frankovich, "Thank God Garland didn't bring any of his men." He signaled Mark and Craig to follow him through the trees to the cabin.

THE CARDS FELT AWKWARD, thick and heavy in Amanda's shaky hands. Trying to shuffle, she nearly dropped the whole deck. She paused for a moment to gain control over muscles that had been refusing to obey her commands. She and the four other players sat at the kitchen table, which was round and so large that it was difficult for Amanda to deal and gather the cards. Every available source of light had been placed nearby. If anyone wanted to leave the room, they had to carry a kerosene lamp with them.

On a small end table placed near Amanda were a water pitcher, a glass and the ebony box, its ornate lid in an upright position. They were using the jade chips, which had been much admired by Septimus Garland. Inside the hidden compartment was the gun Cal had given her. She regretted she had forgotten to mention it to Mark or to tell Cal where she'd put it. Knowing the pistol was close at hand made her feel better, even though she doubted an opportunity would arise for her to use it.

"Who's turn is it?" Jesse Hite asked. He was dressed in a poplin safari jumpsuit that unflatteringly revealed his paunch. If he'd worn a pith helmet, he could have hunted lion on the African veld. The other man, Orson Adler, wore a plaid wool shirt and corduroy pants that were still stiff and new. The four men had arrived with heavy aluminum briefcases filled with cash. These cases were now secured to the men's chairs with thick chains and locks.

Rob Quintero was a small man with a receding hairline. His black glittering eyes reminded Amanda of jet buttons she'd found on an old dress. Despite his diminutive stature she didn't underestimate his potential for violence. She suspected that his temper could easily be aroused.

Septimus Garland was the surprise. He looked ordinary...like a friendly postman or small-town hardware store clerk. But whenever he glanced in her direction she felt a frisson of fear climb her spine. He seemed to exude evil, as if all the crimes he'd been involved in had been absorbed into his skin.

"You've shuffled those cards ten times, Miss Kirk," Adler said. "Let's play poker."

She glanced up. "Sorry."

Cal stepped closer. "Finish this hand, then take another break."

Amanda nodded and had Hite cut the cards. "Mr. Quintero, it's your choice of game." How different this all was from when she played poker with Mark on the ship. Then the sensual sound of the cards drifting across the felt-covered table, the clicking of the chips, the fresh sea air coming in through the open porthole had created an ambience of excitement. But it had been Mark's presence that had caused her elation and aroused senses. This game was like the hundreds of others she'd played over the past year. Except the stakes were much higher.

"My turn?" Rob asked, suddenly aware that everyone was waiting for him. "Five-card stud," he answered in a gruff growl, and again glared at O'Grady, who leaned against a nearby wall. Liston had just gone outside for his turn at patrol.

When Garland and Quintero discovered that Cal had brought along bodyguards, they'd come close to refusing to play. Hite and Adler had also objected, but not nearly so vociferously. Only Cal's diplomacy and reasoning had calmed the men's nerves. He had explained that the guards were present for protection. Everyone had brought huge amounts of cash. The house was isolated, and this was Nevada, after all. Who knew what types of people were wandering around in the mountains? Or what player had casually mentioned the big game with Amanda Kirk to one of his cronies. That last possibility was dismissed as impossible. None of the men had told anyone, they said. Finally Cal's words seemed to reassure them and they stopped complaining. Only Rob acted disgruntled whenever he saw the two guards, but he kept his mouth shut.

Amanda knocked on the table to indicate that the pot was right and began to deal. Since they'd started to play three hours before, the stakes had only been moderately high, but she knew that would change. Everyone was taking this time to learn what kind of players the other men were. Hite and Adler had steadily lost. Frequently they dropped too soon, or they bet wildly on hands they had little chance of winning. Amanda had thought they'd be better players.

In that instant, as if the thoughts had been boiling away in the back of her mind, everything became clear. She had finally figured out Rawlings's plan. But why hadn't she seen it before? Both she and Cal had been stupidly naive.

Amanda turned her cards over, indicating she was dropping out of the hand, but continued to deal, making sure the bets were correct. It was all so simple, she thought, and so diabolical. Hite and Adler were ringers, paid by Rawlings to pretend to be two big-time gamblers whose reputations were known to Garland. They'd been invited to play to give the stamp of legitimacy and to put the ever-cautious Garland's mind at ease.

If Garland and Quintero won, Rawlings would wait until just the right moment, then he'd deliver his knockout punch. His revenge could be a reenactment of what they had done to him.

Her next thought chilled her, but she was positive none of her emotions showed on her face. Rawlings had to know what would happen if Garland lost and walked out of here alive. Garland had worldwide resources and would hunt Rawlings until he found him. But Rawlings wouldn't stupidly place himself in that kind of position. So the logical step would be for him to go for the ultimate revenge—death for his enemies.

She shivered with fear when she thought about what would happen to the witnesses. No matter how she tried she couldn't deny the images that formed in her mind or shake her feelings of impending death.

ALL EVENING wind and rain had lashed against the windows. Thunder bounced around the mountains, so loud that it seemed to shake the house on its foundation. The storm's fury only made Amanda more tense. For the thirteen hours they'd been playing she'd lost more than she'd won. The card god who had always treated her so well had now deserted her.

At midnight she asked Cal for two aspirins and more water. She sat on the straight-backed oak chair with a pillow under her, another behind her, but still her back ached. As she swallowed the capsules, she coughed. Her throat was raw from the smoke of the fireplace. The wind kept shifting, causing a downdraft that filled the room with the acrid smell of burning wet wood.

Whenever she'd suggested they quit playing and begin again in the morning, Garland and Quintero had refused. They were like addicts. Each time a hand was dealt, their eyes shone with an excitement she'd never seen before. Neat stacks of jade tokens and Cal's colored clay chips stood in front of each man. Amanda tried to calculate their winnings but found she couldn't concentrate on the numbers long enough to arrive at a total.

The insane part of the whole situation was that nothing they were doing made any difference. She might as well end this pointless game by gathering all the money and handing it over to Quintero and Garland right now. Then Rawlings could direct his final act. But she had to continue going through the motions, pretending distress when she lost, smiling in triumph at the few hands she won.

Finally it was time for another break. Amanda dropped her head forward and tried to massage her stiff muscles. What was Mark doing? And her father? The day must have been as terrible for them as it had been for her. They'd been cooped up with Frankovich and Rawlings in that tiny cabin for fifteen hours.

"I've had enough," Hite said after glancing at his gold watch. He threw his cards onto the table. "Mr. Norton, cash me in."

"Me, too," Adler said, standing. "I'm cleaned out in more ways than one."

Garland looked at Quintero and smiled. "Looks like we're the big winners."

"I don't want to stop," Rob said, sounding like a petulant child. "Norton, we'll rest for a few hours, then go on with the game." The words were a statement of fact, not a request.

Amanda glanced over at Cal, only now realizing just how exhausted he must be. He'd been tireless, fetching drinks and food, serving as banker, keeping track of the money. She felt admiration for him, even sisterly love. That would never change. He would resent any feelings of pity, but she couldn't curb her compassion for this man who'd been her best friend.

"No, we'll quit," Cal said to Rob. "The bank's nearly broke. The game's over."

Rob stood, his face flushed. "Damn it, I said—"

Just then the door opened, letting in a draft of cold air that fluttered the cards to the floor. Rawlings entered, followed by Craig and Mark. Frankovich came in and shut the door. The four men stood in a line, as if on parade. They were wet and windblown.

Mark's gaze sought Amanda's. His reassuring smile looked a little forced, but she had to give him credit for trying.

Rob was the first to react. "What the hell's going on?" His mouth literally dropped open when he recognized Mark, and his eyes filled with hate. "What are you doing here?" he demanded, moving toward him.

Garland also stepped forward, acting as if he couldn't quite see what was going on.

"Get back," Liston said. "Both of you."

Rawlings laughed. "This is even better than I'd hoped."

"Rawlings!" Garland shouted, looking as if he were having a heart attack. "You mean . . . ?"

"You've been set up, Garland," Rawlings said with unmitigated glee. "And there's not a damn thing you can do to get out of my trap."

CHAPTER SIXTEEN

AMANDA SILENTLY accepted a cup filled with hot chocolate from Frankovich. Rawlings had ordered him to make and serve whatever anyone wanted. The man moved from her range of vision as he continued to hand out mugs of coffee and mixed drinks.

Every muscle in her body felt numb. Her reserve of strength was leaving her, making it nearly impossible for her to function. All she could think about was the pounding pain in her head. She sipped the too-hot liquid, set the cup on a side table and plopped down on the sofa. A cloud of dust enveloped her, making her cough.

She knew she should be concerned about the events that had occurred in the past half hour, but she couldn't generate much interest. Nothing seemed to matter anymore.

After the emotion-filled moments when Garland and Rob first came to the realization that they'd been taken in by Rawlings, everyone seemed to have settled down. The two men who'd been playing the part of Hite and Adler were paid off and left in one of the cars. O'Grady and Liston looked tired but continued to stand guard over a locked metal strongbox filled with everyone's money.

Only Rawlings showed no signs of fatigue as he continued to orchestrate his little drama. "Okay, everybody," he said, standing in the center of the room. "I've got a proposal that's going to make all of us very happy...." He looked over at Mark and Craig. "Well, almost all of us."

Rob glanced at the silent Garland. When he realized he would receive no help from that quarter, he turned back to Rawlings. "What do you mean?" Rob was no longer the self-assured, contemptuous gambler. His shoulders were hunched, as if he, too, didn't have the strength to stand straight. He'd spent the time since Rawlings and Mark had entered the room directing a hate-filled gaze at the two men, especially Mark.

"It took me a long time to set all of this up," Rawlings began. "Using Norton and Amanda as lures succeeded better than I'd hoped." He stared at Garland, then at Rob. "For years I've planned how I was going to get my revenge against you two. I've even been perfecting my knee surgery techniques using a power drill."

Rob became visibly pale, looking as if he might be sick.

Rawlings threw his head back and laughed. Just as suddenly he stopped, again assuming his somber expression. Only his eyes told how much he was enjoying his own production. "But now I've got a better idea. As much as I like inflicting pain, I like money better."

Amanda knew her guess had been right. Rawlings was going to get the most mileage out of his revenge by blackmailing his two enemies.

"Come on, Rawlings, get to the point." Garland's act of indifference had changed to an attitude of impatience.

Rawlings nodded. "By an odd set of circumstances I was able to obtain some documents about you two that

I know the FBI and the attorney general would be interested in seeing. You two have been very busy since you met at the Kentucky Derby all those years ago. Your business arrangements include various crimes—bribery, conspiracy, fraud in securing Pentagon contracts. I've probably missed a few minor violations, but there's enough to send you both to a federal pen forever."

"I don't believe you!" Rob shouted.

"Then let me give you a few names of top brass so you'll know I'm not just blowing smoke."

As Rawlings began listing names, Mark crossed the room to sit beside Amanda. He said nothing as he listened intently. Where had Rawlings obtained his information? Mark wondered. Had someone examined Rob's safe, someone who knew how to bypass the complex security system? Mark realized how easily Philo had found all the right documents, the most incriminating papers. After they were microfilmed, Philo had returned them in just the right order. Mark knew everything had gone too smoothly. Could Philo hate the Quinteros so much that he'd sold that information to a man like Rawlings? If so, then why had Philo done the same for Mark? Was he covering all his bets, making sure Rob came to justice one way or another?

"The proof against you two is in a bank vault in Los Angeles," Rawlings said. "A most reputable and trustworthy attorney has explicit instructions on what to do with that safety deposit box in case of my unexpected death."

"Rawlings, you're bluffing," Rob said with a sneer. "You haven't got anything on us."

"Shut up, Rob," Garland growled. He glared at Rawlings. "We've got the picture. Now tell us what you've got in mind."

"In the morning I want Quintero to fly us to Sacramento. At a bank there each of you will arrange for a million dollars to be transferred to my account in Switzerland. And, of course, I'll keep the stakes you two brought."

Rob laughed derisively. "And why the hell should we give you all that money? If we don't, are you going to kill us? You wouldn't get away with it. People know where I am."

"You're so stupid, Rob," Garland said. "Rawlings didn't set all this up just to murder us." He inhaled deeply and asked, "What else do you want?"

"I'll be fair. I've got an exchange program all worked out."

"What do we get in exchange?" Rob asked, sounding like a child.

"Just sweet revenge," Rawlings said. "When everything's been done to my satisfaction, Quintero can have Banning, and I'll give Craig Ross to you, Garland."

"Ross?" said Garland, and stared at the tall blond man, recognizing him for the first time. "My God, Rawlings, I've got to hand it to you. I can hardly believe what you've pulled off."

Amanda started to stand, but Mark held her back and shook his head in warning.

Cal and Craig didn't move from their chairs. Only a dim light from the lamps penetrated that part of the room, making it difficult to see their faces.

"And no one has to know what happened to them," Rawlings said, obviously pleased with his plan.

"Craig's disappearance can't be reported. After all, he's already officially dead. His wife doesn't know where he is. She could easily be convinced that he became despondent and killed himself. She's got control of the company, so she's happy."

Rawlings looked at the end of the room where Mark and Amanda sat. "Banning was brought up here without anyone's knowledge. He was alone when he came to Tahoe." Rawlings shrugged. "He'll just vanish. Those kinds of things happen all the time in the wilds." His smile grew broader.

"What about you and your three friends?" Garland asked. "And Kirk and Norton?"

"My silence and my men's, of course, is guaranteed. If you two get caught, then you could blow the whistle on me. We'll work something out about Cal and Amanda later."

"What if we don't agree to your terms?" Rob asked.

Rawlings's happy smile disappeared. "Mark's been checking you out, Rob. He knows everything's not kosher at Orion. He'd be interested in buying the information I've got on you."

After a moment's silence, Garland stood. "Well, it all seems to be in order." He now acted the role of a businessman who knew he'd been beaten in a deal and was trying to make the best of a bad situation. "Craig Ross cost me a hell of a lot of money, but I'll sleep better knowing he didn't get away with it."

Rob slowly got to his feet. He said nothing for a moment, as if controlling his anger enough to speak. "I had Mark right where I wanted him. His silly mother agreed to give him and Diane a cash settlement to get him out of Orion. Everything was all worked out."

"That would have cost more than what you'll be paying," Rawlings said in a reasonable tone of voice, as if addressing a stubborn child. "So you're getting off cheap. And this way Mark Banning will never mess with you or Orion again."

The words seemed to please Rob. He walked over and poured himself a shot of bourbon, downing it like a practiced drinker. His hatred of Mark shone from his eyes. He acted as if he could hardly wait to kill his meddlesome stepbrother.

"Oh, Mark." Amanda's whisper revealed her alarm. She reached out and took his hand.

He offered a smile of reassurance. Only then did he realize that he felt no fear. Since he'd first met his stepbrother, he'd never been able to consider him as a threat. Rob had always been a sneak and a bully, more bombast than action. But with Garland backing him he could be dangerous. And he certainly hated Mark enough to kill him. Despite what Rawlings said, Amanda and Cal were also in jeopardy.

Rawlings joined Garland and Rob at the table and began talking in low tones. Cal and Craig sat in the large upholstered chairs pulled up close to the fire. The three guards were stationed around the room, one near the door. Since it had started to rain, no one had gone outside to patrol.

Mark continued to hold Amanda's hand in his. She was trembling. "It's okay," he said quietly. He pulled her against him and wrapped his arm around her shoulders. He shifted so that he could look directly at her face. Her cheeks were pale, emphasizing fear-filled eyes that were underlined with dark smudges.

If Amanda was getting ready to panic, he could handle her two ways. He decided she needed his get-tough approach. "You're not going to fall apart on me, are you? I didn't think you were the type who cried or screamed hysterically in crisis situations."

Amanda pulled her shoulders back in defiance. "I'm not!" The words were whispered but strong. "How can you ask something like that? I'm just tired."

Mark nodded. "You've been very brave. But it'll soon be all over."

Tears blurred her eyes. "I don't like your choice of words." She attempted a smile.

Mark laughed. "Good point." In a whisper he added, "I worked out an escape plan with Cal and your father, so be ready for anything."

"When?" she asked, wishing there was time for him to go into detail but knowing he couldn't, not with Rawlings continually glancing in their direction.

"Rawlings and the others will go to Sacramento in the morning," Mark whispered. "He'll leave two or three of his goons behind, but that will be our best chance. Watch for my sign. Do you understand?"

She nodded. "In the hidden drawer of the box you gave me is a handgun," she said, barely moving her mouth. "The safety's off, ready to shoot."

"Does Cal know about it?"

"He gave it to me, but I haven't had a chance to tell him where it is."

Within minutes everyone in the room found places to sit or lie down. The flames in the kerosene lamps had been lowered so that only a muted glow filled the room. The noise of the storm increased. Thunder bounced around the mountains. Rain and hail drummed on the corrugated metal roof, sounding like buckshot. Wind rattled the windows, as if demanding to be let in.

Mark pulled the blanket over Amanda, snuggling her under his arm. "I wish we were alone," he whispered.

Amanda nodded, remembering their night at the inn.

The loud sound of a chair scraping across wood made them both jump. Amanda sat up and watched as Rawlings stood and moved away from the table where he'd been sitting. He lifted one of the lamps and held it in front of him as he headed across the room.

"Amanda, I think you'd better go to bed." He headed for the stairs. "I'll light your way up." His tone was neutral, his face expressionless. At the railing he paused and waited for her.

She almost laughed at his preposterous suggestion. Instead, she stared at him with all the hatred she could muster.

Before she could speak, Mark said, "She's not going upstairs, either with you or alone." He glanced over at the window. "It'll be light in a few more hours. We'll all wait here, just one big happy family."

Rawlings looked angry, and Mark decided he'd better focus the spotlight on someone other than himself or Amanda. Rob was the most likely candidate. "Yes, just one big happy family," he repeated in a louder tone, gazing around the room. "It reminds me of the joyful times we had at the Banning house after the parasite Ed Quintero and his freeloading son moved in."

"You bastard," Rob said, getting to his feet. "I'll kill you right now."

"Cool it, Quintero." Rawlings set the lamp down on a small wooden table and moved across the room, his limp even more noticeable. "Everybody's got to stay nice and calm. You can't get your hands on Banning until I have proof the money's been deposited in my account."

"But at least let me—"

"Shut up, you fool," Garland shouted at Rob, grabbing the back of his jacket and pulling it so forcefully that it almost tore. "Sit down!" When Rob obeyed, Garland looked at him steadily. "Now tell me," he said in a controlled voice, "how did Rawlings get that information about our military contacts? I know it didn't come from my organization."

Rob began to sputter, claiming his innocence, trying to prove no one at Orion could have obtained the documents.

Mark knew Rawlings wouldn't expose his source, not unless he could make a profit out of the deal. Leaning his back on the sofa, Mark grinned at Amanda. "Isn't this fun? Just like the movies. The bad guys fighting with the bad guys while the good guys look on."

Garland's accusations and Rob's protestations of innocence continued, getting louder and more heated. Rawlings finally took charge. "Damn it, Quintero, be quiet. Both of you. Or I'll have Frankovich make you shut up."

After that the tension seemed to ease, but everyone knew what the morning would bring.

Mark again drew Amanda back under his arm, tucking the blanket around her. "Get some sleep." She nodded and closed her eyes. "I love you," he whispered softly.

She sighed, then heard nothing more.

NEAR DAWN Amanda awoke. Her head lay at an awkward angle on the back of the sofa. She straightened her spine and tried to stretch out the knot in her neck. Mark was absent from the room, but she felt no alarm. She could hear him talking to Cal as they made coffee in the kitchen. Rawlings was the only other one not in the room, but she could hear the antiquated water pipes and knew he was taking a shower. O'Grady still dozed by the fire.

Her father sat in a chair across the room. He glanced over at her, stood and came to sit on the sofa. He didn't touch her, as if afraid she'd reject his gesture.

"We've got to talk," he said in a low voice. "How much do you know about what I've done?"

"Almost all of it except...except why." She purposely kept her tone free of condemnation. Considering her own actions during the past few months, she had no right to pass judgment.

"You should understand my reasons. You knew how much trouble the company was in. I had to do something to save it."

"Gambling's always a good way," she said, unable to keep the sarcasm out of her voice. His pained expression made her regret her words. "Sorry," she said in a low voice. "Tell me what happened when you played against Garland."

Craig inhaled deeply. "That night was one of those times when I couldn't do anything wrong. Even when Garland and I played the last hand for double or nothing, I knew I would win."

"How did you get away from Garland?" Before he could answer she continued, speaking in a rush. "After a big game with Rawlings, Garland's men found him, took his money and beat him. That's why he limps and why he set all of this up—to get revenge."

Craig smiled. "If you can believe it, I climbed out of a small bathroom window, carrying all that cash in a pillowcase. It must have been a sight to see." His tone proved just how much he had enjoyed his little escapade.

"You make it all sound so simple."

"Surprisingly it was. Before the game I'd planned to go to Rio on business. Even had the plane ready. I got to the airport, left the money in a locker, mailed the key to your mother and just took off."

"Did you crash on purpose?"

"God, no! That was the most horrible experience of my life. I didn't get my face changed just so I wouldn't be recognized. It was a mess. I don't remember how many operations I had."

Amanda could now see tiny scars cleverly hidden in the natural lines of his face. Whoever had done the surgery was a master.

Craig rubbed his right cheek, as if remembering the pain he'd had to endure. "Bill got a doctor for me. When he told me what he'd have to do to my face, I saw a way to hide from Garland. I knew he'd never let me get away with the money, but I thought I could play a waiting game. The feds were breathing down Garland's neck. It was just a matter of time before they found enough on him to put him away for life. Then your mother would meet a man who bore an odd resemblance to her dead husband. We could be reunited and I could take over the company again."

"Piece of cake," Amanda said ironically.

When she didn't continue, Craig said, "Damn it, Susan, don't act like that. I was born poor and I sure as hell wasn't going to die poor. I worked my guts out for that company. I just couldn't sit back and let it go down the tubes without at least trying *something*. The money boys had turned their backs on me. I was desperate. I took the chance on gambling with Garland and Quintero, won a bundle and everything seemed to be working out all right . . . until Rawlings's man spotted me in the Dallas airport. Then somehow Rawlings got on your trail, and we've both ended up here."

She could tell he was waiting for her to explain the sequence of events that had led her and her two suitors, Cal Norton and Mark Banning, to that remote cabin in the Sierra Nevadas. But right now she was too tired to explain.

"Mother doesn't know where you are, does she?" Of all the people involved, Amanda felt the most sorry for her. Just when everything looked as if it was going to work, Craig had again vanished, leaving her with nothing.

"I still don't know how I was spotted," he said.

"You were just in the wrong place at the wrong time. The gold doubloon gave you away. One of Rawlings's men saw you and remembered how you always fiddled with that coin."

Craig shook his head. "Well, I'll be damned. I always thought Garland would get me." He smiled. "I wondered why Rawlings seemed so pleased to take the doubloon away from me." He looked over at Amanda. "Your mother spent months trying to find you, then gave up, deciding you were dead."

"I've got a lot of explaining to do," Amanda said.

"We all do, honey." He took her hand.

Amanda swallowed to ease the lump in her throat. Tears formed, nearly blinding her. Just then Rawlings reentered the room.

"The bathroom's empty," he said to Amanda. "But you'd better hurry before the rest of the crew gets moving."

Amanda quickly stood. Without bothering to speak she ran out of the room and down the hall to the bathroom. Once inside the closed and locked door she at last gave in to her misery.

"THE STRONGBOX GOES with us in the chopper," Rawlings announced. He'd impatiently waited while everyone got dressed and ate a rushed breakfast. Now they were ready to go to Sacramento. "Liston, you and Quintero carry the box down. Frankovich, you and O'Grady are to stay here. I'll take Liston, and let's see..." He looked around the room, studying Craig, Mark and Cal. Finally he smiled and said, "Amanda will go with us."

Amanda saw the three men start to protest, but she quickly said, "Yes, I'll go." Her expression served as a warning to them not to argue with Rawlings. She knew it would do no good. Each of the captives had a role to play in his little drama. Nothing could change the scenario that had so carefully been created.

"We'll be back in about four hours," Rawlings said to Frankovich. The huge man had been placed in charge, much to his obvious delight. "Garland and Quintero have agreed that if anybody causes trouble, you've got permission to shoot to kill." The orders were casually spoken, as if he were saying it was okay to give them all a haircut. Frankovich looked pleased.

Rawlings took Amanda's arm and followed Garland to the door. Before leaving she turned for one last look at the men she loved. Her father gave her a thumbs-up signal. Cal winked at her. Mark's mouth formed the words, "I love you."

Amanda smiled but said nothing. She turned and let Rawlings lead her down the rough path toward the clearing. All morning she hadn't allowed herself the luxury of wondering if Mark's plan had even a remote possibility of success. She had become a mere participant, willing to obey whatever orders were issued. She had no control over her own destiny, a position she didn't like, but there was nothing she could do to change it.

CHAPTER SEVENTEEN

THE TRIP TO Sacramento was uneventful. They went to a bank in a rental car, and while Rawlings went inside with Garland and Rob, she waited in the car, guarded by Liston. When the three men reemerged from the bank, Rawlings looked well pleased—so Amanda assumed he was now two million dollars richer.

Once they were back in the helicopter, Rob again took the controls. During the entire trip, Amanda felt as if she were in a daze.

Suddenly she realized the helicopter was now making wide circles. She forced herself to look out the window. They were above the clearing near the lodge. From what she could tell, Rob was checking out the field before landing. She saw Frankovich wave from the edge of the trees.

"It's okay!" Garland shouted to Rob. It was the first time he'd spoken since leaving Sacramento. "Go on down."

Rob maneuvered the helicopter away from the field, made a wide swing, again rose in altitude, then began his descent. Amanda's heart and stomach turned over.

Let the helicopter crash. Her thought shocked her. But it would solve so many problems for everyone. Better to die this way than to watch Cal and Mark and her father be killed. Mark could put his plan in effect; they'd overpower the guards and get away.

Rob set the machine down like an ungainly bird landing on its precarious nest. Before the rotors came to a full stop Rawlings opened the side door, dropped the stairs and gestured for her to go first. She did, holding her blowing hair as she hurried away from the craft. For a moment, flying pine needles and dirt blinded her. Finally she was able to look around. Frankovich was still standing at the edge of the small field. There was something odd about him. He acted nervous, not his usual cocky, confident self. He didn't approach the helicopter, but stayed in the same spot. He wore his leather holster, but she couldn't tell whether his gun was in place. His eyes kept shifting to the left, then to the right.

Amanda turned around. Rob, Garland and Liston were just emerging from the helicopter. All three men kept their heads low. Amanda studied the trees that surrounded the clearing. Something caught her attention. She focused on an unusually large pine behind Frankovich. Again she saw something—an arm clad in a white shirt waved at her for a brief moment. Instead of a gesture of greeting the arm moved sideways, as if warning her to move out of the way. But the action was so brief and indistinct that it could have been a bird fluttering to the ground.

As she heard Rawlings and the rest of the men come up behind her, she headed across the field, keeping her eyes directed at the place where she thought she'd seen the signal. If Mark had been able to carry out his plan and get control over Rawlings's men, he might be behind that tree. What did he want her to do? Get out of the way so he would have a direct shot at Rawlings?

In the next instant Frankovich dived under some nearby bushes. Without thinking, operating purely on instinct, Amanda dropped to the ground and began to roll down the slight incline, covering a surprisingly long distance before she heard Rob shout something she couldn't hear. When she felt she was far enough away, she got to her feet and ran.

The sudden bursts of gunfire were deafening in the quiet air. As much as she wanted to stop to see what was happening behind her, she continued to run, heading for the little cabin. Her heart beat in a rapid staccato; breathing became difficult. A scream of terror threatened to erupt from her throat, but she was panting so hard that she couldn't make any sound. She heard more gunshots, sounds that compelled her to move even faster.

She found the cabin but didn't go in. Instead, she circled it cautiously, heading toward the back of the main house. She now understood what had been going on at the field. Frankovich had been forced to wave the helicopter in while Mark, Cal and her father waited in the trees.

Suddenly someone grabbed her arm. Before she could turn or scream, the man clamped a hand over her mouth. Her knees became weak with terror. She tried to twist around, planning on injuring her assailant with her knee. But all she accomplished was to tear her silk blouse and hurt her arm. During the silent scuffle, she tried to figure out who her attacker was. It certainly wasn't Liston or Frankovich; they were back at the field. And it wasn't O'Grady, unless he'd borrowed somebody's blue poplin Windbreaker. Besides, this man reeked of strong tobacco, and O'Grady didn't smoke.

"Stop fighting and I'll let you go. But promise you won't scream."

Amanda nodded. When she was at last free to step back, she swiveled around and saw a stranger. "Who are you?"

"I'm Amos—a private investigator hired by Mr. Banning. You're Amanda Kirk. I saw you and Mr. Norton leave the lake house." Before she could respond, he asked, "What's going on? I just got here and saw the chopper land. Then all hell broke loose." He paused, as if to listen for more gunfire. But not even the usually noisy birds and squirrels made a sound. "Who was doing all that shooting?" He didn't look at her but continued to scan the area around them.

"My father, Cal and Mark are at the field." She next described the men who had just arrived. While she spoke, her mind busily added up the elements. Mark must have made arrangements to hire a private investigator to protect her while he was in Philadelphia. Somehow Amos had found the remote cabin and was here to rescue all of them—if it wasn't too late.

"Did you come alone?"

"Yes, but a couple of sheriffs are on their way. I requested medical help, but I'm not sure we'll get any. Maynard and another man named Philo are coming, too. Somebody should be here soon."

Amanda wondered who Maynard and Philo were but didn't want to take the time to ask. She began to walk out of the trees. The man took her arm and held her in place. "You stay right here. When it's safe, I'll come back for you."

Before she could protest he ran off. She remained by the tree while she counted slowly to one hundred, then she headed for the house. She figured that was where Mark and the others were most likely to go if they'd lost the battle at the landing field.

CRAIG CAUTIOUSLY stood up. He'd been crouched behind a large pine tree during the shooting. "Did you see where Rawlings went?" he asked Mark, looking around. "And where's Cal?"

"Rawlings took off to the left, the same way as Amanda. Cal went after them."

Liston and Rob were now standing by the helicopter, their hands at the back of their necks. Both men had surrendered the minute the battle had begun. Beside them lay the body of Garland. Frankovich also lay on the ground. In all the confusion, Mark didn't know who had actually killed him. Rawlings had opened fire first, directing his shots at the trees. At the wrong moment Frankovich had stood and gotten caught in the cross fire.

Mark grabbed the clothesline he'd found in the house. "Cover me," he said to Craig, and headed toward Frankovich. When he confirmed the man was dead, he went to the helicopter and retrieved Liston's weapon from the place where it had been thrown. He shoved the heavy gun into his waistband.

Mark then looked at his stepbrother. Robert Quintero was a changed man—shaky, older looking, seemingly smaller in stature. Rob kept his gaze focused on Garland, as if he couldn't believe the man was actually dead.

When Rob realized Mark was tying his hands behind his back, he said, "We can make a deal, Mark. Let's talk—"

"Shut up. We'll talk later." After securing Rob and Liston to the helicopter, he ran back to Craig. Amanda would have been proud of her father. He'd been brave and cool under fire. If it hadn't been for Craig, Mark doubted they'd have won this phase of the war.

"I'm going to look for Cal and Amanda," Mark said, hurrying past Craig. "Go on up to the house. But be careful. Rawlings is still around somewhere."

"You, too," Craig called after him. "Don't hesitate to shoot first. He's going to be all the more dangerous now that he's alone."

Mark didn't pause long enough to comment. He just waved Liston's Magnum and continued toward the old cabin. In his pocket he carried the small handgun he'd found in Amanda's box. The tiny weapon had made it possible for him to overpower Frankovich and O'Grady at the house. Mark realized just how well his plan had worked. He still felt surprised that they'd been so successful—almost successful, he quickly added. They still had to contend with the most treacherous and unpredictable man of the lot.

AMANDA STOPPED running and listened. She thought she'd heard her name, but the wind whistling through the tree branches created a low, whining moan that sounded almost human. Dappled sunlight on the uneven ground played tricks on her mind, giving the appearance of shadowy men jumping out at her. She convinced herself that she was just being silly, seeing ghosts behind every tree. She again headed for the back of the house, trying to avoid tripping over the foot-long pinecones that littered the field.

To her left, in her peripheral vision, she saw Cal running toward her. His long legs covered the ground in easy strides. She smiled and started to call out to him, but the words stuck in her throat. First she heard the loud crack of a shot from her right. In the same instant she saw the splash of red below Cal's shoulder. What looked like a carnation boutonniere formed just above his heart. He stumbled and placed his hand on his chest, but continued to head in her direction, holding a hand out toward her, a gesture of supplication. She could see his mouth moving, but nothing reached her ears. His eyes were filled with pain.

From the ring of trees Rawlings came into her view. If she'd had a weapon, she would have used it on him. Instead, she had to watch as he raised his gun and aimed it at Cal, preparing to deliver the coup de grace.

"Rawlings, don't!" Amanda shouted. The man's gaze changed direction. Slowly he adjusted the gun's angle, now pointing it at her. He was going to kill her, and she had no defense. Running would be pointless; he'd just shoot her in the back. Cal, now standing straight but still holding his shoulder, came between her and Rawlings. He was acting as a shield.

"Cal! Get out of the way." Her plea was drowned out by a sharp explosion that seemed to come from many different directions. Cal fell forward, landing first on his hands and knees, then dropping to the ground. Was he dead? She had to do something to stop Rawlings from shooting again.

She started to rush him, then stopped. Rawlings wasn't taking aim at her or Cal. His face revealed a totally surprised expression. His hands no longer held the gun but were gripped against his stomach where a crimson stain spread across his shirt. He acted as if he couldn't believe he'd been shot. He fell slowly, then lay still, gasping for breath.

Amanda heard someone behind her.

"I told you to stay where you were," Amos said in a loud, accusing voice. As he spoke, he dashed over to Rawlings, kicked away his gun, then returned to Cal, feeling his pulse. "Rawlings only hit him once in the shoulder. The second shot you heard was mine."

In the next instant Mark was there, pulling her into his arms. "Amanda!" He was so out of breath that he had difficulty speaking. "Are you all right?"

She silently drew away from him and sat down by Cal, gently lifting his head into her lap. "Get something to stop the bleeding," she shouted to Mark. "Please help him. We can't let him die!" She placed her hand against Cal's cheek. His eyes were closed, his face totally drained of color. "Oh, Cal, don't die. I love you. I love you!"

FOR MARK, the next hour was a nightmare. The only bright spot was the arrival of Maynard and Philo, two paramedics and two deputy sheriffs. One medic immediately took charge of Cal, who now lay on the sofa near the fireplace. Amanda hadn't left his side. The other man dressed Rawlings's wound but refused to offer his opinion on the man's chances. The deputies began their investigation by talking to Rob, Liston and O'Grady, who shared a bench at the table. They were handcuffed together. Maynard and Amos stayed on the deck, talking, while Philo smoked.

From the moment Mark had heard Amanda tell Cal that she loved him, everything became a blur, a surrealistic play in which he performed his role like a robot. He encased his emotions in a shell, trying to protect his heart from any more pain. At first he tried to convince himself that Amanda's confession of love was a spontaneous reaction to seeing Cal wounded and to the other terrifying events of the day, but he at last decided she'd spoken the truth.

No matter what had happened between him and Amanda or the feelings they had for each other, he was the loser. It would be impossible to contend with a man who had been her mentor, her constant companion, her protector and now her savior. All of those elements were more important than a brief affair with a man she'd met on a ship.

What if Cal died? Mark wondered, hating himself for asking the question but realistic enough to admit that the man's death was still a very real possibility. Nothing had been said about his condition. If Cal died, Amanda's natural reaction could possibly be never to forgive Mark for being the one to live.

"Hey, Mark," Rob called out.

Mark had been standing in front of the window for a long time, totally unaware of everything except his own thoughts. He turned around and faced Rob.

"Come here." To a degree Rob's normal superior attitude had returned. After Mark walked over to him, he said, "We can work out a deal."

"No, Rob. There's nothing you can say that would make me change my mind about you." Mark suddenly realized the irony of the situation. His smile was bittersweet. "Rawlings is probably dying. Everything he had on you is in a box in L.A. Your fate will be decided by Rawlings's attorney.'' Seeing Rob's stricken expression made Mark laugh out loud. "And if the attorney doesn't have enough to hang you, I do.'' He returned to his vigil by the window.

Philo entered the room, spoke quietly with the sheriff and the medics, then came to stand beside Mark. "You all right?''

Mark ran his fingers through his hair. "I'm okay. What's going on?''

"Rawlings just died,'' Philo said without expression.

"Oh." Mark knew he should say more, but he was unable to express any emotion. He glanced at the back of the room, toward Amanda. "How's Cal?''

"He's going to live, but the wound was close to the heart. He needs blood and an operation. Sheriff's going to take you up on your offer to fly him out of here. You'll go to Sacramento. As soon as you've got the chopper ready, you can leave.''

"Why not Reno?" Mark asked. "It's closer.''

"UC Med Center's got a heliport and a special trauma unit. The hospital's waiting for you.''

Mark nodded and headed across the room, then stopped and turned to face Philo. "You let Rawlings have copies of the incriminating evidence against Rob and Garland, didn't you?''

Philo's gaze shifted away from Mark's. "Yeah. A few days before you contacted me, that guy over there—'' he pointed at O'Grady "—came sniffing around. Somebody had told him how much I hated the Quinteros.'' Philo shrugged. "I wanted to get those bastards one way or another. What Rawlings got, you got. I guess I should have gone to you first, but, well, you know how it is. Rawlings paid." Philo had the decency to look ashamed. "It all worked out okay, right?"

Mark took a moment to study his father's friend. In the past month he had met more people filled with greed, hate and revenge than he'd ever known before. But he couldn't blame Philo. A man bent on retaliation was apt to do anything to attain his goal. Receiving compensation just made revenge that much sweeter. Given the identical set of circumstances, Mark decided he might have acted the same way.

"Yes, everything worked out fine." Except for his relationship with Amanda, he thought, and headed for the door to get the helicopter ready.

CHAPTER EIGHTEEN

CAL LAY STRETCHED OUT on the padded floor of the helicopter, surrounded by long rolls of blankets to keep him in place. A long IV tube led to a bottle hanging from the side of the craft. The medic stayed nearby, checking Cal's vital signs. After Mark sat at the controls, Amanda reluctantly climbed into the passenger seat, helped by her father.

"When we leave here for wherever the sheriff takes us, I'll bring your things." Around Craig's neck was the gold doubloon and chain. Perhaps her father's good luck would return, Amanda thought.

While Mark checked out the instruments and familiarized himself with the controls, Amanda combed her still-damp hair. She'd taken a shower and changed her bloodstained and dirty clothes, even though she hadn't wanted to leave Cal that long. The medic had insisted that his patient was going to live. Getting herself cleaned up would be psychologically beneficial. He also pointed out that she might be at the hospital for a long time. Now she was glad she'd obeyed the man.

"Okay," Mark said, "here we go." He had on his headset to listen to any air traffic in the area.

Amanda shut her eyes. Once they were off the ground and ascending, she sighed her relief and focused her gaze straight ahead. Looking out the side window was more than she could stand.

This was her first chance in hours to think about Mark. She felt totally confused by the way he'd been treating her since she'd left Cal's side. Mark was acting like a stranger, a passerby who'd offered help at the scene of an accident. He was solicitous, in a detached sort of way, but he avoided looking directly at her. What was wrong? Could a man who had vowed his love suddenly change his mind? Was he turned off by everything that had happened? She looked over at him. But he kept his eyes firmly fixed on the instrument panel.

AT NINE THAT NIGHT Amanda and Mark stood as the tired-looking surgeon entered the waiting room to make his report. Mark put his arm around Amanda's waist just in case the news was bad. They were both feeling light-headed from donating blood.

"That bullet came close to your friend's heart. He's lucky."

"Oh, thank God," Amanda whispered, leaning her weight against Mark.

"The shattered bone and torn ligaments of his shoulder will take a long time to heal, but with more surgery and physical therapy he'll probably regain full use of his arm. His size and strength worked in his favor. He's still in intensive care, but if you're Amanda, you can talk to him. But you've only got a few minutes."

She looked over at Mark.

"Go on. I'll wait here."

When she stood by Cal's bed, she softly said his name.

He opened his eyes and smiled. "You saved my life."

"You saved mine, too."

"Then we're even." He shifted his position, closed his eyes for a moment in pain, then again stared at Amanda. "I guess the Kirk and Norton partnership is dead," he said hoarsely. His meaning was perfectly clear.

She nodded. "I'm sorry, Cal. It was just—" She paused, unable to go on.

"Just one of those things."

She couldn't tell if his expression was a smile or a grimace of pain.

"Before we left the dock in New York I had a feeling we shouldn't go on that trip." He lifted the hand that had no tubes attached. Amanda grabbed it and held on tight. "It's time I went back to Wyoming, anyway."

"Oh, Cal, I—" Tears formed, making it difficult for her to speak.

"Hush, my darlin'. I'm not being brave. I just want all of it to be behind me."

"Miss, you'll have to go now." A stiff and starched nurse stood on the other side of the bed.

Amanda bent down and kissed Cal's forehead. "I'll come by in the morning."

He nodded, closing his eyes.

When she rejoined Mark, she'd gained some control over her tears.

He held a slip of paper. "The hospital got a call from Maynard. Want me to read the message?"

"Yes." She found a box of tissues on a nearby table, wiped her eyes and blew her nose.

Mark unfolded the paper and began to read. "Amos and I are in Carson City along with Craig. The sheriff

is trying to straighten all of this mess out." Mark held
his hand up to stop Amanda's questions. "You and
Miss Kirk have been given permission to stay in Sacramento tonight, but you're to report to the Nevada district attorney's office in Carson City tomorrow at one
o'clock p.m." Mark looked up. "That's all it says." He
turned to Amanda and sighed. "I'm glad we don't have
to go back tonight."

"What are we going to do?"

"I've got everything arranged. When I took the
chopper to the airport, I rented a car and got a room at
a hotel in the downtown district." Just before leaving
the airport he'd remembered the strongbox full of
money sitting in the helicopter. In all the confusion
everyone had forgotten about it. He'd put the box in a
locker, the key in his pocket. Now he wondered what the
fate of all that money would be. Part of it probably belonged to Orion; as banker, Kirk and Norton had put in
a big stake, so some of it belonged to them. The courts
would have to decide what to do with Garland's and
Rawlings's shares. Since the poker game was illegal,
there were ramifications to all of this that Mark didn't
want to deal with right now.

He took Amanda's arm and began to walk. "Let's get
out of here."

Too tired to argue, she let him guide her through the
quiet hospital corridors and into the car. Even though
he had continued to act coolly distant, she appreciated
his moral support. She decided they would discuss everything in the morning when they could both think
clearly.

THE HOTEL MARK had chosen was white brick and had been a private home during the last century. After he unlocked the door and let her enter, he handed her a large paper bag. Inside were two toothbrushes, paste and shampoo. "Airport shops don't carry much," he explained. "I didn't know what else you'd need."

"This is fine. Thanks."

They both spoke formally, as if they were two strangers placed in an uncomfortable situation. The small room held a king-size bed, which didn't leave much space to move around. But the light-colored walls and large areas of glass covered with airy lace curtains gave the appearance of openness. Mark adjusted the window to let in the fragrant breeze. Camellia bushes filled the yard. Roses on trellises climbed the outside walls of the three-story building. "At least it's warm in this part of California," Mark said, breathing in the balmy air.

Amanda stood by the bathroom door, but didn't enter. For the past few hours Mark had avoided looking at her. There was no mistaking his coldness. Why was he angry? Finally she could wait no longer to ask her question. "Mark, what's wrong? Have I said or done anything that—"

"Yes, you have." In three steps he was beside her. "I have to know right now if you're in love with me or Cal."

Amanda frowned, puzzled by his angry words. "But I thought you knew how I felt about you."

"That doesn't tell me what I want to know. What is he to you?"

"He's my friend." She spoke quietly, still confused.

"He's become more than a friend. He saved your life. When he was hurt, you said you loved him."

Now she remembered. "I thought you'd learned on the ship not to jump to conclusions."

Mark's familiar frown appeared. He looked doubtful, as if he couldn't believe what she was saying. "Do you mean you don't love Cal?"

"Mark, I do love Cal, but you see, I'm *in* love with you. When Cal saw you arrive at the cabin, he knew you and I belonged together. He realized then he'd lost out. He'd waited too long."

"What does that mean?" Mark's voice was a soft growl.

"Since we first met, he's been in love with me. But he never felt he could declare his love, because—" She hesitated. She couldn't reveal Cal's secret without his permission. "Well, it's complicated and someday I'll tell you all about it."

Mark tried to assimilate what she'd just told him. "Say it again," he ordered.

"I love Cal like a brother, but I'm in love with Mark Banning," she said with a smile. "Fate or destiny, karma or kismet—whatever it's called these days— brought us together on that ship."

Mark grabbed Amanda around the waist, pulled her against him and kissed her deeply.

When his kiss ended, she asked, "Think you can afford to spend the whole night?"

"I think I can afford the rest of my life—if you'll marry me."

"Oh, yes, Mark. I will."

PENNY JORDAN

Sins and infidelities...
Dreams and obsessions...
Shattering secrets
unfold in...

THE HIDDEN YEARS

SAGE — stunning, sensual and vibrant, she spent a lifetime distancing herself from a past too painful to confront... the mother who seemed to hold her at bay, the father who resented her and the heartache of unfulfilled love. To the world, Sage was independent and invulnerable—but it was a mask she cultivated to hide a desperation she herself couldn't quite understand... until an unforeseen turn of events drew her into the discovery of the hidden years, finally allowing Sage to open her heart to a passion denied for so long.

The Hidden Years—a compelling novel of truth and passion that will unlock the heart and soul of every woman.

AVAILABLE IN OCTOBER!
Watch for your opportunity to complete your Penny Jordan set.
POWER PLAY and SILVER will also be available in October.
